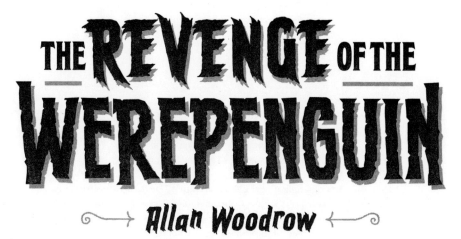

THE REVENGE OF THE WEREPENGUIN

Allan Woodrow

illustrated by Scott Brown

VIKING

VIKING

An imprint of Penguin Random House LLC, New York

First published in the United States of America by Viking,
an imprint of Penguin Random House LLC, 2020.

Text copyright © 2020 by Allan Woodrow
Illustrations copyright © 2020 by Scott Brown

Visit us online at penguinrandomhouse.com

LIBRARY OF CONGRESS CATALOGING-IN-PUBLICATION DATA IS AVAILABLE
ISBN 9780593114230

Printed in USA   Set in Bell MT Std   Book design by Kate Renner

1   3   5   7   9   10   8   6   4   2

To K. L.,

who believed in werepenguins before anyone else did.
—A.W.

For Berkeley Breathed.

Of the heads on my personal Mount Rushmore of influences,
Mr. Breathed's looms largest . . .
—S.B.

CONTENTS

PROLOGUE

Formerly Known as the St. Aves Zoo

A chill trickled down my back. My spine froze, my legs shivered, and my fingers felt like ten creaky icicles. I twisted the temperature knob in the shower and silently cursed my broken water heater. But while the water grew warmer, my brain still felt the harsh cold brought on by my memories of the boy and the penguins, a tale so filled with horror that I had barely slept since I had heard it months before.

Every night since had been the same: I would awaken at midnight screaming for Iggy, the stuffed iguana I'd hugged as a child. Then I would lie awake for hours, continuing to scream. The man who lived in the apartment above me would also lie awake for hours, or so he told the landlord before I was forced to move to a place with a thicker ceiling.

The worrying had aged me. Not only was my voice hoarse from screaming every night, but my hair had turned white, and my face had grown deep wrinkles. My fingers had grown deep wrinkles, too, but that was because I was taking a very long shower.

I knew what I had to do. First, I needed to turn off the water. Then, I needed to travel to the St. Aves Zoo and visit the penguin exhibit. I needed to find the penguin caretaker. I needed to hear what happened next in his long, dark story.

I soon found myself driving down the winding avenue that led to the St. Aves Zoo, armed with a briefcase filled with tissues. People tell me that, because of my severe animal allergies, I should never have started a job working with zoos. "Nonsense," I tell them. "I am not allergic to all animals, only those with fur. Or legs." In another life, I might have worked at an earthworm farm.

But that was neither here nor there. As I stepped out of my car, I sneezed and wiped my nose on my briefcase, before opening it to grab a tissue. It was already dusk; the trip had been a long one. I stared at a menagerie of idle trucks, cranes, and bulldozers.

Earlier in the day, these vehicles must have been loud

and the action chaotic. Now all was still except for an angry ostrich hopping around the vast parking lot. Any workers who had been here before were gone, as were the walls of the zoo. The entrance sign lay on the ground along with broken wire fencing and crumpled gates. I stared down at that sign, now with a big crack down the middle:

WELCOME TO THE ST. AVES ZOO. HOME OF THE WORLD FAMOUS ST. AVES PENGUINS.

"What's going on? Where is everyone?" I asked a tall man scurrying across the lot. He wore a safari hat, a tan hunting jacket, and a long frown.

"What does it look like?" the man replied, his frown sinking deeper into his chin. He adjusted his monocle. "Everyone is gone for the day. They will finish demolishing the zoo tomorrow."

"The St. Aves Zoo has closed? Why?"

"Why did the *Hindenburg* burn? Why did the *Titanic* sink? Why did the Great Chicago Fire take down a city?" he asked.

"Electrostatic discharge, an iceberg, and Mrs. O'Leary's cow," I answered.

"Exactly," said the man. The angry ostrich dashed toward us on its thin gray legs and pecked him.

I thought about assisting the monocle-wearing man as he sprinted across the parking lot, trailed by that deranged bird. Being pecked by an angry ostrich is no laughing matter, or at least only sort of a laughing matter. But I had more pressing concerns. I hurried into the zoo, leaping over a stack of iron posts that had once been part of the front gate and racing down a winding cobblestone path.

I knew the route well, having walked through this zoo months earlier, and every night in my nightmares since. In those dreams I would sprint past Lion Lane and Alligator Alley, past Bison Boulevard and Hippo Highway and, finally, down Penguin Pass. At the end of the pass, among faux glaciers, wacky fish slides, and ceramic walrus statues,

was the world's greatest collection of penguins. But, in my dreams, I did not find a bounty of cute waddling birds. Instead, my nightmares were infected by an abnormally large creature with blood-red eyes, bushy eyebrows, twin horns, and a desire to eat me.

A werepenguin. A creature born to terrorize the night.

The penguin exhibit I found now at the St. Aves Zoo was not the one I had dreamed of, or remembered from my previous visit. The walrus statues were gone, as were the slides. The faux glaciers were broken apart so they looked more like giant faux ice cubes. There were no penguins.

The penguin caretaker, the man I had met during my last visit, stood next to a small maintenance shack, one of the few buildings left standing. He shook his head and

gripped some of the strands of black hair on his mostly bald head. He was still short and round. He still wore, as he had when I last visited, a long black overcoat, a black scarf around his neck, and a white shirt, so that, if you squinted, he looked like a penguin.

As soon as I saw him I waved, then sneezed.

"Hello, friend," he said. "It is good to see you again." He smiled at me but could not completely hide his distress.

"What happened here?" I asked, sniffling and gripping my tissues tightly.

"A zeppelin crashed into us, all of the zoo's money was lost at sea after a freak iceberg boating accident, and one of the cows burned down half the zoo."

"So I heard. But what will become of you and your birds?"

The man sighed. "Your guess is as good as mine, my friend. My birds are zoo penguins. They are not used to foraging for food or battling sea lions. But I will do what I can to help them. In a way, they are my family."

I had been commissioned by a large zoo, a new zoo, to find the best creatures in the world for its collection. That was what had brought me here previously. I had not succeeded in procuring the St. Aves penguins then, and had not yet found penguins of equal quality.

So perhaps my coming back here had been fate! I

could give these penguins a home. I could provide the St. Aves chimpanzees a home, too, and the St. Aves llamas, elephants, hyenas, okapis—although I wasn't sure what okapis were—and all the other animals. Each and every creature would have a new place to live.

Well, every creature except that mean-spirited ostrich in the parking lot, unless it took anger management classes.

No, even it!

"Where are the penguins now?" I asked.

"In a refrigerated storage facility near the boatyard. I will join them in the morning. But where we go from there, I do not know."

"Perhaps I could be of service to you. Do you recall why I was here last? I can escort your penguins to my zoo."

The man arched his eyebrows. It was an impressive arch, and I was jealous because I have never been able to create eyebrow arches with any skill. Still, I took his expression as a good sign.

But before I would give his penguins a home, I needed something first.

"I must hear the rest of your story," I said to him. When he looked puzzled, I continued. "You told me of Bolt, and how he was adopted by an evil baron and turned into a werepenguin. But the story ended with him swimming off with his penguin colony, doomed to be a werepenguin forever."

The man nodded. "I remember." He briefly turned away and shook his head as if to say, *How could I forget?*

"I must know the rest," I answered. "Tell me the entire story, and then I will take you, your penguins, and all the other St. Aves animals to my zoo."

"Even the mean ostrich?" he asked, and I nodded. "Your offer is beyond generous, but I cannot accept. For it is a long, dreadful story. A story best left untold; a story I would rather forget than repeat. Ask anything else of me. But do not ask me to tell *that*."

I folded my arms and stomped my foot, the latter of which was a mistake since my shoes had thin soles and I stepped on a sharp rock. "That is the price of admission. You must tell me what happened after Bolt fled Brugaria."

"Please. Anything else."

But my tightly folded arms showed that I would not budge from my request. I stared at him firmly and then sneezed, but dared not wipe my nose and break my stern gaze.

The man bowed his head. "I will tell you about the revenge of the werepenguin. But your hair looks whiter than I remember, and the rest of you seems more wrinkly.

Let me ask you this: Have you had nightmares since you saw me last?"

"Every night," I admitted. "And I also take very long showers."

"After hearing the rest of my tale, you may never fall asleep again."

1.
My Life as a Penguin

It was a city of snow: the glaciers were its skyscrapers, the floating ice sheets its roads, and the thousands of penguins barking along the seashore its remarkably well-dressed, tuxedo-clad citizens.

Humboldt Wattle—people called him "Bolt" back when there were other people around to call him anything—was almost thirteen years old but not quite, and he was a penguin, but also not quite and certainly not at that very moment. He sat in the snow on top of a small hill, wearing only a pair of old sweatpants and a thin T-shirt. That outfit would be quite insufficient to keep anyone else comfortable on this frozen tundra, but Bolt was cozy. He couldn't feel cold.

However, he *could* feel the thoughts of his penguin brothers and sisters waddling along the shore, although he was not one of them. Not truly. He would never lay an egg, or at least he hoped he wouldn't. He would never molt. He would never dive, beak-first, into the near-freezing sea during the afternoon. Instead, he would only dive, beak-first, into the near-freezing sea at night, under a full moon. But those nights were the only times he didn't feel like an outsider! For on those nights, Bolt would swim with his family, yowl with them, and play with them.

It was too bad that full moons were so few and far between. The rest of the time, Bolt was merely human, or at least mostly so. For Bolt still had penguin blood surging inside him, which meant he could talk with the penguins, and read their minds.

But there was something deep inside the birds, a barrier that was hard and round and slightly crusty, and no matter how much Bolt tried to penetrate that crust, he couldn't quite do it. Before joining this colony, before even coming to Brugaria, Bolt had been an unwanted orphan. It seemed that, no matter what he did or how far he traveled, he would never truly feel like he belonged somewhere, at least not completely.

That was part of his curse: the curse of the werepenguin.

As Bolt sat on his snowy hill, he rubbed his fingers against a slim gold chain around his neck. That chain had once held a killer whale's tooth, but the tooth had been lost when Bolt fought the Baron, the diabolical despot who had bitten Bolt and transformed him into a penguin monster. Bolt had won the battle, and now he sat here while the Baron's remains sat inside the stomach of an orca.

After their fight, Bolt had led the penguins here, hundreds of miles away, and far from other people. Word of a young werepenguin who treated penguins not as his servants but as his family had spread far and wide. The tale had been told from the glubs of fish, the chirps of birds, and the legs of ice crickets. And so the penguin colony had grown.

Bolt stood up, stretched his legs, and waddled down the hill. His walk was part penguin and part human, just like the rest of him.

"Good afternoon," barked a nearby penguin. Bolt couldn't bark like a penguin, not in his human form, but he thought the words *Good afternoon to you*, and the penguin smiled, as best a penguin can, which is not much of a smile at all.

Penguins show their emotions through their eyes, mostly. Beaks are not very expressive.

As Bolt walked through the colony, nodding and smiling to his brothers and sisters, he heard a human shout. It took him a few seconds to realize he wasn't imagining it. There it was again: a girl's voice, calling out in the distance.

No, that was impossible. The colony was at least fifty miles from any human town.

"Bolt!"

Or maybe it was possible.

Bolt turned and there, in the distance, stood a girl, waving. A short penguin sat next to her.

Bolt ran toward the figures, his bird-blood-powered legs skimming across the ice with more traction than if he wore snow boots. He saw the girl with the waving hand, a girl who was about Bolt's age with blonde hair held up with bobby pins, collapse, first to her knees. Then the rest of her buckled and flopped to the ground like a dead fish. The small penguin beside her gave a doglike howl.

Bolt squatted on the ice next to the fallen girl, his cold-impervious hands holding her nearly frozen fingers.

"Bolt, we found you," said Annika, her voice a whisper, a small but desperate smile on her ashen face as she closed her eyes and lost consciousness.

2.
Alive and Coughing

olt lived in a small igloo, which he'd built with help from many penguins in the colony. Penguin wings can't scoop snow well, but are excellent for patting down lumps and smoothing gaps.

The igloo had just one big round room and, since it was carved from snow and ice, lacked basic amenities such as heat or plumbing. Now that he had a visitor, Bolt wished he had done more decorating. A small ice table held a pink vase with some green wisps of seaweed that tried to pass themselves off as flowers. On the ground, in the corner, was a sleek stainless-steel toaster that might have made wonderful toast if there had been an electrical outlet. And if Bolt had bread.

The waves from the sea brought gifts like those on

occasion. The clothes Bolt wore, for example, had been in a washed-ashore suitcase. The toaster and vase had floated to their beach in a small wooden crate.

Annika lay on Bolt's snow bed. She wore black-and-white tattered lederhosen, the traditional penguin-like garb of the Brugarian Forest Bandits. Bolt had piled his two blankets atop her.

A small groan floated from her bluish lips. Bolt tucked the edges of the blankets around Annika to keep her warmer. Soon, her blue lips looked less bluish. Some pink returned to her pale face.

Seeing Annika reminded Bolt how much he missed being around people, and especially Annika, who might have been his only human friend in the world. He brushed his hands through a curl of hair that had fallen out from one of her bobby pins.

"Bolt?" Annika's voice, although soft and quiet, surprised him. "I'm so glad we found you . . ." Annika coughed, deep harsh coughs. Bolt gripped her hand and she squeezed back.

"Why are you here?" Bolt asked. "How did you know where I was?"

Annika coughed again, then flashed the hint of a smile.

Bolt was happy to see that smile, and returned it. He had not been happy in a long while, he realized. He had not been unhappy, either. He had just felt . . . mostly nothing.

He had just lived. But *just* living isn't doing much living at all.

"My papa and I . . ." Annika began, and then coughed again. Some spittle landed on Bolt's cheek. She looked away and bit her lips, as if organizing a jumbled heap of memories into one. She nodded, seeming to make up her mind on what to say, then shared her story.

3.
Annika Shares Her Story

"After we defeated the Baron, or I suppose after *you* defeated the Baron," said Annika, "all of us bandits thought we would continue robbing carriages and kidnapping people. Life would be happy again. Fun."

"Maybe not so happy or so much fun for the people you robbed and kidnapped," Bolt pointed out.

"Maybe not." It seemed difficult for Annika to speak, her voice thin, her bones creaking like a rusted wheel. It pained Bolt to see her this way. "But after the Baron was defeated," Annika continued creakily, "we became friends with the villagers. The bandits and villagers were like one big family. Have you ever kidnapped or robbed your family?"

"No," admitted Bolt, who had never kidnapped or robbed anyone.

"It's not happy or fun for anyone. And bandits rob. That's what we do!" She raised her voice, but then erupted into a series of coughs. Once they subsided, she cleared her throat. "If I was going to become the greatest bandit of all time, I needed practice kidnapping and robbing, right?"

Annika had often told Bolt she wanted to be the greatest bandit of all time. Her father, Vigi Lambda, was a bandit legend.

"So, I decided," continued Annika, "or rather, Papa and I decided, that I would go somewhere else to learn how to kidnap and rob. I wasn't sure where I was going, but after a couple of days I had already robbed two small carriages and kidnapped the daughter of a rich merchant. I had to let her go because I didn't have a pencil or paper, and everyone knows you can't kidnap someone without leaving a ransom note. It's sort of the whole point of the thing." She let out another loud, raspy cough. Bolt grabbed some snow from the floor of his igloo, clenched it in his hand, and dripped the water into Annika's mouth. She croaked, "Thank you."

"Sorry I don't have any water glasses. I wasn't expecting company today. Or ever."

"I'll steal some for you sometime," Annika promised. "On my third day I saw a carriage. It was a huge, extra-fancy carriage. I had my knife and I had my bobby pins,

although bobby pins aren't particularly useful in a robbery, and I was hiding behind a bush when a group of penguins captured me."

"Penguins?" Bolt gasped.

Penguins didn't capture people. Penguins were good-natured creatures, eager to give a stranger a helping beak, or a sympathetic wing around the shoulder. Only the Brugarian penguins had been different. The Baron had twisted their minds, corrupting them. But Bolt had defeated him.

"I don't understand," said Bolt. "Why did they capture you?"

"I was outside the city of Sphen. You've heard of Sphen, right?" Bolt shook his head. "It's a teeming fishing city, much bigger than Volgelplatz, that's surrounded by mountains on one side and the Deader Sea on the other."

"Deader Sea?"

"It's like the Dead Sea, only deader. The Earl of Sphen lives in the huge Sphen Castle in the middle of the city. You've heard of *him*, right?"

"If I had heard of the Earl of Sphen, I would have probably heard of the city of Sphen."

Annika again coughed and gagged. Bolt bent down to crush some more floor water into her mouth, but she waved him off. "I'm good," she insisted. "But the Earl of Sphen is anything but good. He rules all the people and

penguins of Sphen with an iron fist. I don't know how he lost his hand, but his new iron one is quite deadly. They say he's . . ." She coughed and this time welcomed the floor water Bolt offered her. Bolt needed to get some snow to repair the divots now covering the ground near his bed. "They say he's . . ." Again, she coughed, and again, Bolt gave her water. "He's . . ." More coughing.

"I'm not giving you any more water until you finish your sentence," said Bolt.

"They say he's a werepenguin."

Bolt gasped even louder than his previous gasp. "I thought the Baron was the only werepenguin. Not including me, of course."

But as soon as those words escaped Bolt's lips, he knew he had never really believed that to be true. Only someone born with a penguin birthmark and then bitten by a werepenguin could turn into a werepenguin. Bolt had that birthmark. It sat upon his neck clear as day, although he didn't like to think of it. The Baron had the mark on his stomach, right above his belly button.

Why couldn't there be others with the same mark?

Of course there are more of us.

Bolt looked up and jumped back. Where had that voice come from? It was as if someone had put headphones in his brain. But that was ridiculous. It must have been his imagination. He pushed the thought away. It was merely his

nerves, which felt particularly fragile after hearing about the Earl.

Annika asked for a few more drops of melted snow and then continued her story. "They locked me in a dungeon in the palace basement. There are other prisoners, too. Most are forced to work in the fish stick kitchens, where they mince fresh fish fillets, dredge them in vats of flour and then egg, flavor them with slightly spicy bread crumbs seasoned with a dash of paprika and garlic powder, and then plunge the fish sticks into oil until they are cooked into crispy yet surprisingly delicate fish stick treats. It's horrible."

"That doesn't sound so horrible," said Bolt, licking his lips.

"The heat is nearly unbearable, and you're forced to make fish sticks for twenty-four hours straight without resting. Other prisoners are assigned equally terrible chores, like waxing thousands of penguin feathers a day. I heard some prisoners have to teach penguins how to bowl."

"Not bowling penguins!" yelped Bolt. "Penguins are terrible bowlers. Their wings don't fit in the finger holes, and their webbed feet ruin the bowling shoes." Bolt cringed at the thought of penguins wearing shoes. What was next, mittens? Penguins were meant to run free, their feet sliding on ice and snow, or wiggling through water. It was one of the true joys of penguin life. "How did you escape?"

"I'm the world's greatest picklock, you know?" Bolt nodded. Annika kept her long blonde hair out of her eyes with bobby pins, but they also made excellent lock openers. "After I got out, I didn't know where to go. You saw that penguin I came with? I found her wandering the mountains outside Sphen. I told her I knew you, and she started yapping like a dog and led me straight here. Well, she kept on chasing her tail, but when she wasn't doing that, she led me straight here. She was so cute!"

Bolt sniffed. He hated when people called penguins *cute*, as if that was all they were, and not smart, loyal creatures with so much more to offer the world than being funny mascots in books and movies.

"I don't understand," said Bolt. "How did this penguin know where to find me? How did she break the Earl's brainwashing control? Why was she yapping like a dog? Your story doesn't make any sense."

Annika shrugged, looked away, and coughed again. "I don't know." For a moment, Bolt didn't believe her. The story seemed so far-fetched!

There had been a time when Annika had decided to trust Bolt, even though trusting someone else was against all bandit rules. He owed her his own trust, too. She was his friend.

Annika coughed a few more times and then said, "Sphen is far away. We had to hitch a ride on a sled, hide in

the back of a carriage, and float on a barge. It took a long time." She choked again, but before Bolt could grab snow to melt for her, her coughing subsided. "And now here we are." She reached out and grabbed Bolt's hand. Her fingers felt warm, and Bolt felt her warmth not just on his skin, but in his heart. "So, will you?"

"Will I what?" Bolt asked.

"Will you go to Sphen? Will you free the penguins? Will you defeat this mad earl and end his evil reign? That's why I came here. So you could save Sphen, like you did Brugaria."

Bolt removed his hand from Annika's grasp and stood up. Bolt was proud of Annika for wanting to free Sphen: bandits were usually kidnapping, not freeing. But *this* was Bolt's home now. He was happy here. Or, if not happy, he was at least safe.

"What happens in Sphen is none of my business," said Bolt.

"Your business is going wherever werepenguins rule. You're brave and mighty and . . ." She never finished her sentence, as a stream of coughs erupted from her throat.

"You're wrong." Bolt wasn't brave and mighty, despite his past bravery and mightiness. Sure, his name, Bolt, was fierce and strong like a thunderbolt. But deep down, Bolt wasn't like that at all.

Annika thrust one of her weak hands into the folds of her jacket and pulled out a small toy with a string around it. "Do you know what this is?"

"A yo-yo?"

Annika grumbled, tossed the yo-yo away, and dug her hand back into her jacket. This time she removed a thick, leather-bound book. "I meant *this*. It's *The Code of the Bandit*. All eight hundred pages of it."

Bolt had never seen *The Code of the Bandit*, the rule book that all Brugarian Forest Bandits lived by. Bolt knew most bandits never read the book because it was long and boring, and most bandits couldn't read very well. Bolt also knew Annika had read it at least twice.

Annika waved the book under Bolt's nose. "The code says that bandits have to be tough and fierce. It says we always need to leave ransom notes when we kidnap people, so you need a pencil and paper. The code also says we have to be honorable. Hiding here with your penguins, while the people of Sphen suffer, that's not tough. That's not fierce. It's definitely not honorable."

"I'm not a bandit," Bolt reminded her.

"You're more than that. You're the chosen one, Bolt. Remember? You weren't chosen to hide here in the middle of nowhere."

The Brugarian Fortune Teller had prophesized that

Bolt was the chosen one, although she had never specified exactly what he was chosen for. Still, it had seemed pretty obvious to Bolt. "I was chosen to stop the Baron. I was chosen to protect the birds of my colony. And that's what I intend to do."

"But what if you were chosen for more than that?"

4.
The Wall

Bolt waited until Annika slept, tucked cozily beneath both of his blankets, before he waddled out of his igloo.

The sun had already set and the moon begun its nightly ascent.

It was a full moon tonight. Although Bolt's heart ached when he thought of Annika's weakened condition, it beat with excitement for the night ahead. For tonight, he would truly feel part of a family. *His* family.

He spied the penguin that had accompanied Annika sitting in the snow, howling at the sky, her azure eyes staring at nothing. Blue-eyed penguins are just as rare as howling penguins, so Bolt approached with caution and curiosity.

The penguin had light specks of gray in her feathers, and a slight upturn to her beak that almost made her appear to be smiling. As Bolt neared, the penguin bounced in place, yapping.

"Hi," said Bolt with a friendly wave. While he said this word out loud, he also reached into the penguin's mind, communicating with her silently. *I am Bolt.*

In response, the penguin yapped and sat up, her wings out like a begging dog. Her penguin yap sounded more dog-like than penguin-like.

"What's your name?" Bolt asked.

"Arf!" The penguin rolled over and squirmed into the snow. She then bounced back on her feet and sniffed Bolt.

"What are you doing?" Bolt pushed her away. "Stop that." This was not appropriate penguin behavior at all. The penguin rubbed her beak against Bolt's hand. Penguins don't have long, smooth tongues, but if this one had, Bolt was certain she would have licked him. "You're a penguin and penguins don't do whatever you are doing. How did you find me? Who are you?"

The penguin howled again, rubbed her beak on Bolt's hand, and then bounced again, yapping and yipping.

"Fine, I'll do it my way." Bolt closed his eyes and plunged into her head, plucking her memories with his werepenguin mind-reading talents.

Bolt shivered as he saw a series of terrifying images:

penguins putting KICK ME signs on the backs of human schoolkids, penguins pulling chairs away just before people tried to sit down on them, and penguins cheating at simple card games by slipping aces under their feathers. Sphen *was* a terrible place.

Entering a penguin's head was like navigating a winding cavern, with each crevice revealing a new and too-often-horrifying scene. Turn left here and watch penguins hurling spitballs at each other. Turn right there and watch a penguin sneezing and wiping its beak on a baby's shirt.

Bolt changed direction inside the penguin's head, slipping down a short slope where he saw a massive penguin army filled with young penguin recruits. They were taught to fight. To hate. To serve. If they failed to follow orders, they were forced to perform dozens of sit-ups, even though penguins have no waists. The Earl's presence loomed over it all. His face was plastered on buildings, hung on posters.

He was a large man; the Earl must have weighed more than five penguins. In every portrait, his puffy cheeks were filled with food, and there were pieces of fish in his scruffy black beard. The man had enormous bushy eyebrows, a thin beak of a nose, and a nest of messy hair sprouting up into the shape of horns. Bolt also had those things, since they were side effects of being a werepenguin. But this man's eyebrows were so bushy they reminded Bolt of twin ferns, his hair horns were so tall they looked like moose antlers, and his nose stood out like a long pencil jabbed into a watermelon.

The Earl stared out with an evil gaze, as if a thousand hungry rats forced their stares into his two red eyes. His mouth was twisted into a sneer so intense it seemed as if he was sneering at other people's inferior sneers.

Bolt wasn't shocked merely at the images he saw, but at what he did not see: the penguin's personal memories, feelings, and emotions. Usually, those were what Bolt found during his brain searches. But here, inside this penguin's head, they seemed gone. Erased?

No. Wait. There was something there, something in a dark, shadowy corner of an otherwise empty space deep inside the penguin's head. Something twitched under a thick gray woolen blanket. Bolt felt cold, and he had not felt cold since he had become a werepenguin.

Bolt hesitated as the sheet twitched. The movement stopped, and Bolt moved closer.

The sheet wiggled. Bolt continued waddling toward it.

The sheet jiggled. Bolt bent down.

The sheet rustled. Bolt lifted it.

A puppy bounced up and then hopped around, yapping. "I'm Pygo! I'm a puppy!"

The ground ripped apart and a large wall rose, a mountainous slab that emerged from the ground with a thunderous and earsplitting roar, separating Bolt from the puppy. It happened in just a moment, Bolt stumbling back, and then there was a wall and he was alone in a small cavern of empty blackness. He shouted, "Pygo?" and his voice echoed back at him.

When he reached inside other penguin heads, Bolt could never reach beyond their own crusty inner shells. But this was different. He had never before felt such a thick, concrete mass keeping him back.

And then Bolt's eyes were open and he stood on the cold, hard ice, Pygo sitting next to him, panting. Bolt tried to dive back inside her head, but he kept bouncing off.

"Bow-wow!" Pygo rubbed her beak on Bolt's leg.

"Stop that. Really."

Bolt stared at the puppy, or rather the penguin that acted like a puppy, and felt his blood tingling. The night

was fully upon them now. Midnight was nearly here. His mind drifted from Pygo and up to the full moon, high above.

Bolt's organs felt as if they were bubbling and swishing and frothing. His face rippled. His stomach flopped over his pants. He yanked off his shirt before it ripped—he didn't own many clothes—and had just enough sense to slip off his sweatpants before a penguin tail shot out the back of him. He was not wearing his sneakers, thankfully, as his webbed feet would have torn through the canvas sides of the only pair he owned.

The world spun and small slivers of blue light exploded in his eyes like an all-blue fireworks show. When the lights settled, Bolt was a penguin.

"I am one of you," he barked.

"Arf! Arf!" sang Pygo.

Bolt raised his beak and barked again, not a dog bark but one that was distinctly penguin, a loud, high-pitched croak that was joined by countless penguins on the shore. These were not the barks of mad Brugarian penguins, or even warped Sphen penguins, but barks of love.

Bolt waddled toward the sea and dove under the dark, icy water. He sucked up a minnow, biting its chewy but tender meat. Unlike other penguins, Bolt had teeth. Fangs. He used them.

What could be more perfect than eating raw fish in a sea with an entire colony of penguins? Why would he ever think of leaving this penguin paradise to journey to a far-away city controlled by an evil earl? Nothing could ever go wrong here.

Then the sea lion came.

5.
Teamwork, Teamwork

Bolt sensed the creature before he saw it, a torpedo within the navy-blue depths heading toward them, its massive gray body three times the length of Bolt, and five times his weight. The sea lion's cavernous mouth was big enough to eat a penguin in one bite.

Penguins splashed their way toward shore, their barks now panicked screams. Bolt felt the same panic, but ignored it as best he could, spreading thoughts of family and love, of togetherness and safety. *Settle down, it'll be OK*, he thought. But his calm did as little to extinguish the enflamed panic engulfing his clan as if he had tried tossing a water balloon into a bonfire. Bolt swam with his family, his fright mounting with theirs, and he was soon leaping from the water and flapping his wings to fly away, although penguins can't fly, at least not without an airplane ticket, and even then, most penguins don't have the required passports.

Behind them, the monster swam on the waves, jaws snapping.

The full moon shone above, bathing the shore as Bolt and hundreds of penguins emerged from the water, scurrying along the icy beach to get away, some mothers and fathers cradling their young, others urging their families to run faster, faster, and the young chicks barking back: "I'm a penguin, I'm waddling as fast as I can."

The monster erupted from the water, snapping and roaring.

Sea lions didn't frequent these shores. It was one of the reasons this home had been so perfect for the colony. Bolt needed to teach this big brute a lesson: no one messes with *my* family.

The beast clamped its jaws shut, nabbing a feather from a penguin in front of it. The penguin scrambled up the icy shore, barking.

No penguin can fight a sea lion alone, not even a werepenguin. But few things are as mighty as a penguin family, fighting together. Bolt barked to the colony: "It'll be OK. Stay with me and fight!"

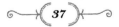

Bolt stepped forward and twenty penguins joined him, surrounding the sea lion in a large circle. The creature turned its head, baring its large, penguin-chomping teeth.

The penguins held their ground. They waited for the signal.

Bolt jumped. He barked. He did a little penguin jig, webbed feet crossing and kicking, but since penguins don't jig well, he just looked silly. Still, it had the effect Bolt had hoped for. The sea lion stared at him, confused. Bolt could not read its thoughts, but he guessed what it was thinking: *This one looks tasty.* And also: *I can jig better than that.*

With the sea lion transfixed by the jig, Bolt closed his eyes. *Now.*

Two penguins behind the sea lion leapt forward. They buried their wings in the soft flesh under the sea lion's back flippers.

Everyone knows sea lions are very ticklish, especially under their back flippers.

The monster giggled, a horrible hyena-like giggle that, mixed with its trumpeting elephant-like roar, sounded like something choking on a tuba. The creature jerked back its head, snapping at its tickling tormentors, but the penguins were already gone, scampering back to their spots in the circle.

As soon as the sea lion moved its head toward them,

two more penguins surged forward. Now it was their turn to dig under the creature's flippers.

The creature, giggling and roaring at the same time, turned its head again, snapping at these new pests. A new wave of penguins rushed forward.

And on it went. Tickle, tickle, head jerk. Tickle, tickle, head jerk.

Now it was Bolt's turn. He rushed forward, toward the sea lion's unguarded rear. Bolt was larger than his adopted siblings, so he tickled under the sea lion's back flipper, but also reached around and tickled under its chin.

The animal bellowed in anger, still giggling but mostly bellowing. No dinner was worth this aggravation.

The beast rose up on its hind flippers like a cornered bear, and spun in a circle. A group of penguins stepped aside as the beast charged back into the water. In a moment it was gone under the waves.

Bolt was confident the sea lion would spread the word to other would-be predators: *Avoid those penguins. They tickle. They also jig, but not well.* The colony would be safe.

Bolt's siblings hooted, high-fived (well, high-winged), and chest-butted one another.

Pygo bounced up onto Bolt's legs, howling at the moon and shaking her tail.

But Bolt did not hoot and slap. He walked away from

the celebration, deep in thought. He had taught his brothers and sisters how to protect themselves. But what about other penguins? Sphen penguins? Who would help them fight?

Annika had asked Bolt, *"What if you were chosen for more than that?"*

What if she was right?

6.
Gentoo

Gentoo Audouin was still six weeks and two days shy of her thirteenth birthday, but she felt older. It was difficult to be a kid in times like these: hard times, desperate times, penguin times.

She closed her eyes while clasping her hands, resting them on her lap as her aunt, sitting across from Gentoo at the kitchen table, recited the evening prayers.

"Thank you for the food on our table, the fish in the Deader Sea, and for letting us survive another day without any penguins chopping us into small pieces. Amen."

Gentoo moved her lips on *Amen* and opened her eyes, blinking. The house was clean, but old and shabby, and the rotting wood and crumbling ceiling timbers emitted dust clouds. The roof creaked and the walls croaked—both from their poor condition and from the family of frogs that lived somewhere within them.

Marguerite Audouin had not quite reached forty years old, but looked older: people often assumed she was Gentoo's grandmother, or even her great-grandmother. Her face reminded Gentoo of a gnarled walnut tree, etched with deep lines, hardened from years fishing under the sun. Even in a city as cold as Sphen, the sun was powerful, although not as powerful as the moon.

Gentoo smiled at her aunt Margie. They shared the same brown skin and white hair, but not many other features. Gentoo's sharp nose was quite different from her aunt's flat one, as were Gentoo's beady green eyes. Gentoo's tall, lanky, birdlike frame—the boys in school used to call her a stork, back when she still attended school—also differed from Marguerite's squatter, shorter stature.

Gentoo glanced at her aunt's plate, filled with a pasty bean gruel. It smelled like garlic—Aunt Margie had added a few cloves to help hide the bitter smell of spoiled thrice-baked black beans. She then looked at her own plate, where a raw trout sat, along with a sprig of parsley placed gently on top of its eyes.

"Eat." Marguerite pointed to Gentoo's plate, which had gone untouched. "It is your favorite, no?"

"Of course." Aunt Margie loved spoiling her, but it made Gentoo feel guilty. She didn't deserve such pampering!

The black beans in the black bean gruel were the only things that should be spoiled in their house.

Gentoo wanted to eat; she had worked a long day on the boat with her aunt, as always. But the fishing had been slow, and their haul had been meager. Fish had always been abundant in the Deader Sea, until recently. "We should save this trout to help pay our fish taxes," Gentoo said.

"Let me worry about that. You just worry about eating."

"But—"

"There are no penguins in this house, Gentoo. They are out patrolling the streets or guarding the fish stick kitchens. We may live in constant fear of them, but here—in our home—we will not. They may take away our food and our dignity, but they will not take away our happiness."

Gentoo bowed her head, nodding. Someday, things would be different.

As she sat, resenting penguins quietly to herself, Gentoo looked closer at her plate and hiccuped in surprise. She hadn't noticed the small dead cricket wedged next to the fish. She picked up the dead bug by its legs. It felt warm to the touch, and smelled, faintly, like cinnamon. "Aunt Margie, we can't afford cinnamon," she protested.

"It's just a pinch."

Gentoo's eyes watered with gratitude as she licked the crusty insect, savoring every grain of seasoning from

its limp body, before dropping it on her tongue. "Do you know what an insect's favorite sport is? Cricket!" Gentoo chuckled.

"Be careful with those jokes."

Gentoo nodded and halted further chuckling. Jokes were outlawed in Sphen. Gentoo only told them to her aunt, or the seagulls on the shore.

Gentoo moved the parsley sprig to the side of her plate and lifted the trout by its tail. She gnawed a fin, and trout juice splattered onto the table.

"Gentoo, where are your manners?" her aunt said in a harsh, reprimanding tone. "You're not a bird, you know. At least not right now."

"Sorry." Gentoo carefully ripped the trout's head off its body, avoiding any more trout juice splattering, and crammed it into her mouth.

Later, after Gentoo cleaned the dishes and she and her aunt played their nightly game of dominoes, Gentoo readied for bed. It was dark outside and inside. They didn't have electric lights—a privilege only afforded the royalty of Sphen—and candle wax was expensive.

So Gentoo brushed her teeth in the dark, then slipped into her nightgown. It was a simple garment, long and pink with a frill on the collar, but not too many frills. The gown had two enormous armholes instead of sleeves.

Gentoo lay in her bed, and her aunt entered to wish her good night and to wrap the chains around her legs and arms. "Are these new?" Gentoo asked. Her aunt nodded. "Did you buy them at a chain store? Ha, ha! Get it?"

Her aunt frowned. "Always with the jokes. But are the chains comfortable?" Gentoo nodded, and her aunt Margie kissed her on the forehead. "Sleep tight and don't let the penguins bite."

Her aunt walked to the door; before she walked out, Gentoo blurted, "I love you. And that's no joke."

"I know," said her aunt with a warm smile. "And I love you, too."

After her aunt left, Gentoo couldn't fall asleep. She kept thinking of penguins. Aunt Margie had declared that the penguins should not prevent their happiness, but how could Gentoo *not* think of their wickedness? Just because she was safe and chained to her bed didn't make the reality of Sphen any less dreadful.

Before long, it was deep in the night, and the full moon was above, its beams shining through Gentoo's drape-free window. Although the Sphen clock tower was far away, in the middle of the city, its clamorous chimes could be heard across all of Sphen. They rang and rang and rang.

It was midnight.

Gentoo's body felt thick, as if mud sloshed heavily

within her. She also felt hot, an uncomfortable heat, like when you hold your fingers near a flame, not quite touching it.

Her body buckled and her face twisted, the bones reforming and the skin pulled tight, like a rubber band. Her arms extended, growing longer and then sprouting feathers. They did not tear her outfit, but instead fit perfectly through the gaping armholes in her gown. Her head whipped back and forth against her pillow, and her thin, pointy nose grew longer and wider, harder and pointier.

Gentoo didn't grow taller; instead she

shrank—not much, but a few inches here and there and especially in her legs, which were soon almost sticks, pink sticks, and her feet morphed until they had but three toes with thick webbing. The chains hung loosely around her body now, but when she sat up, they splintered in half and fell to the ground with a clang.

She hopped to the window and pecked the glass with her beak. It swung open from its hinges. A moment later Gentoo was outside, spreading her wings and soaring high above the earth, eager to join her feathery friends in the Deader Sea.

She didn't worry about penguin soldiers anymore. Instead, Gentoo basked in the beauty of flight.

"Ha, ha!" she cried. "Look at me now!"

Being a were-gull was grand!

7.

A Break in the Action

"Wait a second," I said.

I was still standing in the partly demolished zoo with the penguin caretaker. The skies had grown darker, and a chill settled in my bones.

"Who's Gentoo?" I asked. "I thought this story was about Bolt and Annika and werepenguins."

"This tale is about many things. Terrible choices. Families in peril. Irritable fruit flies."

"Irritable fruit flies?"

"Well, maybe not those," the man admitted. "Still, stories are what they are. Some characters come, some go, and others remain."

"And this were-gull girl?"

"Her role in our long and dreary tale will be made clear eventually, although not for a long eventually. I ask for your patience, although we will check in on her from time to time. But perhaps I should tell you her story and go back, way back, to before Gentoo was a winged seagull creature, when she was just a normal girl. Her small family was poor, but they were rich in love, and isn't that all that anyone really wants?"

"Actually, lots of people want to be rich in money, too. But please tell me her story."

8.
Gentoo and Her Story

Gentoo's parents had died years before, during the penguin riots, a time when people still dared fight against the Earl and his many soldiers. Gentoo had been very young, but had heard stories of brave people uniting to take a stand against their oppressors by locking the doors of the bowling alleys and refusing to hold Friday night fish fries.

That was a different time, though. No one dared fight against penguins anymore.

Her parents had been heroes, fighting to free Sphen! Still, Gentoo didn't like to think about them. It made her too sad. Maybe that's why Gentoo liked telling jokes. It was far better to laugh than to cry.

After her parents died, Gentoo went on long walks

along the shore at night. The sounds of the waves calmed her sadness and frustrations. They seemed to speak to her, as if the waves lapping and her heart beating were in rhythm, together. She had an odd bird-shaped birthmark on the bottom of her foot—Gentoo was convinced it was shaped like an eagle—and walking along the shore made it tingle.

The lock was broken on Gentoo's bedroom window, so it was easy for her to sneak out after bedtime. It was not safe to walk alone in Sphen at night, where patrolling penguin soldiers might terrorize you for no reason. But there was a small abandoned cove where hardly anyone ever went. Gentoo often walked there, alone.

Gentoo didn't enjoy keeping secrets from her aunt. She only kept two: her nightly walks, and that she didn't always clean behind her ears when bathing.

For many years, Gentoo ventured out for nightly strolls through the vacant cove, often admiring the laughs of the seagulls that danced amid the roar of the waves. Gentoo knew most people found seagulls annoying and dirty, but she loved to watch them. She loved their laughter.

One of those nights, the shore was darker than usual: the full moon, so bright it usually lit the entire city, hid behind a cloud. It was an ominous sign. The darkness concealed the seashells, and Gentoo stepped on a sharp one, yelped, and then tripped over a small log.

Gentoo landed on the sand, and when she stood up, she kicked the log because it was a stupid log that made her trip. The log groaned and Gentoo yelped again. It wasn't a log, it was a leg, and attached to the leg was an entire person.

A thin old woman lay on the ground, stinking of seaweed and fish. She wore a long white dress, torn and dirty, and waterlogged from the sea. Oddly, it did not have sleeves, but instead had two large armholes.

"Sorry for kicking you," said Gentoo. "I thought you were a log."

"Come closer," the woman rasped, her voice hoarse and gravelly and a little spooky.

"I'm fine right here," Gentoo mumbled. The cove, despite its isolation, had never scared her before. But she was scared now.

"Move closer!" the old woman shouted, a surprising strength in her voice despite her frail appearance, and Gentoo found herself stepping forward.

"Closer!" the woman shouted again, and Gentoo came closer until she knelt on the sand. "Closer!"

"I can't get any closer without banging my head on you."

"Closer!"

Gentoo did as she was told, and banged her head into

the old lady's head. Gentoo was now so near she could see blood staining the woman's dress. "What happened?"

"I was harpooned. My kind are sturdy, but not harpoon-proof. Have you ever been harpooned?"

"No."

"Consider yourself fortunate, then." The woman grabbed Gentoo's arm, pulling her closer so that they banged heads again. The woman's mouth was only millimeters from Gentoo's face. Her breath smelled like spoiled fish but, surprisingly, the smell did not disgust Gentoo. Instead, it seemed to stir something inside her, an inner yearning for . . . she didn't know what. Her birthmark tingled.

"Do you know what I am?" the woman demanded.

"An old lady who has been harpooned?" guessed Gentoo. "Who likes to wear odd, sleeveless dresses?"

"Well, yes. But I am also something else." And it was then that Gentoo noticed one of the woman's arms was not a human arm, but a bird's wing. Seeing a lady alone on the beach, harpooned, who was part bird, should have sent Gentoo running away in terror. It would have sent most people running away in terror. But something made Gentoo stay. "I have been waiting for you," rasped the old woman.

Gentoo didn't understand. Waiting for her? How?

"I knew you would be out here," the woman continued. "I could sense it. I only have a little bit of time left. I believe I am the last of my kind."

"What kind is that?"

The woman didn't answer her. "If I die here, we will be gone forever, unless I pass on my talents. But I can only pass them on to someone with a birthmark the shape of a seagull."

Gentoo patted the lady on her head. It was a gentle pat, a caring pat for a dying woman, but also an apologetic one. "I have a birthmark, but it's eagle-shaped. Sorry."

"There are no such things as eagle birthmarks!" the woman shouted, her voice once again powerful. "Yours is that of a seagull!"

She maintained her grip on Gentoo's arm so that Gentoo could not run away.

"You will take my place," said the woman. "You just need to agree. It is my final wish."

The woman was near death, that was obvious, and Gentoo knew it was impolite to deny a dying person's final wish. She shrugged and said, "I agree."

The clouds drifted from their moon-blocking ways, and the beach was aglow in light. Gentoo stared as the woman transformed, her skin rippling, her face twisting. Her one human arm grew into a second bird wing, her legs seemed to shrink, and her feet turned into pink,

three-toed, webbed seagull feet. The woman was no longer a person but a bird, although a very large bird with bushy eyebrows and feathers that sprang up on her head and looked like twin horns.

This creature, which was now the largest and ugliest seagull Gentoo had ever seen, plunged its mouth into Gentoo's neck.

Gentoo did not realize the curse of the were-gull was now hers, and hers alone. That realization would come the next evening, when the full moon rose and Gentoo flew to the sea and laughed with her new seagull friends for the first time.

9.
A Farewell to Fins

More than a year later, and hundreds of miles away, Bolt stood in front of his igloo. It wasn't much of a home, but he would miss it. He had particularly grown fond of the toaster. He considered bringing the appliance on the trip, but decided against it; they probably wouldn't pass any random electrical outlets on the journey to Sphen.

A sparkly backpack with a rainbow and a baby unicorn on it, a gift from the waves, was strapped to Bolt's back. It was packed with raw fish for the journey. Bolt knew the fish might spoil, but rotten, stinky fish tasted even better than the fresh kind.

Annika had declared she would find her own food

along the way and she was not about to eat stinky fish that had been sitting in a backpack.

"More for me and Pygo, then," said Bolt. Then he paused. "She eats fish, right?"

"And puppy chow."

The entire colony had gathered, thousands of penguins, their wings linked. Bolt had hoped to slink away, unnoticed, but that was not to be.

Last night had been the final full moon of the month. The evening had been more festive than sad, as Bolt had devoured fish and romped under the waves with his brothers and sisters. But now Bolt was nearly overwhelmed with grief. He sniffed and tried hard not to sob. If he sobbed, he feared his brother and sisters would sob, and once penguins start to cry, it's hard for them to stop. Bolt felt their sadness just like he felt all their emotions, which made his own sadness even sadder.

Ferguson spread his wings. A little shorter and fluffier than the other penguins, Ferguson was Bolt's closest penguin brother. When they had first met, in Brugaria, Ferguson had been a Baron-controlled ruffian, rummaging through a stolen bowling bag for some flounder chips. Bolt hadn't even known his name then! Ferguson laid a wing on Bolt's shoulder.

"Brothers," Ferguson barked.

Always.

Annika tapped her foot impatiently and Pygo jumped in place, yapping. "Just a few more minutes," Bolt said to Annika. "Or maybe a few more hours? Tomorrow? Maybe you need a few more days to recover?"

"I'm fine," she harrumphed, foot tapping. "Let's go."

Bolt regretted that Annika was a fast healer, but nodded. His place was not here, hiding. It was out in the world, protecting penguins. Bolt tried to keep his thoughts to himself, but his remorse and misgivings were louder than he realized, and Ferguson shook his head.

"Go," the penguin barked. "Save Sphen. It is what you are chosen to do."

But what if I wasn't? Bolt sent his words into the air and into Ferguson's head. *I can't break up our family.*

Ferguson wrapped his fins around Bolt. "Even far away, you will always be one of us."

Bolt embraced Ferguson one last time while Annika grunted, "C'mon already. The people of Sphen aren't freeing themselves."

Bolt released his hug and marched forward. It took all his strength to walk away. It was as if he was dragging a heavy brick behind him.

"Hold on," said Annika, bending down. "You're dragging a heavy brick behind you."

With a small knife, Annika cut a twine of seaweed that had twisted around a brick and Bolt's foot. When Bolt stepped forward again, the heavy physical weight had lifted, though not the emotional one.

Pygo ran in place next to Bolt and Annika, yapping and sniffing the trail ahead.

"You're a penguin, not a puppy," said Bolt, trying to reach into Pygo's mind but once again hitting a solid wall.

As Bolt continued onward, he hoped he would see Ferguson and the other penguins again but, deep in his heart, he was afraid he never would.

10.

Ransackers

Bolt's feet hurt. His sneakers had been a gift from the sea, but not a very generous gift, as the rubber on the bottoms was worn and there were holes on the sides. He knew he was doing the right thing, but that didn't make his feet hurt less, or his heart ache less.

But how could he not go? Annika was a ruthless bandit, and yet she was marching back toward Sphen to help the people and penguins. If she was going, Bolt couldn't very well stay behind.

Their journey took them from the seashore through a massive forest, across a vast field of snow, over a wide frozen lake, around a towering volcano, up and down an imposing mountain, and into a large, festering swamp.

"Let's stop for a minute," suggested Bolt, eager to rest his feet, but also to eat.

"But we've only gone through a massive forest, across a vast field of snow, over a wide frozen lake, around a towering volcano, up and down an imposing mountain, and into a large, festering swamp," protested Annika. "We haven't even reached the immeasurable firepits or the endless caverns."

Bolt sat down, anyway. He unzipped his backpack and pulled out some raw fish, tossing a silver, rubbery trout to Pygo, who sniffed it, barked, frowned, and then ate.

Bolt threw one of his fish high into the air and opened his jaws. The long fish somersaulted before landing in his mouth. His stomach growled with delight. Or maybe that was Pygo, growling at a squirrel in a tree. Regardless, Bolt swallowed the fish whole. "Delicious."

"Disgusting, you mean," said Annika.

She sprang to her left, her movements so nimble and quick that Bolt barely had time to register her spring, let alone the knife flash that followed. Annika held up her blade, a lizard impaled on its tip. "A much tastier lunch than some nasty fish," she announced.

Soon, the lizard was roasting over the flames of a small fire. "Sorry for the pungent smell of roasted lizard," said Annika as the gag-inducing fumes wafted through the air.

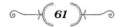

Few odors are stronger than that of burnt iguana skin.

Now it was Bolt's turn to groan. "Disgusting."

But Annika appeared to enjoy her meal. And a few minutes later, after stomping out the fire, the trio were on their way again.

Bandits are trained to walk silently, and Annika was a superb bandit. She walked as if on air. Somehow she even avoided leaving footprints in the snow. Bolt, on the other hand, seemed to kick every piece of rubble, crack every pane of ice, and leave prints twice as big as his feet.

"You'd make a lousy bandit," snapped Annika. Bolt had no intention of becoming a bandit, so he didn't mind that he'd make a lousy one.

They continued to walk silently, or at least without talking, because only Annika actually walked silently. They ambled through the immeasurable firepits, although they turned out to be quite measurable and were crossed in about a half hour. Eventually they reached a gravel road, but one with well-worn wheel marks and hoofprints upon it.

They were finally near civilization. Bolt bit his fingernails. He suddenly felt sensitive about his bushy eyebrows, alabaster skin, and horn-spiked hair.

He slowed down until Annika snapped, "Why are you slowing down?" She shook her head. "No one cares about

your eyebrows, white skin, and horn hair, you know."

"That's not why I slowed down," muttered Bolt, but Annika just rolled her eyes at him.

Soon they saw a wooden post sticking out of the ground with a wooden board nailed to it. Words were written on the board with splotchy white paint:

Welcome to Fischerdorf
Population: ~~*1126*~~
~~*482*~~
~~*156*~~
Way less than that
Warning: No penguins allowed, and that means you!
(If you are a penguin)

Bolt put his hands on his hips. One of his big toes popped out of a sneaker hole. "Can you believe that sign? It's awful."

"I know. They can't even count how many people live here," agreed Annika.

"Not *that!*" He pointed at the words *No penguins allowed.* "That's penguin discrimination!" His face flushed and he was suddenly filled with a nearly overwhelming urge to run into the town and start pecking people.

Oh, if only he had a beak just then!

"They probably don't really mean it," said Annika. "Let's check out the town. Maybe they have a restaurant. I'm so hungry, I could eat a penguin." She smiled, sheepishly. "Not that I would. It's just an expression."

"It's not a very nice expression," Bolt grumbled, before turning back to the sign and counting to twenty.

Sometimes, when he had still lived at the Oak Wilt Home for Unwanted Boys, one of the boys would get upset. It was easy to get upset when you discovered dead roaches in your meat loaf at dinnertime, or woke up in the middle of the night to find moths landing on your head. "Count to twenty," Bolt would say, knowing that after you had counted to twenty, the anger would subside.

Now, infused with his werepenguin blood, Bolt found himself counting to twenty quite often.

Bolt hated that part of himself, the angry evil werepenguin part. Werepenguins are prone to raising armies, ransacking seafood shacks, and causing trouble. Bolt's evil inclinations often churned through his veins, urging him to the dark side of werepenguin-ism.

Anger is good.

"What? Did you say something?" he asked Annika.

"No. Come on. I'm hungry." She rushed ahead, toward the town.

Bolt shook his head. He was hearing things. But that

voice had sounded so close! It must just be his nerves. Going far away to fight a werepenguin was quite nerve-racking.

Bolt suggested Pygo wait outside the town, where she wouldn't be seen, remembering the sign's warning. Annika thought he was overreacting, but agreed.

As Bolt escorted Pygo into the forest, he reached into her mind, hoping to pluck her thoughts. But the wall inside her brain was as impenetrable as ever. "What's blocking me?" he asked her, but Pygo merely nuzzled Bolt's hand. Bolt reached down and scratched behind her ears, or at least where her ears would be if penguins had ears. Pygo growled happily.

A minute or so later, Annika and Bolt entered the town, which was just around the bend. They followed a dirt path around a few shops. The stores were small and needed painting, but the only thing remarkable about the town was the silence. It felt deserted.

Bolt looked in the store windows: one store sold drums, one sold firecrackers, and one sold chain saws. They only made the silence more disturbing.

They spotted a small diner. It smelled like freshly made pancakes. Once, Bolt would have been delighted at the aroma of pancakes. Now it merely made him hope they made pancakes from dried fish blubber, but he doubted they did.

They heard a murmuring of people, agitated whispers and a few sobs mixed in. They followed the sounds, walking past the diner and down an alley between a discomfitingly quiet trombone store and an eerily silent gong shop.

A group of twenty or thirty people had gathered in front of a seafood shop, or at least what was left of one. It was as if a hurricane had twirled inside the place, shattering the plate-glass window and scattering ice and fish bones into the street. Inside, light fixtures hung loosely from the ceiling, attached by only a few dangling wires, and shelves had been toppled.

"They come down from Sphen, you know," said a woman in the crowd. "Why won't those horrible beasts leave us alone?"

"Not all penguins are horrible," responded a man.

"Name one penguin that is not a vicious ransacker of fish stores," the woman demanded.

"I can't, but that's only because I don't know any penguins by name," said the man.

Bolt could barely speak. He had not seen evil penguins for a long time, and he was still far from Sphen. Could the Earl's powers reach all the way out here?

How powerful was this earl?

We are all powerful.

"What did you say?" Bolt gasped.

"Nothing," said Annika. "Shh!"

Bolt shook his head. Just more nerves rattling in his head. "We should get out of here," he said, uneasy at being so near so many penguin haters.

"Let me steal some food from the diner first, I'm starving."

"Steal?"

"I'm a bandit. Bandits steal stuff."

Bolt knew it was in Annika's nature to rob, just like it was in Bolt's werepenguin nature to want to rule the world. But she needed to curb that impulse, just like he curbed his own evil desires. "You can't go around taking things all the time."

Annika's smile drooped. "But I can keep these, right?" Annika thrust her hand into her jacket pocket and removed a purse, a wallet, a silver wristwatch, a rubber duck, and two fuzzy banana slippers. "People staring at broken sea-food stores aren't paying attention to their pockets."

"Put them back," Bolt demanded.

"But . . ."

Bolt gave Annika a harsh stare. She sighed and dashed into the crowd of seafood-store mourners. When she returned a minute later she was empty-handed. "I really could have used a pair of fuzzy banana slippers," she said with a sigh. She marched toward the restaurant. "Anyway, let's eat. And *you're* paying."

Luckily, Bolt had some coins in his pocket: they had been in his pants when the pants first washed ashore.

"They should outlaw penguins," said one of the women who was standing near the seafood shop, loudly. "The world would be better without them."

"You can say that again!" said another woman.

"OK. They should outlaw . . ."

Bolt blocked out the rest of the woman's voice. Feeling his anger returning, he clenched his fists and counted to twenty. When that didn't help, he counted to twenty again.

The anger finally subsided after he counted to 280.

11.
You've Been Warned

Bolt and Annika sat at a small booth inside the diner. There was only one other customer—a man at the counter sipping coffee. They paid no attention to him.

After sitting for a few moments, Annika slipped a spoon into her jacket pocket. Bolt cleared his throat; Annika grunted and returned the spoon to the table.

They read their menus, and Annika's disappointment in not stealing the diner cutlery quickly gave way to joy. She kept pointing and smiling. "They have fried chicken! Sausage! Toasted meat strudel!"

None of that sounded appetizing to Bolt, who closed his menu with a frown. "Not even a single raw trout," he grumbled.

A waitress approached them. The short, round woman gave them a friendly smile. A rainbow-colored bandanna held back her bright red hair, matching her rosy cheeks. "Welcome, kids," she said, handing them each a glass of water. "I haven't seen you two here before. You must be from out of town."

"We're passing through," said Bolt.

"We love all strangers here!" She seemed so genuine and friendly, Bolt regretted leaving Pygo outside. Maybe he had been wrong assuming everyone hated penguins in the town. "We love all strangers," she repeated, "that is, unless that stranger is a penguin or someone who is traveling with a penguin. Then we hate them."

Bolt lost his grin. His voice turned into a low growl. "Not all penguins ransack and terrorize, you know."

"And not all rattlesnakes will bite your toes, but that doesn't mean I'm about to keep a rattlesnake in my sock drawer," the woman declared. She pointed to the menu. "Now, what can I get you kids?" She stared at Bolt for a moment. "Hmmm," she said, tapping her chin. "Horn hair, bushy eyebrows, and pale skin. You remind me of something."

"I can't imagine what that could be," said Bolt, shifting nervously. The woman shrugged, and Annika ordered one of everything on the menu. When the woman walked away, Bolt groused, "The Earl is giving penguins a bad name."

"You'll stop the Earl, and things will change."

"I hope so," answered Bolt, confident neither that the rampant hatred of penguins would end so easily, nor that he would defeat such a powerful werepenguin.

The shadow of concern and worry cast over Bolt was soon replaced by the smell of sausages. The waitress returned with plates of pancakes and bacon, French toast, and blueberry muffins.

"This looks delicious," said Annika. "Hopefully it'll get us all the way to Sphen."

The waitress, rather than setting the plates gently on the table, dropped them. They shattered on the table and the floor, and some shattered on the table and fell on the floor, where they shattered again. Broken ceramic plate pieces mixed with maple syrup, and pieces of glass swam in orange juice.

The waitress stared at Bolt and Annika, her mouth agape, her arms shaking. When a sound finally emerged from her throat, it was a tiny high-pitched squeal, like helium from a balloon. Then the squeal became words, frightened words. Her lips trembled and she gurgled, "Y-you sp-spoke of Sph-Sph-Sph . . . ?"

"Sphen?" guessed Bolt. The woman nodded. "That's where we're going."

The woman's eyes bulged with fear. "You cannot! You must not!" The woman continued shaking, and her voice

rose into an even higher squeak. Bolt's legs began to shake, too. "They say the Earl is as evil as a rabid vampire bat, as ferocious as an irritated ostrich, and as power-hungry as a panda."

"Few things are as ferocious as an irritated ostrich," Annika muttered. "But you sort of lost me with the panda."

"Panda bears are the most power-hungry creatures in the world," said the woman, still trembling. "But the Sph-Sph-Sph . . ."

"Sphen?" guessed Bolt.

". . . penguins are worse than pandas. They say the penguins will twist off your ears, and eat you with their morning granola."

Annika crossed her arms. "They don't even have granola in Sphen," she said with a huff. "I know. I've been there."

"You've been to Sph-Sph-Sph . . . ?"

"Sphen?" said Bolt.

The woman screamed, gasped, and then gasped again. Her eyes rolled back into her head and she fell over. She landed amid the fallen food and broken plates. She lay on the ground, unmoving, in a small puddle of maple syrup.

"I think she fainted," said Annika.

Bolt's heart pounded and his arms twitched with fright as the woman's words lingered in his head. He had seen many people faint when talking about the Baron of

Brugaria, but he had never sensed as much terror as the waitress had shown when talking about Sphen.

Bolt slid out of the booth and knelt next to the waitress to make sure she was breathing. She was. As Bolt checked her pulse, arms still twitching, a finger tapped his shoulder. The man who had been sitting at the counter stood over Bolt. He was thin, his black hair stood nearly straight up, and he had sagging bags under his eyes. He twitched even more than Bolt. "I couldn't help overhearing you are traveling to Sph-Sph-Sph . . ."

"Sphen," said Bolt, now getting a bit tired of finishing everyone's sentences.

The man spoke in a furtive whisper, although there were no other people in the room to hear. "I'm heading there. I'm not going *into* Sph-Sph-Sph, well, you know. Going into that cursed city would be insane. But I'm riding near it. I can drop you off at the edge of the Calamity Mountains. It's just a short walk down from there."

"Thank you," said Bolt. He bit his lip and added, cautiously, "We have another friend with us. She's waiting outside. Can she come, too?"

The man nodded, and continued whispering. "Sure, but you'll all have to sit in the back of the wagon. There's no room in the cab up front. But be warned. If you enter Sph-Sph-Sph . . ."

"Sphen," said Annika.

". . . then you will never leave alive," finished the man.

"We can take care of ourselves," Annika hissed, and then adjusted one of her bobby pins.

"Perhaps," said the man. "Or perhaps Sph-Sph-Sph . . ."

"Sphen," said Annika with a sigh.

". . . will take care of you."

12.
Inside Annika's Head

The wagon bounced violently every time its wheels hit a pothole along the dirt road, which was pretty much constantly. Annika also bounced, landing on her back with a BANG! on the wagon's hard wooden bed. Again. And again. Andagainandagainandagainandagain.

Annika took a sip of cider from the canteen she held. The waitress at the diner had recovered from her fainting as they were leaving, learned they were leaving for Sphen, fainted again, recovered again, and then given them a basket of food for the trip and two canteens of cider.

While providing a basket of food was generous, her reasoning that "Everyone should have a final meal" wasn't reassuring.

Annika removed a golden pocket watch from her

pocket. She had plucked it from the driver of the wagon. She didn't care what time it was—it was dark, late, and they'd arrive in Sphen the next day, or so the man had said, or rather he'd said they would arrive in Sph-Sph-Sph the next day, and Bolt had finished his sentence. Annika had swiped the watch because she was a bandit, and that's what bandits did. She didn't regret that; bandits didn't regret stealing things.

But there were other things she regretted, things much bigger than swiping a watch.

How could she not feel regret? Sure, bandits stole and kidnapped, but they always kept their word, at least usually, and they didn't cheat, unless they were losing, and even then, only sometimes. Bandits had honor. And nothing about what she was doing was honorable.

But what choice did she have but to lie to her best friend?

She told herself that bandits weren't supposed to have non-bandit friends at all. *No friends, unless they are bandits!* That was not only written in *The Code of the Bandit* but starred, circled, and underlined. Bandits had to stay loyal to one another, and friends outside the clan could put a bandit in a sticky situation. Hadn't that been why she had gone to Sphen in the first place, because kidnapping and robbing the people of Brugaria had seemed so wrong,

after the bandits had befriended so many of them?

So she and her father had left the Brugarian forest in search of new carriages to rob and kidnapping victims who weren't also dinner guests. They had robbed two carriages and were preparing to rob another when a gang of Sphen penguins discovered them.

If she had been alone, Annika could have escaped. But her papa had been too slow—was he getting old?—and Annika had doubled back to help him. She had then been easily overpowered. Annika and her father had been thrown into separate cells in the dungeons below Sphen Castle.

If Annika had been able to pick her lock, as she had told Bolt she had done, she might have been able to escape and then rescue her father. But Sphen locks are unpickable. Everyone knows that.

The penguin soldiers were cruel, and so were the human prison guards. Annika told one of the guards about Bolt. She hoped the guard might stop yelling at her if he knew Annika was friends with a werepenguin. Instead, the man poked her in the eye and hauled her into the Earl's grand throne room.

She could still picture the scene vividly:

The Earl sneered from his gilded throne, a large throne for an incredibly large, powerful man. His iron fist

gleamed from the sunlight pouring in through a series of windows at the very top of the room, positioned to let in the glow of the full moon at night.

Annika eyed the Earl's fist warily. She had heard he could cut down a tree or break down a wall with a single swat. She had been warned never to give him a high five.

A pile of dead fish lay by the Earl's feet and he sucked on a fish carcass as Annika knelt between two penguin soldiers. He peered down at Annika with deep red eyes nestled under two enormous bushy eyebrows. His hair was twisted up to resemble horns, and between the hair horns sat a large golden crown studded with rubies. A long black beard grew from his pasty face; the beard was also twisted into two horns. "One of my prison guards says you are friends with Bolt Wattle?"

"Molt Twaddle? Never heard of him," said Annika,

chin up and defiant. Bandits never gave information when imprisoned, at least not willingly.

The Earl sucked on another fish, and some fish slime coated his beard, which he didn't wipe off. "Do you think I'm a fool?"

"I can't say. We don't know each other very well." She puffed out her chest and glared at the Earl.

The Earl frowned and flicked a fish bone. It bounced off Annika's cheek. She didn't even flinch. "I need you to bring Bolt Wattle to me."

"I don't know who you're talking about," sniffed Annika.

The Earl pounded his iron fist onto the armrest of his throne, and the wood splintered in half. "I don't have patience for this. Bring in the prisoner!" Two more penguin soldiers entered the throne room, dragging a dirty, tall prisoner behind them.

"Papa!" gasped Annika. She had not seen him since they had been locked up, and though it had been only a few days, he already looked weak and thin. "What have they done to you?"

"Nothing, my darling Annika," he said, but the bruises on his face told a different story.

"You will help me," said the Earl to Annika, and then he pointed at one of the tuxedo-clad men in the room. "Take the prisoner's neck measurements." The man rushed over, his wing-tip tuxedo shoes slapping against the marble

floor, his boutonniere flopping to the ground. He held a measuring tape, and wrapped it carefully around Vigi Lambda's neck. "Seventeen and a half," said the man.

"Are you measuring me for a new bow tie?" asked Vigi Lambda, flashing a smile. "I could use a new fancy bow tie."

"We're measuring you for a noose," said the Earl, sucking on another fish. Vigi's grin faded away. "We will hang you at the end of the month. That is, unless your daughter brings Bolt Wattle to me first."

"What do you want with Bolt?" Annika asked, her voice higher and shriller than she liked, her defiant glare gone.

"That's for me to know and you to find out." The Earl picked up another fish carcass and sucked on its fin. Then he flicked the skeleton at Annika again, but it missed her.

"I don't know where he is," moaned Annika, trying to keep the panic from her voice.

"Not my problem," said the Earl. "Bring him here, or your father will swing from the gallows."

Annika had considered attacking the Earl right then and there. Maybe she could have defeated him. A bandit needed confidence, and Annika had lots of confidence. But a bandit also needed to be realistic. You could be confident that you could kidnap an entire village at once. But then, to be realistic, where would you put them all?

And who would be left to pay the ransom?

Besides, if she brought Bolt back, that didn't mean she had to turn him over. Bolt was mighty and strong. Well, he was neither of those things, but Bolt Wattle the were-penguin was not the same as Bolt Wattle the person.

Maybe he and Annika could fight. Together.

Yes. That's what she would do. She vowed to herself to fight. With Bolt.

So Annika had left the city, but with no idea where she was going. She had wandered the mountains outside Sphen for half a day, lost, when she heard something growling behind a tree. At first, she had thought it was a wolf. Or a stray dog. She had approached carefully, her knife clutched in one hand, and a bobby pin in the other. Bobby pins made poor weapons, at least compared to knives, but she gripped it anyway.

A penguin leapt out from the foliage, barking. Annika thought she would need to fight this penguin, but the bird didn't seem vicious. It nuzzled its head against Annika's leg, which was not normal penguin behavior. It seemed harmless. Friendly, even.

Penguins weren't allowed in the mountains, so Annika assumed the penguin was running away from Sphen, too. And the penguin growled happily when Annika scratched under its neck, which was very cute.

The rest of Annika's adventure had been exactly as she

had described it to Bolt. The penguin seemed to under-stand what Annika wanted to do, and had known how to find Bolt. She didn't know how the penguin knew.

When Annika found Bolt, she considered telling him the truth. "My papa is trapped, and if you come with me and turn yourself in, he'll be freed. Although, actually, I thought we could fight the Earl instead. Honest!" What if Bolt didn't believe her? What if he had refused to come? She decided she just couldn't take the chance.

But Bolt would come if Annika appealed to his love of penguins. Bolt might not have been brave or cunning, but he was selfless and true to his word.

Besides, she wasn't lying to Bolt, not exactly. She just wasn't telling him the entire story, and that wasn't the same thing as being untruthful.

Another pothole interrupted Annika's thoughts, and her body leapt up, and cider spilled on her lederhosen. Up above, the moon rose.

Bolt stirred, opening one eye and looking up into the sky. "Good thing there is no full moon tonight," he yawned. "I don't want to turn into a werepenguin. I just want to sleep." Then he added, "The moon was full every night in Brugaria. Wasn't that strange?" He yawned and closed his eye, and was soon back asleep.

Annika nodded, regretting yet another secret she had kept from Bolt.

13.
It's All Downhill from Here

The horses trotted through the night, the quakes and thuds of the wagon waking Bolt every few minutes. His mind raced with images of rampaging penguins. He saw the Earl in his head as clearly as he had seen it in Pygo's, right before he had been shut off from her memories: the massive face, the immense power that radiated from him, and the bits of fish in his beard. The closer they got to Sphen, the more real that picture seemed to become.

Werepenguins are meant to rule! The world is ours!

His eyes opened with a start. "Who said that?" But no one was there. His brain was playing tricks again, his worry creeping up.

And he had plenty to worry about! Not only was the Earl powerful, but Bolt remembered how tempted he had been to fight alongside the Baron all those months ago, and how easily the Baron had twisted Bolt's mind, bringing out the evilness from within Bolt.

Bolt was stronger now. But was he strong enough to resist that temptation?

With all these thoughts and worries in his head, Bolt remained awake for quite some time. But eventually, he fell into an uneasy sleep. He dreamed of monsters and were-creatures and bowling penguins.

Bolt awoke again when his body flew up in the air after the wagon wheels hit a particularly cavernous pothole. He opened his eyes and saw sunlight.

"Good morning, Sleeping Beauty," said Annika with a yawn. "Pygo and I woke up three dozen potholes ago." Bolt wondered if his eyes were as bloodshot as hers.

They rode along a narrow winding road through a mountain range, but the horses soon slowed and stopped. They must be near Sphen: Bolt could feel an angry and violent cloud of penguin hatred bubbling in the air, the corrupted thoughts of thousands of birds. He tried to sense the Earl, perhaps pick out the source of all that disturbance, but the hatred was so thick he could barely wade through it. He coughed and dislodged a nugget of loathsomeness from his throat, but there were plenty of evil

nuggets of loathsomeness still hovering in the air around him.

"I feel cold," said Annika, as if even she could sense the dense, frigid despair around them. Only Pygo seemed unaffected, panting and bouncing on the wagon bed.

The horses neighed and snorted, their legs marching in place. They did not like stopping here.

The driver shouted to the group from his cab up front. "This is as close as I get. If you're foolish enough to go to Sph-Sph-Sph . . ."

"Sphen," said Bolt.

The man nodded. ". . . then get off now. The faster I get out of here, the better. Not better for you, mind you. No, things are going to be horrible for you pretty much from here on out."

Annika leapt easily off the side of the wagon, but Bolt had to carefully wobble himself over, as did Pygo. No sooner had they touched the ground than the man cracked his reins, and the horses broke into a gallop, their hooves spraying dirt behind them.

For a moment, Bolt wished he was still on the wagon, but the moment passed. It was far too late to change his mind now. He was just glad Annika was with him. She made him feel braver than he was.

Even with her here, though, Bolt felt a wave of fear washing over him as he gazed across the edge of the

mountain and the grayish hue that floated above the city. Sphen was bigger than Bolt had pictured, with hundreds of houses and buildings stretching out between the mountain and, on the other side, the Deader Sea. Every house was gray. The trees were also gray. And the lawns. And the flowers.

"So this is Sph-Sph-Sph . . ." Bolt said, now unable to finish the word himself. "Looks like a happy place." He gulped. "For a goblin." Bolt would have been far happier fighting a goblin than entering this city.

He bit his bottom lip as the group began their descent down the mountain and into the gray land below.

14.
Gentoo and The Beautiful Seagull

On the other side of Sphen, Gentoo stood on her family's small fishing boat, *The Beautiful Seagull*, which her aunt had named after Gentoo. It was Gentoo's job to untie the nets, secure the tiller, and raise the mainsail, although her aunt would cast the nets, set the course, and take care of most of the smaller details. At that moment, however, her aunt stood on the pier, talking to two members of the human pier patrol and three penguin soldiers.

The pier patrol officers wore the same traditional Sphen uniforms as all the human traitors who worked for the Earl: black tuxedos with tails, white bow ties, and cummerbunds. They looked like penguins from far away, which, Gentoo supposed, was the point. Their black tuxedo shoes, however, made chasing criminals difficult, and their boutonnieres tended to fall off. But, even Gentoo had to admit, they must be the world's best-dressed patrol officers.

To complete the outfit, the men wore orange beaks strapped around their heads. The beaks were not just for show, however. They were made of wood and could be removed and used as a weapon. Most of the people of Sphen had been bonked on the head by a wooden beak for some reason or another, at least once.

The real penguins, like all the penguins in Sphen, scowled, their contempt for humans practically oozing from their blubber. That contempt was as much a part of their uniform as the tall black bearskin hats on their heads and the black sashes across their chests.

Gentoo knew her aunt was upset. She could not hear the conversation, but her aunt kept pounding her fists, which she did when she was upset, or when she was flattening pizza crust.

Gentoo scanned the pier. Other fisherfolk, near their own boats, were involved in similarly animated conversations with beak-clad pier patrolmen and their penguin masters. One fisherman, someone Gentoo didn't recognize but who seemed younger than most of the others,

looked particularly upset. He didn't pound his fists when he talked, but he jabbed his finger, and one of those jabs accidentally poked a penguin. Gentoo winced even before the penguin's mighty wing crashed down on the man, who yelped and fell to the ground. His yelp reminded Gentoo, and all the fishing people nearby, that disobedience would not be tolerated.

Gentoo turned away and looked over the water. The sea was where she longed to be, with the fish below and the clouds above. A group of seagulls skimmed the sea surface and each dove down, suddenly and without warning, before flying back up carrying a small bug or perhaps a fish in a beak. Gentoo was jealous. She closed her eyes and greeted them, speaking to the seagulls telepathically, and they replied, "Ha! Ha!"

A seagull always sounds like it is laughing, and they often are. Seagulls have wonderful senses of humor. It was one of the many reasons Gentoo loved them. It was also why she loved telling them jokes, even if jokes were illegal in Sphen.

Gentoo spread her arms wide, and birds landed on them, their talons clinging to her limbs, their wings beating against her face. She reached her mind out to other birds, and they also flew to her and sat on her arms. Two more birds, and then two more, three on her shoulders,

two on her head, and others squeezing in wherever they could. More birds came, more and more and more, but there was no more room on Gentoo, so many flapped just above her.

Hello, my friends! She spoke to them silently. *If you call a gull over the sea a seagull, what do you call a gull over the bay?*

It was an old joke, but it still made her giggle.

The birds called back aloud—garbled and a little confusing, since seagulls have a hard time keeping a train of thought—*Ha, ha! A bagel! Get it? Bay-gull? Ha, ha! We love you! Zebra-lined monkey breath!*

Gentoo closed her eyes and returned their affection, ignoring the zebra monkey thing, as the breeze from their wings blew back her long white hair.

"What are you doing?" Aunt Margie's voice cut through her revelry, and Gentoo opened her eyes to see her aunt still standing on the pier watching her, frowning. The human traitors and the penguin soldiers also stared, gasping at the spectacle of a girl covered by seagulls.

For a second, Gentoo panicked. No one but her aunt knew of her special abilities. What would happen to her if her secret was discovered?

But the humans laughed, apparently amused that a young girl was being attacked by seagulls. The penguins laughed as well, which was unfortunate because their laughs

sounded like out-of-tune trumpets. This merely made the human officers laugh louder.

"Help me get this boat out to sea," said Aunt Margie as the gulls fluttered away. "The penguins have raised their fish taxes again. It's getting harder and harder to find fish! But heaven help us if we don't meet their quota."

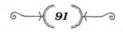

15.

The Sphevil of Sphen

Bolt wasn't quite sure how they managed to climb down the mountain. But they did, although twice Bolt had to grab Annika's arm to keep from falling.

At the very bottom of the mountain was a dirt path. Bolt took a deep breath. The air seemed to curdle from the harsh odor of dead fish. It was so thick, Bolt's eyes watered, and so did his mouth. He longed to run into the city and start licking things, basking in the rich fishy-ness.

"I forgot how much this place stinks," said Annika, pinching her nostrils.

"Isn't it wonderful?" asked Bolt, licking his lips. The delightful stench almost calmed his fragile nerves.

Bark! Bark!

Two penguin soldiers approached, their tall bearskin caps wiggling on their heads as they waddled closer. Bolt froze, as did Annika. Bolt's heart thundered inside his chest. Pygo was too busy sniffing a flower on the ground to notice.

"Just act like you belong," Annika whispered to Bolt. Bolt nodded and smiled. He whistled merrily. Annika jabbed him in the ribs. "What are you doing?" she hissed.

"Acting like I belong?"

"Then don't whistle. People in Sphen don't whistle, and especially not merrily." The soldiers neared, Bolt's fear ebbing thanks to Annika's cool facade. Bolt smiled and Annika again jabbed him in the ribs. "What are you doing? People in Sphen don't smile either." Bolt frowned as deeply as he could. "Better."

The penguin soldiers glared at Bolt, and also at Annika and at Pygo, who had stopped sniffing flowers and now stared at the soldiers, her face seemingly frozen in terror. One of the penguins barked, viciously.

You didn't need to speak penguin to understand what the soldier wanted, although Bolt did speak penguin:

What are you doing here? Humans aren't allowed outside the city. And neither are penguins. And why is this penguin sitting like a puppy dog?

The other penguin barked, just as viciously. *Let's*

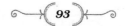

throw them all in the dungeon. I don't like puppies.

Annika stood, ready to pounce, her hand moving to the knife in her belt. But Bolt reached inside the heads of the two soldiers, to calm them. Unlike Pygo, they did not have impenetrable walls in their heads.

But Bolt sort of wished they had.

The hostility! The anger! It was so thick! Bolt had to peel back onion-like layers of hate inside their heads, each layer revealing another layer of terrible thoughts. These penguins would do anything for the Earl: maim and pummel; spit and snort; ransack seafood stores and fisheries.

Bolt couldn't peel past the oniony layers fast enough, layer after layer after layer.

There. A soft lining of warmth, of true, natural penguin-ness. These penguins were still penguins underneath everything. With enough time, he could dice those oniony layers and restore their peaceful natures, but for now, he just needed these soldiers to leave them alone.

You are wanted back at the castle. Go!

The penguins looked around, as if trying to determine who spoke to them. But they didn't move.

They are having a fish stick party at the castle! Hurry!

That seemed to jar them. The penguins looked at each other, barked, and turned. In an instant they were waddling back toward the city as fast as they could.

"Nice job," said Annika, removing her hand from her knife.

Bolt wiped a bead of sweat from his forehead. "That was more difficult than I thought it would be." He smiled, so as not to show his worry. If he struggled controlling two penguins, how could he stop a horde of them?

Annika had already taken a step forward and Bolt followed. "Let's go, girl," he said to Pygo. He didn't hear a response. Bolt spun around.

Pygo was gone.

Bolt scanned the area looking for her, but saw no sign of their penguin friend. "She was just sniffing a flower a moment ago." He closed his eyes to sense her, but felt nothing.

"Maybe she ran away?" Annika guessed.

"Maybe." Bolt couldn't shake the memory of that look of terror he had seen in Pygo's eyes. It was the same terror he had seen in the eyes of the waitress at the diner. "Should we look for her?"

"No. It might be better if Pygo stayed away," said Annika. "She's a penguin deserter. I don't know what they do to runaway penguins in Sphen."

Bolt nodded. He and Annika would be locked up if they were caught, but Pygo's penalty could be far harsher. "I just hope she's OK."

"We're the ones entering Sphen," said Annika. "I think we have more to worry about than Pygo does."

Bolt nodded, ignoring his trembling legs as he followed Annika down the path and toward the cruel, sad city of Sph-Sph-Sphen.

16.
Inside Pygo's Head

17.
Unwelcome Strangers

The path grew colder and the winds fiercer inside the city limits of Sphen. It was late afternoon by the time Annika and Bolt walked along its streets, past tall concrete buildings, pockmarked and gray, the winds biting at their faces. Bolt didn't mind so much; he could imagine far worse things biting his face.

They passed people, but not many, all wearing gray wool coats and fuzzy black Russian ushanka hats. The people walked slowly, as if weighed down by years of oppression and horror. As Annika had said, no one smiled or whistled merrily, or even looked capable of smiling or being merry.

While the people seemed grim, the penguins soldiers, which were everywhere, were even more so. They snarled.

They snapped. They glared with beady, violent eyes. Bolt hunched as he walked, lowering his head so as not to draw attention to himself.

"It's so quiet," he said. "It's like everyone is training to become mimes."

"Was that a joke?" asked Annika warily. "Jokes are forbidden here."

They turned a corner and entered an open-air market. The crowds were denser now, people packed together except for a splattering of open circles around each penguin soldier. The people didn't dare crowd a penguin. At least there was noise here, compared to the dreary silence of most of the city, as merchants sold their wares. But the place still seemed drab and depressing.

"Welcome to Sphen, strangers," said an old woman with leathery, wrinkled skin standing behind a counter that was lined with buckets of ice. "I know you are strangers because you do not walk as if weighed down by years of oppression and horror." She pointed at one of her ice buckets. "Would you care to buy dinner?"

"All you eat is ice?" asked Annika, squinting at the buckets.

"Of course not, dear. I sell fish." She dug her hand into a bucket, wiggled it under the cubes, and then lifted a thin, tiny guppy. "A fine guppy. Just fifty flumkins."

Bolt didn't have any flumkins, or even know what a

flumkin was, but it sounded like a lot of money for just one guppy. "You're joking, right?"

"Are you accusing me of breaking the law and joking?" demanded the woman, and Bolt quickly apologized. "With the terrible fish shortage, I'm lucky to have seafood today, at any price." She leaned over. "But come back tomorrow. I may have a sardine." She rubbed her fingers together. "Although it won't come cheap, honey."

Bolt and Annika bid goodbye to the old woman and continued walking into the market. Bolt was horrified at hearing about a fish shortage, and surprised. The Sphen air stank of fish! How was a shortage possible?

They passed another merchant's table with a sign advertising *Pure Gold Jewelry*, but Bolt noticed all the samples on the table were black: black necklaces, black earrings, and even black diamond rings.

"The jewelers paint all their gold," explained Annika. "Colors are illegal in Sphen. They are even worse than telling jokes."

As Bolt looked around, he now realized why everything appeared so drab. Not only did all the people wear black and gray overcoats and hats, but all the street signs were black-and-white. Near them, a rug merchant sold only black rugs and white rugs. A games dealer offered only chess sets. A fruit and vegetable market provided white onions, cauliflower, black-eyed peas, and really old, blackened bananas.

They continued walking, eventually leaving the market behind, and heading farther and farther into the city. The streets became grayer and grayer and the air got colder and colder and the odor of dead fish grew smellier and smellier. The number of penguin soldiers grew thicker, too, seemingly now on every corner. They seemed to sneer more, and glare more, and the people looked even more miserable.

Bolt and Annika crossed the street and passed a saloon named the Tipsy Penguin. The swinging saloon doors revealed a dark, smoky interior. Bolt spied a long wooden bar inside, and a small room next to it. He caught but a brief glimpse, but that glimpse left him feeling queasy. That small room was filled with penguins sitting at a table, playing poker.

Bolt pressed his lips together to keep from crying out. Penguins didn't play cards! Penguins didn't gamble! It was an abomination, and it took all of Bolt's inner strength not to run inside the saloon and bark at the birds: *Have you no decency?* He counted to twenty.

He was getting tired of counting to twenty.

They continued on, and after a few minutes, Annika gulped. "The Sphen Castle is over there." She pointed to

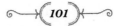

a tall spire rising up only a few blocks ahead. Bolt was the one who usually gulped, so hearing Annika gulp was unsettling. If something made Annika, the world's greatest bandit, nervous, it must be something truly worth being nervous about.

Every part of Bolt screamed: *Turn around! Go! Run away! Bolt, Bolt!* But he ignored the panic building inside him and continuing plodding forward, although the weight of oppression and horror had grown so heavy that each step was a struggle, as if he was pulling a cinder block behind him.

"Hold on, you're pulling a cinder block behind you," said Annika, bending down and cutting a small rope that had wrapped around Bolt's leg, and was tied around a cinder block. "What's with you and dragging heavy objects? First a brick, and now this."

But Bolt couldn't answer. His mouth didn't seem to work, so thick was the cloud of fear and terror blowing into him from the castle ahead.

No Humans Allowed

As Bolt and Annika neared the castle they saw signs posted on the sides of buildings or standing on metal posts. They all said the same thing:

Stop. Go back. No humans* allowed in the castle, or around the castle, or even looking at the castle.

*Traitorous human patrol officers in tuxedos excluded.

Annika hesitated for a moment. It would be easy enough to shout out, get caught, get brought to the Earl, turn Bolt in, and free her father. She even opened her mouth to cry out, before slamming it shut, a little too fast, and biting her tongue. Sure, she was a bandit. Sure, a bandit looked out for other bandits before anything else. But one look at Bolt, her best friend, and she lowered her head. She would fight, as she had vowed to do.

They would hatch a plan. They would find a way into the palace. And they would defeat the Earl, and free her father and all the people and penguins of Sphen.

Succeeding was highly unlikely, but a bandit befriending a werepenguin was highly unlikely, too.

She hid in the shadows with Bolt, walking as quietly as they could to avoid detection. For Annika that was very quietly, but for Bolt, less so. Now they knelt behind two aluminum trash cans at the lip of an alley, across the street from a black iron gate that wrapped around a moat that in turn wrapped around the tall and majestic Sphen Castle. The water in the moat was ink black.

The palace was grand and imposing, with a large clock tower and a spire that rose so high it seemed to disappear into the gray clouds above. Just being this close to that building sent shivers of horror, regret, and guilt running up and down Annika's spine.

The penguin soldiers were as thick as the stench of fish in the air, a dozen of them marching up and down the drawbridge, back and forth.

"That's the only way in," whispered Annika. Bolt watched the soldiers. Getting past them seemed impossible.

"How did you escape from the castle? You couldn't have slipped past all these soldiers."

"Pure luck, I guess," fumbled Annika, trying to ignore the guilt she felt from lying to Bolt. "All the penguins closed their eyes and I snuck past."

"Closed their eyes?"

"Right." She looked away. *Don't feel guilty. Don't feel guilty.* "They, um, were playing Red Light, Green Light. It was a long game."

"Penguins don't play Red Light, Green Light."

"Did I say Red Light, Green Light? I meant hide-and-seek. Sphen penguins love that game," she mumbled. "But it was a one-in-a-million chance."

"One-in-a-billion is more like it," said Bolt, shaking his head. "Let's just hope your luck continues. Maybe we can swim across the moat."

Just then, as if mocking Bolt's suggestion, a monster leapt from the dark water, gray and long and muscular, with a sleek, massive head and sharp teeth lining its colossal mouth. The creature snapped at some of the penguin soldiers marching on the bridge, missed them all, and then landed back in the water with a resounding *splash!* The water drenched the bridge.

"Oh, right. There are leopard seals in the moat," said Annika.

Bolt froze, as terror swept across his face.

The soldiers, who had seemed unafraid of anything a moment ago, were clearly terrified, too. Their organized marching had turned into random scampering.

"Leopard seals are the fiercest enemies of penguins," muttered Bolt, breathing heavily. "There's no way we're swimming across it."

Annika gazed at the castle, deep in thought, scratching her chin. "Just do your mind-control penguin thing, then. You know, tell all the penguins about family and love and peace and all that nonsense. And we'll walk in."

Bolt shook his head. "Do you ever think of your brain as an onion?"

"No. Never."

"Well, it is. Layers over layers over layers. And the layers in these Sphen penguin brains are coated with more hate and corruption than I've ever seen. If I missed just one layer in one penguin, we'd be caught for sure. Besides, even if we somehow got past the penguins, how could I fight the Earl? I don't even have a weapon."

"Would any of these help?" asked Annika. From her pockets she removed a soccer ball, a tuning fork, a turkey baster, three pairs of pantyhose, and a wind-up chicken toy.

"I thought you were going to stop stealing things."

"If people don't want things stolen from them, they shouldn't carry them in their pockets." She sighed under Bolt's harsh gaze and lowered her head, once again reminding herself not to feel guilty. Bandits didn't feel guilty! "I'll try harder."

As she stuffed the objects back into her pockets, the soccer ball slipped from her normally deft bandit hands. CLANG! It landed on the lid of the trash can next to them. BANG! It bounced off the lid and landed on the lid of the second trash can.

"These are loud trash cans," Annika yipped.

A human patrol officer had been walking by, and the man wheeled at the noise, his tuxedo tails lifting as he spun, his wooden beak askew, his boutonniere slipping to the ground.

As Bolt and Annika gulped in unison, the man shouted and pointed at them. "Hey! Only traitorous human patrol officers in tuxedos are allowed this close to the palace!" He blew a policeman's whistle. Even if someone had not heard the trash can clanging, they could not miss the whistle's high-pitched siren wail. The penguins on the drawbridge stared. So did a dozen other penguin soldiers marching down the street.

Annika kicked over the trash can nearest her. It rolled forward, toward the patrol officer. Then she booted the

soccer ball that now lay by her foot, and it flew straight into the air before bending and smashing into a penguin's face. The ball stuck on the bird's beak and immediately deflated.

"I used to play forward on the Brugarian Forest Bandit soccer team," Annika explained to Bolt.

Bolt bolted, and so did Annika. The patrol officer chased after them, blowing his whistle. Each time he blew, more penguins joined the chase.

They dashed down the streets, no longer confined

to shadows, a dozen pairs of webbed feet flopping on the ground along with loud clopping from fancy wing-tip tuxedo shoes. More whistles blew, more penguins barked.

Bolt grabbed one of the straps of the backpack he still wore, so it wouldn't swing as he ran. The two friends turned the corner, where people walked glumly. Annika was an expert crowd runner, but Bolt stayed on her heels, hopping when she hopped, spinning when she spun, and diving under someone's legs when she dove. The penguins and tuxedo-clad patrol officers were not as nimble and, occasionally, Annika heard a shout and a crash behind them, followed by grunts and angry barks.

She overturned a fruit cart, blocking the way of some of their pursuers. "Sorry for upsetting the apple cart!" she shouted to the cart's owner.

Up ahead, a horse was attached to a small wagon filled with hay. Annika kicked the bar connecting the horse to the wagon, which rolled in front of the horse and blocked the street.

"Sorry for putting the cart before the horse!" cried Annika.

Bolt spied a mountain of old furniture, mostly wooden tables and broken chairs, awkwardly piled on top of each other. He rushed around it.

"Why didn't you topple that tall pile of old wooden furniture?" asked Annika.

"I couldn't think of a pun," admitted Bolt.

He soon heard a crash followed by the sound of furniture collapsing and someone shouting behind them, "Looks like someone turned the tables on us!" said Annika.

"Good one," said Bolt.

Even with apple carts and wagons and large mountains of broken furniture in the way, they could still hear the sounds of people and penguins chasing them. Annika turned to look. There had to be thirty patrol officers and penguin soldiers running and gnashing teeth or beaks.

A couple of officers shouted, *"Stop at once!"* and *"You'll be sorry when we catch you!"*

"Why would we stop if we'll be sorry when they catch us?" Annika asked.

Bolt agreed the conflicting orders were confusing.

They turned a corner, and Bolt shouted, "In here!" while pointing to a dark alley. They veered into the alley only to realize, almost immediately, that the alley had no trash cans, and was a dead end.

"I don't know what I was thinking," said Annika, cursing to herself. She knew better than to turn down an alley without checking it first. *The Code of the Bandit* had an entire section titled "Why You Should Never Run into a Blind Alley."

"Sorry," said Bolt, although it seemed like they would both be very sorry in seconds, as soon as their pursuers swarmed into the alley.

"I still have a turkey baster!" Annika exclaimed, pulling the cooking utensil from her pocket. The world's greatest bandit would never go down without a fight. Bolt groaned, but before another groan could float from his gullet, a door next to them opened and hands tightened around their shirt collars. They were both yanked inside a room, and the door slammed shut behind them.

19.
Another Break in the Action

The winds, colder than I expected, wrapped around my face like an ice scarf, which made me wish I was wearing a scarf, although not an ice one. The penguin caretaker coughed, and so did I. The sun had set over the horizon, and my stomach protested the late hour. I had not eaten dinner.

The caretaker arched an eyebrow at the sound of my grumbling stomach. "Care to eat?" He pointed to a plastic tub behind him stuffed to the brim with raw fish, chilled in ice. "The penguins won't be eating it. I could also tie the ice cubes together to make you a nice ice scarf."

"No thank you." I never ate raw fish unless it was atop sushi rice. "Do you have any funnel cakes?"

"The problem with a zoo that is being torn apart is that there are so few snacks."

So there I stood, stomach groaning in harmony with the low irritated moan of an irritated flightless bird in the distance. "The angry ostrich," I said.

"You've met?" asked the penguin caretaker, and I nodded. "He's upset that the zoo has closed. But he's always been bad-tempered. He can't help himself, I'm afraid. We are who we are, after all. Some of us are angry ostriches. Others are out-of-work penguin caretakers."

"And others of us are werepenguins," I added with a wink.

The man nodded. "So true. But we are all many things, are we not? No one can be defined simply by one's anger or one's career path or even one's curse. The only thing we cannot be is someone else."

"I was once a ghost for Halloween," I added, although I wasn't sure if that's what the man meant. "But the hour is late, and growing later. Please continue your story."

"Are you sure? My story is far more disturbing than a Halloween ghost." Once again the screeches of the angry ostrich blew by us, along with another blast of frigid air. "Some people say that ostriches keep their heads in the sand when they are frightened. After hearing my tale, you may wish to do the same."

"Unlikely." I had always been afraid of burying my head in dirt and suffocating. But I did not speak of this lifelong fear. Instead I merely said, "The sooner you continue, the sooner our night will end."

The man opened his mouth to speak, but then closed it, and then opened it, and then closed it, as if uncertain where in the story he should continue, or perhaps he was pretending to be a fish. "Let's take a break from Annika and Bolt, and catch up on young Gentoo."

20.

Gentoo and the Fish Taxes

Gentoo threw the bowline around one of the pilings on the Sphen pier. The day's fishing had
been disappointing again. It seemed like only
months before, because it was only months before, when
she and her aunt would return from their fishing expedi-
tions early in the day, their nets crammed with the riches
from the sea. Today, they fished on the boat for eleven
hours and caught three dozen scrawny catfish.

As Gentoo tied the ropes securely, checking to make
sure they were knotted as tightly to the boat's cleats as
they were to the pilings, she heard members of the Sphen
pier patrol approaching, along with penguin soldiers.

Gentoo glared at the men and their fancy patrol tuxedos. She hated the penguins as one would hate anything

unpleasant, such as a canker sore or banging your knee on a coffee table. But she had a special layer of hate for the humans, like banging against that coffee table and then tripping.

"Gentoo!" barked Marguerite Audouin, breaking Gentoo's concentration on the men's conversation. Her aunt dragged a net filled with the fish they had caught. "Help me unload our meager catch, and stop daydreaming. It's already dusk and I still need to make dinner, buy new chains to tie around you tonight, and fix a leaky pipe in the bathroom."

"Yes, Aunt Margie." Gentoo grabbed the netting from her. "You don't have to buy chains, you know. I mean, you could just let me roam around outside as a hideous seagull monster all night."

"No!" her aunt cried, pounding her fist into her palm, so Gentoo knew she was upset. "What would happen if you were discovered? I shudder to think about it!" Indeed, her aunt shuddered for a great many seconds and even pulled on her hair in anguish.

"Please don't shiver and pull your hair," said Gentoo. "Your hair has so many hairs plucked out as it is." She reached out and smoothed her aunt's messy curls. She wished Aunt Margie weren't so easily anguished.

Her aunt grumbled. "We're out of bait. You'll need

to run to the store tomorrow and buy more." She then stepped down from the boat, but she was shuddering so much that, when she stepped onto the landing, she shook right into a penguin soldier.

"Please forgive me, oh mighty, merciful penguin." Gentoo's aunt cleared her throat and recited meekly, "I am a poor human thing, not deserving of a penguin's wing." It was a poem that all the people of Sphen were taught to say if they ever upset a soldier.

Despite the poem, the penguin soldier shoved Marguerite to the ground with its wing.

Gentoo opened her mouth to shout, but swallowed the wail before any sound escaped, fearful of doing anything that might encourage the penguin to push her aunt again. Instead, she covered her mouth to halt her cries as the penguin laughed, which came out like a whale blubber snort with plenty of spit. It was quite disgusting, and Gentoo cringed as the penguin laughed again, spit raining on her aunt, still on the ground.

As the penguin soldier below continued to laugh grotesquely, Gentoo looked up at the gulls flapping in the air around her; as always they were close by. Her eyes narrowed and she spoke silently to her feathery friends.

See those laughing penguins and men? Want to play a joke on them, even though jokes are illegal?

In an instant, the gulls, a dozen of them or more, sped toward the bullying humans and penguins. Marguerite Audouin, who was starting to stand, ducked out of the way.

The birds hovered above the pier, flapping their wings in the faces of the penguins and men, feathers knocking off hats, and well-aimed gull droppings splattering tuxedo jackets. The men waved their arms to beat off the birds, cursing at them, while the penguins barked and covered their heads with their wings.

The seagulls laughed, *Ha, ha!*, a cacophony of bird cries and wing flaps. They shouted: *Anything for you, Gentoo! . . . Right between the eyes! . . . Hairbrush peanut monsters!* As always, some of their thoughts were jumbled.

"Gentoo! Stop that!" Gentoo had not heard nor seen her aunt get back on the boat, but Aunt Margie stood next to Gentoo now, hands on hips, brow wrinkling with anger. Meanwhile, the traitorous humans and the penguins raced away, down the pier, shooing and swatting, cursing and screaming, as more seagulls flapped and laughed after them.

"Gentoo! I said *stop!*" cried her aunt.

Gentoo's shoulders sagged, and her connection with the birds snapped. The birds lost interest in their prey and flew away.

"What were you doing?" her aunt growled. "You know better than to draw attention to your condition."

"Sorry, Aunt Margie," said Gentoo, her voice cracking, her eyes staring at her feet.

"If you're done goofing around, help me finish docking the boat for the night."

Gentoo nodded. If only she could do something to free her people! But what could a were-gull do against such evilness, other than encouraging harmless wing flaps and increasing tuxedo dry-cleaning bills?

21.

Blackburn the Pirate

Bolt and Annika stood in a small, squalid apartment that smelled like mold. The few pieces of furniture were torn, scarred, or leaning oddly. A large skull and crossbones flag hung on one of the cracked walls, and a dozen model ships in bottles sat on shelves. Bolt always thought ships in bottles were interesting—how did they get those models inside a bottle?—but these ships were very, very tiny and the ends of the bottles very, very wide.

But mostly Bolt stared at the man who had whisked them inside the dark apartment. He was a big man, a man who might have been powerful once, but now was more flab than muscle. He wore a thick black frock coat, and a scabbard hung from his belt. A long hoop earring dangled from his left ear, and a gray-and-black tricorn hat sat on his head.

There was no doubt about it: this man was a pirate.

"Hush now, children," the pirate whispered. Patrol officer shouts, mixed with angry penguin barks, filled the alley along with the clamor of footsteps. Bolt stood, rigid at attention, frightened for his life.

After a few moments, the footsteps outside trailed off, as did the shouts and barks. "That was a close one, eh?" asked the pirate. "Borscht!"

"Why did you grab us?" Annika asked. She backed away and held up her fists, ready to fight. "What do you want from us?"

"Is that the thanks me gets for saving yer lives? I want nothing, although I'm always happy to accept gold. That's the customary gift for someone who saves yer life. A few gold coins, or even a golden tooth." He smiled, and Bolt noticed a tooth missing. "I lost mine a ways back. The life of a pirate is rough, it is."

"I have no gold," said Bolt. "Or extra teeth."

"And ye, missy?" asked the pirate, jabbing his thumb at Annika.

"I have a tuning fork, a turkey baster, some pantyhose, and a wind-up chicken toy," she said. "I had a soccer ball, but that's gone now."

"A shame. I have always wanted me own soccer ball," said the pirate with a frown. "It's hard to play soccer with a wooden leg, though."

"You have a wooden leg?" asked Bolt, surprised. The man stood so straight, and his legs seemed to be the same size.

"No, I'm just saying it's hard to play soccer with one."

"Why did you save us?" Annika asked. She had not lowered her fighting fists.

The man ran his fingers through his long black curly hair. He had incredibly thick black sideburns, the thickest sideburns Bolt had ever seen. "I saw ye were in trouble. Not that I help people in trouble, mind ye. A pirate don't help people in trouble. But we pirates have no love for rules, or laws, or penguin soldiers. Borscht! But let me introduce meself. I am Blackburn the Pirate. Ye've no doubt heard of me?"

"I've heard of Black*beard* the Pirate," said Bolt.

The man shook his fist in the air. "Curses! Everyone has heard of *him*. But I can't grow me a good beard, and lord knows I've tried." He pointed to his face. "Ye have, however, noticed me impressive and plush sideburns?"

"They are very nice sideburns," agreed Annika.

"They're me calling card, and why I am known as Black*burn* the Pirate, scourge of the seven seas! Most pirates only stick to six of the seas, you know. But I've

been to all seven, which is quite impressive. Borscht!"

"Um, why do you keep saying *Borscht?*" Bolt asked. "I thought pirates said *Arrr!*"

"I will never say *Arrr,* not including that time just then. No, I only say *Borscht!* It's part of what makes me special, me calling card in addition to me wonderful sideburns." He stood taller, his chest out. "Borscht!"

Bolt admired the man's sideburns once again. It didn't seem like the man intended to rob or harm them, so Bolt relaxed, although just a little—pirates, even friendly ones, were still dangerous. "But if you're such a great pirate, why are you living here?" Bolt scanned the cramped, dirty room.

The pirate shook his fist again. "I'm down on me luck, lad. I meant to stop in this horrid city for one night before heading out again to sail the seven seas, but penguins took me ship. I just need a boat and I'll be off to resume me sea-faring life. Me stay in Sphen will be a short one, I hope."

"How long have you been here?" asked Annika.

"Twelve years, or thereabouts."

"Not a very short stay," said Bolt.

"Perhaps. But soon I will reclaim me fame as the most fearless pirate that ever lived! Well, soon-ish, anyway. I don't have a deadline or anything." He stood up tall and puffed out his chest. "Borscht!"

The man caught his reflection in the cracked mirror

on the wall, and adjusted his hat and fluffed his sideburns. Annika pulled Bolt away to whisper to him.

"Just think," said Annika, her eyes wide, her voice trembling with excitement. "Me, the greatest bandit that ever lived, meeting the most fearless pirate that ever lived. What are the chances?"

"He doesn't seem all that fearless," said Bolt.

"He's just down on his luck." They both looked back at the pirate, who was still fluffing his sideburns, apparently lost in thought.

"I bet someone that fearless, and with such great hair, could help us defeat the Earl," said Annika.

"Those *are* impressively plush sideburns," admitted Bolt. "But why would he agree to help us?"

"You heard what he said. Penguins took his ship! I bet he'd love to get revenge." She ignored Bolt's skeptical frown and nudged his shoulder. "I'm a great judge of people. Trust me." She turned back to Blackburn and cleared her throat.

The pirate stopped fluffing his hair and smiled at them. "Are you two done conferring?"

"For now," said Annika. "We're going to defeat the Earl and free Sphen. Will you help us?"

The pirate stared at them with a frown, but that frown quickly turned into a loud, boisterous laugh. "The Earl is way too powerful. Ye must be joking!" He immediately

stopped laughing and added in a whisper, "Which is quite illegal in Sphen, ye know."

"I'm not joking," said Annika. "We're going to fight him. You could fight him, too."

The pirate laughed again, before clearing his throat. "I may be down on me luck, living in a squalid apartment, and without a ship for twelve miserable years, but I'm not *that* desperate."

"I told you so," Bolt whispered to Annika.

"But you're a fearless pirate," she protested.

"And it's far better to be a fearless pirate than a dead one. Pirates aren't heroes. Borscht!" Blackburn removed a small leather-bound book from his inside jacket pocket and waved it in the air. "This is me *Pirate Handbook*. All pirates live by its code. It's long and boring, but I've read it twice, anyway." Annika clapped with delight at those words. "The handbook clearly states that pirates cannot be heroes."

"I'm a bandit. A Brugarian Forest Bandit!" Annika bubbled with so much excitement she couldn't stop tapping her feet. "We have our own code, so I can totally relate. One of our rules is that I'm not allowed to make friends with someone who isn't a bandit." She put her hand on Bolt's shoulder and squeezed. "I've broken that one, but sometimes rules are made to be broken."

"Just like a peanut shell," said Blackburn. "Have ye

tried to eat one? Not so good. But break one open and ye find those little edible pea-sized nuggets inside."

"So you'll help us?" Annika asked brightly.

"Do I look like a peanut shell?" asked the pirate. "Besides, I'm allergic to peanuts, missy."

Bolt was about to whisper *I told you so* again, just in case Annika hadn't heard him the first time, when she shouted out, "We'll give you gold, then."

The pirate's mouth had been curled into a mocking smirk, but at the mention of gold, his expression grew serious. He straightened. He gazed down at Annika. "Gold, ye say, missy?"

"Yes, gold. An entire chest of it." She added with a hiss, "And stop calling me *missy*."

"It's a term of pirate endearment. But I thought all ye had was a tuning fork, a turkey baster, some pantyhose, and a wind-up chicken toy. Where would someone like ye get a chest of gold?"

"My father is a great bandit. If you help us, he'll get you enough gold to buy a pirate ship." Then she added, "Borscht!"

The pirate eyed Annika, sizing her up. "It's a tempting offer. But how do ye plan to defeat the Earl? Many have tried but all have failed. Why will ye succeed when no one else has?"

"I just will." Annika beamed with so much confidence, Bolt almost believed they could defeat the Earl, and that maybe they had a plan and her father had a chest of gold.

"Twelve years is a long time to remain landlocked," said the pirate with a sigh. "Perhaps it's time to try to change me luck meself." He held out his hand. "I'll do it. But me price is *two* chests of gold, a soccer ball, and a new gold tooth. And I get to call you *missy*."

Bolt said nothing as the pirate and Annika shook hands, sealing the deal. He didn't think Annika could get her hands on even a single chest of gold. But Bolt kept these worries to himself, preferring to believe that Annika's promise wasn't purely false bravado. Annika was many things, but Bolt knew she wasn't a liar.

22.
The Code of the Bandit

As Annika shook the pirate's hand, she threw Bolt a big smile, a winning smile, a smile overflowing with bandit confidence, even though she didn't feel much confidence underneath her swagger.

She didn't have chests of gold to pay Blackburn, and from the questioning glance her friend threw her, Bolt knew it.

Of course, she would only have to pay the pirate if they were successful in their mission, which was far from certain. But she felt their chances were better with a fearless pirate than without one. She would gladly enlist all the fearless people in the world if she could to free her father, whether they were fearless pirates or fearless Vikings or fearless ballerinas.

She had never met a fearless ballerina, but that didn't

mean they weren't out there, dancing violently.

And if they failed? She looked at Bolt with lingering regret. He had no idea the Earl was expecting him.

Her shoulders sagged. She was nothing but a liar, first to Bolt about, well, everything, and now to Blackburn about chests of gold. Bandits didn't lie, at least not usually. It was bad enough that she and Bolt were friends, which was against all bandit rules, but now this? What would she do next—write letters of apology after robberies? She would never be the greatest bandit of all time at this rate.

"Are you OK?" Bolt asked. "You look sad."

Annika coughed and looked away. "It's nothing."

Bolt put his arm on her shoulders. "I'm not sure if this pirate can help us, but I'm proud of you for trying. I used to think bandits couldn't do heroic deeds, but I was wrong."

Annika coughed and looked away again. Bandits didn't feel guilty. That was in the code, too, although at the very end and in a footnote.

Annika and Bolt sat down at the cramped kitchen table, where Blackburn was already sitting. He gave them both a tall mug of brown cider. "Grog," he said. "Have some. It'll grow hair on yer chest." He drank his mug in one gulp and then refilled it from a tall pitcher.

Annika pushed her mug to the side, as she had no desire to grow hair on her chest. Bolt took a sip, cringed, and pushed his aside, too.

The pirate downed another mug of grog, poured himself more, and stared at Annika with narrowed eyes, as if trying to read a secret etched in the lines of her face. "Tell me, missy," he said. "Why do ye want to free the people of Sphen? I thought bandits only cared about kidnapping and robbing."

"Because it's the right thing to do," said Bolt, smiling at Annika. Annika nodded back, but without conviction, trying to ignore that horrible and lingering guilty feeling.

The pirate guzzled his mug of grog and burped. "Well, I suppose the *why* matters far less than the *how*, aye? The Earl of Sphen is well protected in the grand palace. We need a plan."

"We have a secret weapon," said Bolt, winking at Annika.

The pirate leaned back in his chair and almost tipped over. "Plunder the poop deck, ye scurvy dog." He cursed at the chair and then stopped leaning. "Anyway, ye won't be the first with a secret weapon, ye know. One fellow, a few years back, brought a flaming catapult to town. That was *his* secret weapon. But catapults are made out of wood, and that flaming catapult was a hill of ashes before it could fire a single boulder. Last year, a mighty warrior came to Sphen. He stood seven feet tall! Oh, he seemed like a powerful adversary. He brought a secret weapon, too. A large cotton ball!"

"What did he do with that?" asked Annika.

Blackburn shrugged. "Nothing. It wasn't a very good secret weapon. Secret weapons aren't necessarily good weapons just because they are secret. On the contrary, they might be secret because they are such worthless weapons that no one wants to mention them."

"Our secret weapon is much better," promised Annika.

"Well, whether it is a cotton ball or flaming wood, it probably won't do any good," said the pirate. "People say the Earl is practically invincible."

"Being practically invincible is not the same as being definitely invincible," said Bolt. He spoke with such confidence, Annika wondered if her own boldness was contagious. Maybe it was.

"Wise words," said the pirate, who then poured himself one more mug of his brownish liquid and drank it in one gulp. "Good grog."

"Why do they call it *grog*?" Bolt asked.

"Because it makes ye groggy." He poured himself another mug, yawned, and offered them some salted biscuits to eat. The biscuits were dry and tasteless, but Annika was too hungry to care, quickly stuffing them into her mouth. Bolt politely declined the meal and instead asked if Blackburn had any raw fish. If Blackburn found this a strange request, he didn't say; he just replied that fish was too expensive nowadays. He and Annika ate in

silence for a while, Annika deep in thought contemplating the mission ahead, the only sound the occasional belch from Blackburn after another swig from his mug.

Finally, the pirate stood up, yawned, and ran his fingers through his dark locks. "I've had too much grog, I'm afraid. Time for me to turn in. One of ye can sleep on the uncomfortable, lumpy sofa and one of ye on the dirty, chipped wooden floor. I know ye claim to have a secret weapon, but even the best secret weapon still needs a plan. I know of someone who might be able to help us, though. We will talk more in the morning." He motioned to the window and yawned, stretching his arms. Annika was surprised it was so late. "Good night. I hope the light from the always-full Sphen moon won't keep ye up." He slipped into his bedroom and closed the door, leaving Bolt and Annika at the table.

"Do you think he can help us?" asked Annika.

"I doubt it," said Bolt bluntly, shaking his head. He looked out a window that revealed the dark night sky overhead. "But did he just say *the always-full Sphen moon*?"

23.

The Always-Full Sphen Moon

Bolt narrowed his eyes as Annika's face turned the color of an overripe beefsteak tomato, and she cleared her throat. "Oh, right. The moon. It's always full here." She coughed, and her face turned a shade darker, this time more like an heirloom tomato. "I didn't think it was worth mentioning."

Bolt bit his lip. The anger, that perpetual darkness he always had to stomp down in his stomach, bubbled. "This place, like Brugaria, always has a full moon? So you knew if I came here I would turn into a werepenguin every night, just like in Brugaria. And you didn't think that was worth mentioning?"

"Well, I can't remember everything." She smiled, as if her forgetfulness was funny, but Annika wasn't fooling anyone, and especially not Bolt. From her still-red face—now so dark that it reminded Bolt of a pomegranate—she was clearly well aware of her deceit.

"Is there anything else you're keeping from me?" Bolt demanded.

"No, nothing," said Annika weakly. "So. Is it midnight yet?"

"Am I a werepenguin yet?" growled Bolt.

"You don't have to be snippy about it."

Silence fell upon them then, Bolt concentrating on keeping himself from jumping off his seat and grabbing Annika's hair and pulling on it. *You are a werepenguin! Destroy all those who stand against you!* spoke a voice in his head.

Bolt hit his ears with the palms of his hands. That voice! Bolt counted to twenty, and the voice seemed to die away, although some of his anger remained.

They went to their beds in silence, Annika taking the lumpy couch, and Bolt the dirty floor. He was used to sleeping on a bed made of ice, so hard ground was not uncomfortable for him. Besides, he wouldn't be sleeping much. Soon, he would turn into a penguin.

His mind drifted in the silence: *Attack! Hurt Annika! Steal fish sticks!*

He concentrated on pushing the voice out—it was getting stronger, louder—but it frightened him, too. He was

able to control his anger, mostly, so why did that angry voice keep coming back?

He glanced at Annika, still angry, but reminding himself that she was his friend. "Why didn't you tell me?" he whispered in the dark.

"I'm sorry," said Annika, and Bolt knew how hard it was for her to say those words. Her voice choked up. "I was afraid you might not come. I just didn't want to take the chance."

"You really want to save the people and penguins of Sphen, huh?"

Annika didn't answer. Silence spread across the room like melted butter on dry toast. She had been brave for returning. Bolt shouldn't let one lie get in the way of their friendship.

He should have figured the moon was always full, anyway. It was the magical always-full moon that had given the Baron his immortality and power. The Earl was likely immortal and ruled the land for the same reason. "Are there other places in the world where the moon is always full?" Bolt asked.

"I don't know." Annika paused for a moment and added, "And that's the truth. But can I ask you something? Is it fun being a werepenguin? I've always wondered." Annika stretched and yawned. It was getting later, closer to midnight. "I think it would be. All that power. All that energy."

"It's not so bad," admitted Bolt. "Apart from the continual anger that floods your brain. And if I'm not careful I tear through my clothes when I transform, which is annoying." He sat straight up, alarmed. "You have to lock me up!"

Annika bolted upright, too. "What do you mean?"

"I'm the secret weapon, remember? Our only hope of defeating the Earl is to surprise him. I won't be a secret if I'm running around Sphen as a werepenguin. He'll know I'm out there. He'll sense me."

"He already knows you're coming," said Annika.

"What do you mean?" gasped Bolt.

"Um, well, r-right." In the dark, Bolt couldn't tell if Annika's face had resumed its pomegranate-like color, but she certainly sounded like it had as she stammered over her words. "I—I mean, I don't know. I'm just assuming. Don't you all sense each other?"

"Only if we're really close," said Bolt. He must have imagined how uncomfortable she had sounded. Besides, he had other things to worry about. He scanned the room, looking for chains or a small prison cell he could be locked inside. He saw neither of those things. He pointed to a small door. "You can put me in there."

"The closet? Will it hold you?"

"Depends on the closet."

Bolt strode across the room, opened the closet door, and peered inside. He winced. It smelled like old gym socks, and piles of dirty clothes sat on the floor along with random pirate gear: half a gangplank, a box of eye patches, an empty rum barrel, and two stuffed parrots. There wasn't much room for Bolt, and it didn't look very hygienic, but he didn't have any other options. He just hoped it would hold him in. He slipped off his backpack and squeezed himself inside, nudging the gangplank out of the way and standing on a pile of bandannas. "Close the door and lock it."

Annika, her fingers plugging her nostrils, stared at Bolt, crammed tightly inside the crowded space. "There's barely enough room for you. You can't even lie down."

"Just do it."

With a reluctant sigh, Annika closed the door, which wasn't easy since Bolt had to shove himself back, into the piles of junk, so the door could shut. Finally, he was sur-rounded by darkness and the smell of gym socks. The edge of the gangplank dug into his side.

Although Bolt was locked inside a closet, his mind was not unlocked from its worry. Also, one of his legs fell asleep and his nose itched, and he couldn't move his arms to scratch them.

And then, it happened. A chime rang, clamoring in

the distance, likely from the giant clock tower on the castle. Bolt feared the loud ring would wake the entire city, and then realized that might be the point. Every night those thunderous bells reminded all the people of Sphen that their nightly horror was about to be set loose. *Stay home! Be scared! The penguins rule!*

After the twelfth chime, Bolt's skin tingled and his blood bubbled. His skin rippled, like waves in a stormy sea. Bubbling blood and rippling skin were not enjoyable things to feel spreading across your body, and Bolt squirmed uncomfortably, although he could only squirm a centimeter or two in the crowded closet. A pain grew in his head, a throbbing in front, but the pain only lasted a moment before his forehead expanded. His nose grew. His arms became wings, his shirt ripped into bare threads around his mutating body. His pants followed. He cursed himself for forgetting to take them off.

There was no room for his belly to expand, not in the closet, and it pressed against the wood. His stomach pushed, the door creaked, and the stomach won, as the wood burst apart. Bolt stepped over the broken slats now scattered upon the floor. He raced across the room, longing to be free. He heard Annika and Blackburn behind him.

"Borscht! Is the boy yer secret weapon, missy?"

"Maybe not so secret anymore."

Bolt leapt at the window, but rather than shattering it, he bounced off. Blackburn had thin closet doors but thick windows. Bolt ran toward the front door, crashing through the wood and into the night.

24.
Those Glowing Eyes

As much as he dreaded the thought of turning into a werepenguin, Bolt would be the first to admit that the after-turning wasn't half bad. As a bird he felt more alive; his senses tingled. He could smell better, see better, and hear better. He waddled toward the shore, the salt from the nearby sea pulling him like a kite on a string.

Unfortunately, pulled kites also get tangled in trees and mangled, but Bolt thought this for just a moment. He was too energized with penguin power to linger on unpleasant kite accidents.

Bolt could sense other penguins nearby, both soldiers and free-range penguins. Everyone burned with the same hostility and Earl-influenced evil.

But their hatred, hatred of people, hatred of all things not-penguin, was not directed at Bolt. Penguins, even crazily deranged penguins, accept one another, unconditionally. That part of their nature is far too ingrained to be eliminated by brainwashing.

Bolt arrived at the shore of the Deader Sea and dove into the water, swimming beside hundreds of other birds. He felt their eagerness to feed—Bolt felt the same urge—but the fish were scarce. Each time Bolt dove beneath the waves, expecting a tasty morsel, he merely got a beakful of seaweed.

Where had the fish gone? Of that, no one seemed sure.

They swam out farther, their blubbery frames immune to the ice cold of the watery depths. Bolt heard a bark, a shout of joy from one of his penguin siblings. A swarm of fish had been discovered. Bolt, and all the penguins, feasted.

Soon their stomachs were full and the true nighttime party began. Penguins boogied to the sounds of trumpetfish, fiddler rays, and bass. Their music would be imperceptible to people, but the fine-tuned hearing of a penguin amplified their strained chords. Bolt did the rumba with a manta, which was all the more impressive since Bolt had never done the rumba before. Apparently, it was instinctual; penguins could rumba. Who knew? He spread out thoughts of togetherness:

I'm Bolt. We are all family.

Thoughts came back to him, a blur of welcoming greetings, but also of violence:

Yes, we are family. Let's find some humans, slap them around, and eat all their potato chips.

Bolt shivered. Penguins didn't eat potato chips! It was merely another sign of how lost these birds truly were.

They all danced and sang together, but the layer of greed and corruption that filled the penguins' heads had no room for love, and a true penguin family felt nothing but love. Well, a penguin family also felt hungry quite often, and indigestion if they ate too fast, but mostly love. Bolt was convinced these penguins could be saved, they could find the path to peace and penguin-ism if the Earl was defeated, but it would not be easy.

After dancing and singing, and singing and dancing, and eating a little bit more as well, Bolt and the penguins swam back to the shore. As Bolt stepped upon the ice and sand, he heard loud humming and squawking. Seagulls! A group of them stood in a large circle. It was an odd sight, as seagulls seldom stood in circles, or any geometric shape. They seemed to be having some sort of meeting. This also was odd, as seagull meetings were seldom this well organized.

Bolt sensed her before he saw her, a vibration in his head warning him: *Something new is here, something interesting.*

She sat in the middle of the gull group, her wings out-stretched, reaching up to the sky. She led the humming, with all the gulls echoing the soft beautiful music trickling from her throat. It was a seagull but twice as large as the others, and also a girl, a human girl. Bolt was sure of it, although he didn't know how he knew. The seagull-girl was draped in a pink nightgown that was way too big for her, her wings sticking out of two holes where the sleeves should have been. Bolt stood, alert, wondering if this was a new enemy, perhaps an ally of the Earl's.

The seagull girl turned her head and stared at Bolt. She had sensed him as he had her. They locked eyes, human eyes, understanding eyes.

Bolt barked. *Who are you?*

His bark startled the seagulls who had gathered around the girl in their circle, and they scattered into the air, wings flapping, creating chaos and confusion. The girl gull lifted up, too, rising higher and higher along with the other gulls, the flock blotting out the moon as they soared up. "Ha, ha!" she cried out, although nothing seemed funny, and jokes were illegal here.

Bolt ran to the edge of the sea, his eyes following the flock, but the night soon swallowed them. He concentrated as hard as he could, sending waves of thoughts in all directions, like a beacon, hoping this human gull might feel the light and shoot back a thought of her own. But he

felt nothing from her. Bolt could not speak to other creatures, only penguins.

Wait. He felt something. But it wasn't from her.

Bolt cursed himself. What had he been thinking, spreading thoughts out into the void? The Earl was out there!

He first sensed the Earl's presence in his neck, where his penguin-shaped birthmark sat, always present, always a warning. It tingled, sending an electric shock into his ears. The strength! The rottenness! The Earl's force, even from this far away, felt harsher and stronger than anything Bolt had felt before. Bolt's legs felt weak from it; he could barely stand.

And then Bolt saw him. On a bluff across the water, far off, two red eyes staring out like twin sparklers before a Fourth of July fireworks show. They sizzled and shone, slits of wickedness. They stared at Bolt across the water, and Bolt stared back.

The penguins on the shore alongside Bolt felt the Earl, too. They jumped up and down, agitated but also fueled by fear and rekindled anger.

The Earl thought: *We are powerful, my siblings! No one can stand in the way of our greatness!*

And the penguins answered back. *Yes, O powerful one.*

The Earl's malicious thoughts slammed into Bolt's brain, hatred and wrath and fish sticks, but not as much about fish sticks as the other things.

Rule with us! the Earl roared, his thoughts aimed directly at Bolt now, the Earl's menacing wishes burying themselves inside Bolt like worms in an apple. Bolt stared at those fierce red eyes and they seemed to narrow. The eyes were smiling. The Earl was smiling.

Rule with us!

Bolt felt a nearly overpowering craving to cause mischief: to spray graffiti on bathroom walls, to jaywalk, and to force human prisoners to wax his wings.

It was horrible. So horrible . . .

Rule with us, boy!

Bolt's mind went soft, like jelly. *Ruling would be nice.*

Yes! Rule with us, Bolt!

No! It took a great reservoir of strength, a reservoir filled with determination to fight back those words. It also took a great deal of that determined reservoir for Bolt to stop his legs from buckling and to move. Bolt ran forward and dove into the water, the cold waves washing off the alarming feelings of violence that had been pumped inside him from those fiendish red eyes.

He swam away from the penguins, away, away, away, needing to be alone, wishing he was back with his colony, far from here.

The thoughts lingered in Bolt's head for a long time, until Bolt had swum so far he was exhausted.

25.

A Penguin Is an Island

When Bolt awoke on the floor of Blackburn's apartment the next morning, he had no recollection of how he'd gotten there. But that was typical. Bolt tended to only remember bits and pieces of his penguin nights, and was almost always surprised to find where he awoke the next day. A big plank of wood had been hammered over a large hole in the front door, but wisps of snow blew in through the cracks. Wet webbed footprints led from the repaired door straight to Bolt. His clothes were in tatters, and he shivered under a scratchy blanket. But it wasn't the cold that made him shiver—werepenguins couldn't feel cold. It was the few memories he held.

Rule with us!

The menace in those words! The force! The Earl's evil ways were planted into Bolt's mind like a stubborn and unwelcome weed. Mind control could take root, just like that.

Bolt also remembered the effort it had taken to cast that maliciousness away.

Rule with us, Bolt!

How had the Earl known Bolt's name? It was almost as if he had been expecting Bolt. But that was impossible.

Bolt had been hearing a voice in his head for days now, maybe longer. He had thought that voice might be the Earl's, but now he knew it sounded different, lower pitched and more intense. Maybe that other voice was just Bolt's fears.

Annika sat at the kitchen table. "Did you have a good night?" she asked.

"Not really," Bolt muttered.

The door to the pirate's bedroom swung open. Blackburn wore the same pirate outfit from the day before, or perhaps he had multiple sets of the same clothes. He tossed a pile of laundry at Bolt. "These aren't fancy pirate threads like mine, but they'll do. Get dressed, and then ye have some explaining to do."

Bolt covered himself with the blanket as he put on his new clothes. Neither the plain black pants nor the matching plain black T-shirt were ripped, and it had been a

long time since Bolt had worn clothes that weren't torn. He would need to remember to change out of them before midnight.

Blackburn and Annika waited for Bolt at the kitchen table, sipping tea and eating English muffins. Neither appealed to Bolt, but he had eaten plenty of fish during the night.

"So, yer a werepenguin," Blackburn said. "It's not a bad secret weapon, I must say. Better than a cotton ball, for sure. But it won't be easy keeping something like that a secret for long."

Bolt nodded, and didn't say anything about the Earl. Why add to Annika and Blackburn's worries? Bolt had enough worries for all three of them. But he did share his other interesting discovery.

"A were-gull?" Annika asked while tearing off a piece of her muffin. "We have to fight her, too?" She put the muffin piece in her mouth.

"I don't think so," said Bolt. "She didn't *seem* evil." He remembered her laugh, which seemed more happy than rotten.

"How can you be sure?" asked Annika, in between chews.

"I can't, I guess," said Bolt. "But she didn't attack me, so that's a good sign."

"That gull creature is the least of our problems," said Blackburn. "Ye still need to stop the Earl."

"You said you knew someone who could help?" Annika asked him, and then began coughing.

"You should finish your muffin before asking questions," Bolt suggested.

"Aye, I know of someone who might have the answers we need," said Blackburn. "Omneseus, the seer. But it won't be easy to get to him." Both Bolt and Annika leaned in to hear more. "Ye've heard of him, aye?"

Bolt and Annika shook their heads.

"Some say Omneseus knows everything that ever was," Blackburn continued. "Others say he just has a really good set of encyclopedias. Who knows? But he will know how to defeat the Earl, and other tidbits such as why people can't keep their eyes open when they sneeze."

"I've always wondered that," admitted Bolt.

"The nose and eyes are linked by cranial nerves, so when we sneeze, the impulse travels to the brain and to our eyelids, which causes us to blink," said Annika. "But some people do sneeze with their eyes open. It's just a myth that you can't." Bolt looked at her, impressed. "We once kidnapped an eye doctor."

Bolt jumped up, fueled by a faint sense of hope that he hadn't felt a moment ago. The Fortune Teller in Brugaria had given him the cryptic clue he needed to defeat the Baron. Seers were like fortune tellers, but better. He strode toward the door. "Where does Omneseus live?"

Blackburn did not leave his seat. "I said it would not be easy to get to him, aye? Omneseus lives on the island of Omnescia. It's a day's journey by ship. Borscht!"

That final *Borscht!* lingered in the air as Bolt stared at the pirate, Annika stared at Bolt, and the pirate stared at his skull and crossbones flag. "I thought you didn't have a ship," said Bolt.

"That's why I said it wouldn't be easy to get to him."

Bolt sat back down, his enthusiasm deflating. He and Annika looked at each other, glum. "But if we get a ship, I can steer it."

"And how are we supposed to get a ship?" Bolt asked.

"I figured if ye had chests of gold and soccer balls lying around, ye probably had yer own ship, too. No?"

"No," Annika groaned, but Bolt groaned louder.

They all stared at one another, no one saying a word.

Annika raised her arms and pumped her fists. "We don't need any seer's help. We'll rush the palace!" Her bandit confidence nearly burst from her ears. "We can take them! We have Bolt, and me, and now a fearsome pirate."

"That's not a plan, that's suicide," said the pirate. He stood up and stared at himself in the mirror, fluffing his

sideburns. "As much as I'd like me chests of gold, I also like breathing. We can't attack the Earl without a plan. If we had a ship, we'd sail off, converse with the seer, sail back, and fight. But without one, we're stuck."

Bolt closed his eyes, his thoughts racing, trying to find a solution to their problem.

"There must be a way," he mumbled. He thought of the palace. The moat. Their walk through town, and all the penguins they saw.

It came to Bolt suddenly. "Tell me," he said to Blackburn. "Are you any good at playing cards? Because I have an idea, and we probably can't lose."

26.
Give That Pirate a Hand

Bolt and Annika led Blackburn down the shadow-covered streets of Sphen, avoiding the glares of the penguin soldiers that stood at almost every street corner. The trio said nothing, except for an occasional "Borscht!" blurted by Blackburn. They went unnoticed.

Blackburn's frock coat pockets jangled with silver and gold coins. They had found some of them in the pirate's sofa cushions and he had agreed, reluctantly, to bring them. But most of the coins came from Annika, who kept running off and returning with fistfuls of them. Bolt didn't ask how she got the money. He didn't want to know.

"You've played poker before?" Bolt asked Blackburn for the fifteenth time.

"Aye, matey. And that's the fifteenth time I've answered the same. Borscht!"

"And you're a good player?" Annika asked.

"For the fifteenth time, aye, missy. All pirates are exceptional poker players. I never lose." He coughed and looked away. "Well, hardly ever."

"What does *hardly ever* mean, exactly?" asked Bolt, watching the pirate suspiciously.

"It means just what I say. I've played cards hundreds of times. Thousands. And I've only lost once."

"When was that?" Bolt asked, a cloud of concern starting to gather inside him.

"Well, that's the thing, aye?" Blackburn said, coughing. His face blushed. "Just so happens I lost the last time I played."

"When was that?" Annika asked.

"Twelve years ago when I lost me ship playing poker."

Bolt and Annika both stopped on the street.

Bolt's mouth dropped open and he stared at the pirate in surprise. The cloud of concern inside Bolt was now a stormy raincloud. "I thought you said penguins took your ship."

"Aye, they took it playing poker. Penguins are excellent

card players, so there is no shame in that. Or at least not a lot of shame."

A sense of unease had pranced inside Bolt's head ever since they had arrived in Sphen, and it flared up now. Bolt took a deep breath and counted to twenty. It was hard to steady himself.

"But it don't matter now, does it?" asked Blackburn. He pointed a stubby finger at Bolt. "Ye said we can't lose."

"I said we probably can't lose," said Bolt. "I did throw in that *probably*. It's like *hardly ever*."

Blackburn scrunched up his lips and stared at Bolt, peering deeply into his eyes. "Let's hope yer *probably* is more certain than my *hardly ever*, eh? We're here."

They had arrived at the saloon Bolt and Annika had passed the day before, where Bolt had spied the poker-playing penguins inside. "Be careful, aye?" the pirate warned them. "If these penguins find out what we're doing, they'll peck us to death, or throw us in the palace moat. Or, most likely, both."

Inside the saloon, a bartender with a long, thin mustache stood behind a long wooden bar. He wore a black vest and bolo tie over a white shirt, and a bowler hat on his head. "Glass of grog?" he asked, holding up a mug of brown cider.

"Don't mind if I do," said Blackburn, taking a step forward, but Bolt grabbed the pirate's arm.

"Perhaps you should skip the drink. It'll make you groggy."

"Aye, yer right," agreed the pirate. Instead of strutting to the bar, Blackburn strode across the room, to where a second man stood next to the open door leading to the poker room. The man hissed at them, muscles bulging from under his black T-shirt. Fish tattoos dotted his biceps and forearms, and when he flexed, it looked like the fish were swimming. They were so realistic, Bolt's stomach growled.

Inside the poker room, six penguins sat at an octagonal poker table.

Bolt felt the urge to yell at them, *Have you no decency? Penguins don't play card games!* He had to remind himself that he wasn't there to thwart the evil swimming in those penguin heads like minnows, but to beat them at their own game, literally.

The bouncer at the doorway cracked his knuckles and spat on the ground. "What do you three fools want?"

"Let me do the talking," Blackburn said to Bolt and then glowered at the man. "I've come to play poker. Let us pass."

The man did not let them pass. Instead, he merely banged his fists together. His muscles twitched. His bicep and forearm fish swam. "This is a penguin-only game."

"My gold is as good as any bird's," snapped Blackburn.

A large poker-playing penguin in a gray hoodie squawked, a tremendous squawk, followed by a bark. It scowled, and it's difficult for a penguin to scowl.

"That's the penguin who took me ship," Blackburn whispered to Bolt, his eyes narrowing. "I'd recognize that hoodie anywhere."

The penguin barked again. It scowled deeper.

The bouncer at the door shouted back, "You sure?"

The penguin barked and the man stepped aside. "I

guess it's OK, then. Play if you want. But if I were you, I'd go home. I've never seen these penguins lose to one of our kind."

Blackburn stepped forward and Bolt followed him, but the bouncer grabbed the boy's arm roughly, dragging him back. "Not you, kid. Players only."

Bolt froze. Blackburn might have been a good poker player, but Bolt was his secret weapon.

If Blackburn shared Bolt's fear, he didn't show it. "Let him go. I need the boy. He's my associate."

"No associates allowed in the gaming room," said the bouncer.

Blackburn cleared this throat. "Did I say associate? I mean, he's me driver."

"Don't allow drivers in there, either."

"Me butler?"

"Nope."

"Errand boy?"

"I don't think so."

"Fortune teller?"

"In a poker room? Definitely not."

"I'm his number one fan!" cried out Bolt.

"Why didn't you say so in the first place?" asked the man, releasing his grip on Bolt's arm and stepping aside. "We always allow fans." Bolt rubbed his arm; the man's

grip had left a red mark. The bouncer shook his finger at Annika, who stood directly behind Bolt. "But not you, girl. Only one fan allowed at a time."

Bolt tensed, expecting Annika to take umbrage at the man's words. Now wasn't the time to fight! But, surprisingly, Annika didn't grab a knife or a bobby pin. Instead, she merely shrugged. "That's fine. I'll go for a walk." She waved to Bolt and Blackburn. "I'll be back in a couple of hours. Good luck."

Bolt's eyes narrowed as he watched her leave. He once again had a feeling that she was keeping secrets from him, secrets even bigger than the always-full Sphen moon.

Bolt shook his head, remembering her bravery for coming back to Sphen. He needed to stop being so suspicious of her.

Blackburn nudged Bolt forward. "Concentrate on poker, boy."

At the table, each penguin chewed on rotten fish and drank murky yellow liquid in tumblers that might have been whiskey, or might have been motor oil.

Blackburn tipped his tricorn pirate's hat. "Top of the morning to ye all."

The penguins snapped their beaks at him and growled.

Blackburn growled right back. Maybe the man *was* as fearless as he claimed. "Remember me?" he hissed at the hoodie-wearing penguin, who sat across from him.

The hoodie-clad penguin spat out a fish bone and yowled. Bolt understood the response: *All you humans look alike to me. But you have very nice sideburns.*

Blackburn and Bolt sat down. There was only one chair, so Bolt had to squeeze himself on the same seat. As a result, he and Blackburn practically cuddled to fit. "Try not to breathe too much on me," grunted Blackburn, half his rear end dangling off the chair.

"The game is Sphen hold 'em," Blackburn explained to Bolt. "Everyone is dealt two cards, facedown. Those are yer cards, and yers alone. Then, three cards are dealt

faceup in the middle of the table. Everyone shares those cards. Ye count the two cards in yer hand, add the three cards on the table, and those five cards are yer hand. And penguins are wild."

"Actually, penguins are quite tame," said Bolt. He glanced at the fierce, angry penguin faces around the table. "At least, usually," he gulped.

Penguins don't have hands, so Bolt was curious how they would deal the cards. One of the penguins held the entire deck in his beak, and he spat each card around the table, one at a time, without even a dribble of spit. It was rather impressive.

Once the cards were dealt, Bolt peeked at Blackburn's hand. A king and a four. Bolt only glanced at the cards before closing his eyes. He peered inside each penguin's head, peeling through the oniony layers to see through its eyes, and see its cards. In an instant, he knew every hand.

Blackburn frowned. "I best fold, aye?"

"No," said Bolt. "Wait."

"No talking during a poker game!" snapped the brawny bouncer at the door.

"I'm just telling him how big a fan I am!" cried Bolt.

"Oh, that's fine, then," responded the bouncer. "Talk away."

Blackburn matched the bet on the table, as did three

of the penguins. Three cards were dealt faceup—a five, a king, and a penguin wild card. That gave Blackburn three of a kind. A minute later, he had won the pot.

And so the game continued. Bolt knew when Blackburn should fold and when he should stay in, when he should raise and when he should call. He knew when the birds were bluffing, and when they had the nuts. Blackburn didn't win every hand—that would have been impossible—but he won many more games than he lost.

Blackburn was dealt two tens.

"Fold," said Bolt, seeing the two aces dealt to another penguin.

After that hand, Blackburn was dealt a nine and an eight.

"Stay in," said Bolt, seeing the poor hands everyone else had, too. Blackburn drew a straight and won a tall stack of coins.

Even without Bolt's help, Blackburn would have won. As he had claimed, he was a talented poker player. He always knew what to do with Bolt's continual comments about which cards were dealt.

"The penguin to your left has an ace high, and the one across from you has two threes," Bolt whispered.

One of the penguins growled at Bolt.

"He's just a fan!" explained the bouncer at the door.

Bolt was careful in his mind reading. He needed to dip into each bird brain but not alert them to his presence. He was like a mind-control spy, sneaking into their skulls and then prancing out, unnoticed.

After two hours, only Blackburn and the gray-hoodie-clad penguin were left. The large bird had played cautiously all morning, except when he was dealing. Then he played aggressively, and seemed to win every hand. He also kept playing cards that were different from the cards Bolt thought he had. Bolt was certain the penguin had dealt himself a five and an eight, a horrible hand, but in the end, the penguin pulled out two queens to win.

There was only one explanation—this penguin was cheating. No wonder he had defeated Blackburn all those years ago! But Bolt couldn't accuse the penguin of such despicable behavior without alerting the room to his mind-reading skills.

Besides, Bolt and Blackburn weren't exactly playing fair, either.

The hooded cheater stuck the deck in his beak and spat out his deal.

Blackburn looked down at two kings. This would have been a great advantage in most hands, especially because the hooded bird held just a three and a six. No. Wait. Now the penguin held two penguin wild cards.

"Fold," Bolt whispered to Blackburn. "We've already won enough money to buy a ship. Let's call it a day."

"Look at me cards. Fold with two kings?"

"Yes."

"A pirate never folds with two kings. It's a rule. It's in me handbook."

"That's a silly rule," said Bolt.

"Is it silly to live free on the sea?" asked Blackburn. "Is it silly to live with honor and respect for yer enemies? Is it silly to yell *Borscht!* all the time, for absolutely no reason?"

"Well, that last one, maybe."

"I won't give this penguin the satisfaction of folding." Blackburn reached for his stack.

Bolt grabbed his arms and yelped, "Stop! Stop!" but the pirate pushed him off and shoved half of his winnings into the middle of the table. "Don't," pleaded Bolt, but it was too late.

The hoodie-wearing penguin chuckled, and the sound reminded Bolt of a fingernail on a chalkboard covered by bees. Like all penguin snorts, it was very disturbing. The penguin pushed in half of his winnings, too.

Bolt tensed.

Three cards were dealt faceup in the middle of the table.

King. Ace. Penguin.

Blackburn had four kings. A remarkable hand. But Bolt knew that the hooded penguin had four aces, which was an even better hand. "Fold," Bolt begged. "We still have half our coins." Maybe they could buy a canoe.

Blackburn pushed in the rest of his coins. "All in."

"But that's all our money!" gasped Bolt.

"Four kings hardly ever loses," whispered Blackburn with confidence.

"I hate *hardly evers*," groaned Bolt.

It was too late to change the bet now. Bolt thought of scooping up all the coins and running through the streets to escape. But he knew that he would never make it out the door in one piece.

Bolt saw their boat disappearing in a puff of smoke. He saw all the people and penguins of Sphen lost forever.

The hoodie penguin pushed in all his chips and snickered, saliva flying from his beak and landing on the table. Bolt was disgusted: the penguin didn't even say *excuse me.*

The penguin buried his beak in a small satchel hanging from the back of his chair. He removed a key, which was attached to a large skull-shaped key chain.

The penguin tossed the key onto the table.

"What's this?" exclaimed Blackburn. "Are ye betting keys now? What do I want with a key?"

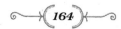

"He has a large sailboat," explained the bouncer at the door. "He's betting his boat."

"Sailboats don't need keys," Blackburn pointed out.

"He's betting a boat, and that really nice key chain," said the man. "Which means if you want to stay in this hand, you'll need to bet something else, or go home a loser."

"All me coins are on the table already," protested Blackburn.

"Never play poker with a penguin if you're not ready to bet everything you have," said the man. "Are you folding?"

"Never," said Blackburn, who jabbed a thumb toward Bolt. "I bet me number one fan." The other penguins leaned forward with interest. "He's worth something, I reckon."

"You can't bet me!" protested Bolt.

"I just did."

"Then I'm leaving," said Bolt, standing up from his chair. After being crammed on a small seat for the last two hours, it felt good to stretch his legs.

The bouncer stepped into the room and pressed Bolt back down, nearly pushing Blackburn off the seat. "You're not going anywhere, kid. Not until this hand is played. What's bet is bet."

Bolt shrank lower in his chair, partly from the weight of the man pushing him down, but also from a desire to

disappear. He tried to imagine what life would be like as the personal property of a penguin. Would he be forced to make fish sticks all day long, like the prisoners in the Sphen Castle? Would he be shackled?

"Four kings," said Blackburn, nudging Bolt over and laying his cards on the table. "I doubt ye can beat that, aye?"

The hooded penguin snickered, and again dollops of spit flew onto the table. As soon as he flipped his cards over, the game would be lost. Sphen would be doomed, and Bolt would be doomed, too.

27.
Hanging Around

Annika knew dozens of different Brugarian bandit card games. There was Gin, which mostly consisted of bandits drinking gin and yelling, and Spit, which mostly consisted of bandits spitting and yelling, and War, which had more drinking, spitting, and yelling than the other two games combined.

The bandits usually played for money and sometimes for air fresheners. But Annika hated those games. Families were meant to care for one another, not fight with one another.

Her distaste for card games was not the only reason she had been delighted to leave the poker game, though. She needed to clear her head and think. Alone. Without looking at Bolt and being reminded she was lying to him.

She should feel proud! She hadn't turned Bolt in to the Earl, had she? She was prepared to sail to an island to get advice from a seer while her father rotted away in a dungeon. Frankly, Bolt should be grateful!

So why was her stomach in knots and her throat tight just thinking about Bolt, and how she was betraying his trust?

Annika walked, pickpocketing an older couple and stealing their dentures out of habit. She kept her head down and avoided eye contact with the hostile penguin soldiers, which were everywhere. Then, she saw a note nailed to a lamppost and froze.

Public Announcement: Hanging Next Friday
Town Square, 10:00 a.m. sharp
We've caught the greatest bandit of all time. He must pay for his crimes!*

    *He must pay and so must you: 5 flumkins per person

Annika ripped the flyer off the lamppost, her hands trembling as she read the words over and over again, hoping that somehow the letters would mutate and change, but of course they didn't.

First of all, *Annika* was the greatest bandit that ever lived, or at least would be soon, so the inaccuracy of the

flyer was disappointing. But seeing the word *hanging*, in print, was far more horrifying. She was supposed to have until the end of the month! Had time really passed so quickly?

She reread the sign, smoothing the crinkles on her leg.

Hanging Next Friday.

She should run back to the poker room and grab Bolt and hand him over to the Earl. She'd save her father. Nothing was more important than family!

She took a deep breath. She had given her word she would help Bolt, and she would. *Next Friday* was still far away. As long as Bolt and Blackburn won their poker game, everything would work out—she would free her father and everyone in this city. Annika didn't care much about saving anyone other than her father, but if an entire city was saved at the same time, then good for them.

"Big hanging coming up," said a girl, pointing to the crumpled sign in Annika's hands. "They're only charging five flumkins a person, too. Usually they charge ten flumkins. They must want a big crowd." The girl was around Annika's age, thin and with the whitest hair Annika had ever seen hanging down from under a black fisherman's cap. Also, oddly, a seagull was perched on her shoulder. The girl stared at Annika, her bright green eyes narrowing, as did the seagull's. "You're not from here, are you? Strangers don't come to Sphen. Not willingly, at least."

"I'm visiting family. Sort of," said Annika, throwing out a smile and trying to look as un-bandit-like as possible. From the girl's and seagull's continued glares, Annika doubted she was succeeding. She coughed and looked away and then stared at a large poster of the Earl hanging from a lamppost, his red eyes staring out from under two enormous, bushy eyebrows, and his mouth twisted in a snarl, or maybe he was choking on a fish bone. It was hard to tell. Annika wasn't afraid of much, but this man scared her. She noticed the girl trembling at the picture, too.

"Is he as horrible as he looks?" asked Annika.

"Shh!" the girl shouted, grabbing Annika's arm, her eyes wide in terror. "Are you trying to get us thrown in the dungeons?" No one appeared to be near them, but she grinned as wide as she could and shouted, "Yes, it's horrible that there aren't more posters of the Earl around!" Seemingly satisfied no one was coming to throw them in a dungeon, she stopped smiling and took a deep breath. "Be careful what you say around here." She jabbed at the poster still crumpled in Annika's grip. "Or you'll be the next one on a hanging poster." She paused. "Although, I suppose since you took down that poster, it is no longer a hanging poster but a non-hanging poster. Get it?" She laughed and then her eyes once again grew wide, worried. "That wasn't a joke." She yelled out, "No jokes here!

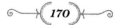

But it's no joke how much I love the Earl!" When no one jumped out to arrest them, the girl breathed easier. "Jokes are illegal," she told Annika.

"I don't care if you joke or not," said Annika. "I'm going to end the Earl's reign, just you wait and see." She stared down at the paper in her hand, a fleeting image of her father in a noose flashing through her mind

The girl shook her head and spoke in a near-silent whisper. "You can't fight the Earl. No one can." The seagull on her shoulder squawked, and the girl's eyes flashed a deep ultra-green for a moment.

"We'll see about that," said Annika, more to herself than to the girl. She glanced back up at the mighty Earl on the poster above her, and her confidence ebbed.

No. She was the greatest bandit ever. And she had a pirate and a werepenguin on her team. How could she lose? She had justice on her side. And good. And truth.

Well, maybe not truth. She thought of her lies and felt her stomach turning again.

"I need to go," said the girl. "I'm supposed to be picking up some bait for our fishing boat. Besides, it's not safe to stop and talk in the street. But take my advice: forget about fighting the Earl. No person can fight him. And no seagull either."

"No seagull?" Annika asked, confused.

"Uh, never mind that," replied the girl, slightly blushing. "Look, I gotta go." The seagull raised its wings and flew off the girl's shoulder, and the girl turned to run off after it.

"Wait. What's your name?" Annika asked.

"Gentoo," said the girl, and then scurried away after the seagull.

Annika watched them both leave, feeling guilty for stealing one of the girl's shoelaces. Why did she continue to steal things like that? Maybe Bolt was right: maybe stealing was wrong, at least some of the time. Just like lying was wrong, every time.

Deep in thought, Annika eventually wandered back to the saloon. She neared it just as Bolt and Blackburn walked out.

Blackburn held a key with a very nice skull key chain. "Perfect timing, missy. We have a ship."

"And a nice key chain," Bolt added. He looked nervous, glancing back at the saloon they had just left. "But if we're going to sail away, we should hurry. Those penguins looked upset. If they realize what we did, we'll never get out of here."

Annika fell in step with them as they hurried toward the pier, not running, but not quite walking either. "Why? What happened?"

"I won," said Blackburn, proudly. "Borscht! And double borscht!"

"No thanks to Blackburn," Bolt added. Blackburn growled but did not argue. "It all came down to the last hand. We were beaten. If that hooded penguin had laid down his cards, we would have lost it all."

"So what happened?" Annika asked.

"I had to dive deep into the penguin's brain with all my penguin mind powers," said Bolt. "There were so many oniony layers of evil in his head!" He shuddered. "I had to peel past all of them, but I did it."

"Did what?"

"Convinced him he had a pair of twos and had to fold."

"And you won back his pirate boat?" asked Annika, barely believing their good fortune.

"Well, no," said Blackburn. "We won a different boat. And I'm sure it's a fine craft. They call it *The Heinous Herring*. Isn't that a wonderful name?"

Annika didn't say anything.

"But if that penguin realizes he was duped, I doubt they'll let us get out of Sphen alive," said Bolt. "So let's hurry."

Bolt quickened his pace, hoping the penguins would never discover their trickery. They had been lucky so far, but Bolt doubted their luck would hold forever.

28.

Yet Another Break in the Action

The penguin caretaker dabbed a tissue to his eyes. He sniffled.

"Why have you stopped telling your story?" I asked. "Few things are more annoying than someone interrupting a horror story with breaks in the action."

"Perhaps," said the man, nodding in agreement. "But then again, it might be better to avoid finishing such a terrifying story." The man blew his nose, the loud honk reminding me of a foghorn. "I don't mean to frighten you. Maybe I should end my tale now."

"I am not frightened," I assured him.

"Then why do you keep screaming in fright?"

"I'm not screaming, I'm exercising my vocal cords." Screams had been blaring in my mind throughout the tale, as every mention of the terrible Earl horrified me, but I thought I had kept the screams inside. Apparently I was mistaken. I trembled and then screamed. "Sorry, more exercising."

"It is late," replied the man, looking up into the sky. "Maybe we should exercise our right to stop telling this story." The moon was rising, a full moon. I knew what that meant, just as I knew who my storyteller must be.

He didn't have to tell me his name. It was as plain as the nose on my face, and as the beak I was certain his would grow at midnight, as quickly as a bolt of lightning.

I smiled at the analogy.

Another scream threatened to spill out. Instead, my lips sputtered. "I have come a long way to hear your story. Tell me all!"

"Very well," the man sighed, stuffing his tissue back into his pocket. "Still, let's take a break from Sphen and go back about two weeks earlier, to when a Brugarian bandit set out to find his missing leader."

I nodded, lamenting the man's annoying habit of zig-zagging back and forth with his stories, which wasn't quite as annoying as his breaks in the action, but still slowed down the pacing a bit too much for my literary tastes.

29.
The Brugarian Left-Hand Man

Far away from Sphen, and many days before Bolt and Blackburn played their risky game of cards, the Brugarian bandits sat in the middle of their cluster of tents, eating barbecued salamander. No one cared for the food. Even thick layers of barbecue sauce could not completely mask the harsh, pungent taste of salamander meat.

The group ate without talking, and not just because everyone had to concentrate on swallowing their salamander without losing their lunch. No, the group had been quiet for days, ever since their leader, the great Vigi Lambda, had left with his daughter Annika in search of people to kidnap and carriages to rob.

Felipe frowned, thinking. Despite being left-handed,

he had been Vigi Lambda's right-hand man, and now, with the bandit leader gone, he was the leader. According to the bandit code, whoever led the group adopted the name Vigi Lambda, but Felipe broke that tradition. Since he was only their temporary leader, or so he hoped, he thought a name change would just be confusing. Finally, Felipe broke the silence. "They should be back by now."

"You're right, Vigi. I mean, Felipe. Sorry. Even though you didn't change your name, I still get confused," said Brutus, who was the biggest of the bandits, but far from the smartest.

The other bandits murmured in agreement. Now that Felipe had mentioned the absence of their leader, their worries spilled out like water from a cracking dam.

"Maybe they're lost!" cried one bandit.

"Maybe they're hurt!" cried another bandit.

"Maybe they learned how to play the trombone and joined a band!" suggested Brutus. The other bandits glared at him. "Or not. Never mind."

"Silence," said Felipe, who used his best *I'm a leader and you're not, although I'm only a leader temporarily* voice, which was assertive, but apologetically so. "There's only one way we will know if they're OK."

The other bandits threw out their best guesses.

"Read the newspaper?" guessed one bandit.

"Visit hospitals?" guessed another bandit.

"Take trombone lessons?" suggested Brutus. The bandits glared. "Never mind, again."

Felipe stood. He had not been chosen as the deputy bandit leader due to his impressive bandit skills, but because he was clever. And loyal. And baked great desserts, although his baking skills weren't particularly relevant just then. He was the shortest and roundest bandit, but he seemed taller under the canopy of leaves and branches that shaded the bandit enclave. "We will only know if they are lost, or wounded, or playing the trombone in a band, if someone looks for them. I've already packed my things and I'll be leaving right after I finish my salamander." He looked down at his half-eaten lizard and frowned. "Or, maybe now."

Robin, who was small but speedy, stood up. He wore a red hood, as always, despite being teased with various fairy tale jokes. "But, Felipe, if you go, who will lead us or bake our desserts? I should leave instead."

"No. I have to go," said Felipe, "because I've already packed my things. Have you packed?" Robin shook his head. "I didn't think so. Besides, I'm the best tracker. I'll be back soon, perhaps with a new soufflé recipe. Now enjoy your salamander meat." From the groans of the bandits, that didn't seem likely.

Felipe soon ventured off, his belongings stuffed inside a bag tied to the end of a stick, which he carried over his

shoulder. He needed to remember to steal some better luggage while he was away. Vigi and Annika were not easy to track—bandits are careful and stealthy—but Felipe was a master of the art. He knew how to interpret broken bush branches and disturbed pebbles. He knew which smashed leaves meant human feet had trod upon them, and which had been smashed by other animals.

He tracked Annika and her father for days, their footsteps winding through forests, stopping near streams, and then continuing onward in the direction of Sphen.

Felipe had not been aware of the evil that haunted the city of Sphen like ghosts in an attic, although he felt its aura of rottenness as he neared. He had not known of the despicable penguin soldiers that roamed the boundary of the Calamity Mountains, either. If he had, he might have approached more cautiously. Or at least he might not have attempted to rob a penguin.

"Give me all your fish sticks," he demanded, popping out from a bush. "And any soufflé recipes you have." He had not eaten for an entire day, and tracking through forests and near streams was tiring, hunger-inducing work.

The penguin merely snickered, and was immediately joined by a dozen others, all snickering, too. Felipe realized he had made a terrible mistake.

A taller bandit like Brutus, or a faster bandit like Robin, might have been able to escape. But the short, squat

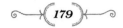

Felipe had no chance. The penguins had him in a headlock before he knew what happened.

It is not easy to put someone in a headlock if you only have wings, but these penguins were ferociously flexible.

Felipe was thrown into a dungeon cell that very day. He wondered if he would spend the rest of his life behind bars and in steamy fish stick kitchens, and never make a soufflé again. He was not aware of Vigi Lambda and Annika's fate, not just yet.

But soon, to his horror, he would discover that he was not the only Brugarian Forest Bandit left to rot below the palace.

30.

The Battle on the Pier

Back in Sphen, about two weeks after Felipe was captured, Blackburn, Bolt, and Annika hurried toward the pier to see their new boat. Bolt kept on sneaking peeks over his shoulder, to make sure no one chased them. So far, so good.

But when they arrived at the harbor and walked to the very end of a long pier and saw their new ship, Bolt discovered he had other things to worry about.

The boat was big enough to fit a half dozen people or more. It had two sails, and a raised deck with a ship's wheel. Someone had painted *The Heinous Hering* on the side of the boat, along with a picture of a dead fish.

But below the picture was a watermelon-size hole.

"That can't be good," said Bolt.

"Aye, it's not a very good painting of a dead fish. And they misspelled the word *herring*."

"That's not what I was referring to," said Bolt.

"It's a fixer-upper, that's all," said Blackburn, scampering up a small plank and onto the ship.

Bolt and Annika followed, stepping on layers of dead leaves and fish bones. Penguins aren't known for their janitorial skills or cleanliness, but the previous owner seemed to have gone out of his way to make this boat disgusting. Seaweed hung on the sails. The sides of the boat were covered in a greenish mold.

The boat reeked of dead fish, and while Bolt enjoyed the aroma, the smell of any sort of death was unsettling. "This ship is a wreck," he said, picking up a lump of seaweed.

"Never say 'ship' and 'wreck' in the same sentence," growled Blackburn.

Annika walked toward the stern of the boat and muttered, "This ship is such a disaster, being in a shipwreck would improve it."

"Borscht! A little mopping will clean this layer of scum right up, and some wood will patch that hole in the side. This is a fine boat, I tell ye. Well, maybe not *fine*. Let's call it *adequate*. OK, that might be pushing it, too. But *The Heinous Hering with One R* will get us where we need to go, and that's what counts." He strode up to the ship's wheel and rested his hands on its spokes, holding

his chin high. With the sun behind him, he looked gallant, pirate-like. "We could use a boatswain and a quarter-master. Maybe some fiddlers—always nice to have fiddlers on board to keep ye entertained. But I suppose there's no room for them, anyway. We'll get to work and set sail in a fortnight."

A roar rose from the end of the harbor.

"Or maybe we should depart now," said Bolt.

Two dozen penguin soldiers, barking and yelling, waddled toward them. Bolt recognized the large hooded poker-playing penguin leading the charge. A few members of the human pier patrol ran with the mob, their wooden beaks clacking loudly.

"Maybe they're coming to wish us bon voyage?" suggested Blackburn.

One of the members of the pier patrol yelled, "There are those poker cheaters!"

"Maim them! Chop off their limbs!" cried another.

"But probably not," admitted the pirate.

Blackburn sprang into action. He was a flurry of movement, running toward the mast and uncoiling rope. "Quick! Unfurl the mainsail! Mincey the lines! Batten the halyards! Lackshire the jibs!"

Bolt and Annika didn't move.

"Stop lollygagging and get to work!" demanded Blackburn. "Don't ye see that mob coming?"

"I've never been on a boat before," admitted Bolt.

"What's a halyard?" asked Annika. "Or a jib? Or anything else you just said?"

"Honestly, I think you made some of those words up," added Bolt.

Blackburn cursed and shook his fist, but continued his blur of activity. He raised a sail and secured it to the bottom with rope. The pirate captain pulled a crank until the mainsail grew taut, and twisted another crank that made the smaller sail grow slack. He kept yelling random things that were gibberish to Bolt, such as "Trim the mizzen!" Then he bounded toward the ship's wheel and shouted, "We're off! Ahoy, matey!"

The mob hadn't quite reached them. Bolt held his breath as the ship began to move.

And then the ship stopped, after only traveling about three inches.

"C'mon, ye old hag!" the pirate yelled, kicking the base of the wheel, which did nothing.

"I'm no expert, but don't we have to untie those?" Bolt asked, pointing to a bunch of ropes still wrapped tightly around a cleat on the pier.

"Didn't I tell ye to unmuzzle the jiggers?" Blackburn demanded.

"Maybe?" guessed Bolt, although if he had heard those words, he had no idea what they had meant.

Bolt bit his lip, limbs quivering, as the penguin group stopped near the end of the pier. Two members of the pier patrol stood at the front, and one of them yelled, "Surrender and no one gets hurt!" and the other shouted, "You'll be sorry!"

"Which one is it?" asked Annika. "Your directions are still confusing."

Blackburn jumped to the edge of the boat and unsheathed a large, sharp blade from his scabbard. The sword was serrated, like a saw. He crisscrossed the air with it, and the blade whistled.

"What sort of sword is that?" Bolt asked.

"A swordfish, of course." To the penguins on the pier he shouted, "I am the fearless pirate Blackburn! And no one ever takes a ship from me!"

"I thought penguins took a ship from you twelve years ago," said Bolt.

"Well, hardly ever," said the pirate. He leapt onto the pier shouting, "We will fight to the death!"

Bolt was a bit uneasy with that declaration. Standing on the boat, he thought about his life, and what little might be left of it. He had once been an unwanted orphan boy, but he had defeated a baron and freed an entire village. He had found a family, even though he never would have imagined that his family would be penguins. And he had made a friend. Maybe a few friends.

He also thought of the things he would never do if they were defeated right now. He would never free the people of Sphen. He would never find another family, a family where he would feel completely whole. He would never eat more fish sticks, which was higher on his list of regrets than he would have liked.

But, to Bolt's surprise, Blackburn was an expert swords-man. He sidestepped a wing and kicked one of the human

patrolmen, who toppled over and splashed into the Deader Sea.

More penguins rushed forward, but Blackburn was quick with his blade. He parried a penguin peck. Another bird spun at him, wings out. Blackburn ducked, kicked, and did a backward somersault.

"Wow, great move!" shouted Annika from behind Bolt.

"Actually, I tripped," admitted Blackburn. "But thanks."

Annika ran in front of Bolt, holding her small dagger. She jumped off the boat and landed soundlessly next to Blackburn.

"Welcome, missy," said the pirate.

Annika sliced and diced the air with her knife. She looked like a masterful fighter, or perhaps like a chef making a chopped salad.

Bolt still hadn't moved. He wasn't much of a fighter, at least in his human form. But he had other means of helping his friends, and he tapped into whatever bravery he could muster to focus and use those powers.

He closed his eyes and reached inside the penguins' brains, sending a flood of thoughts across the pier.

Stop! We are your friends. I am family.

His cries echoed inside the bird brains. The penguins were too angry and vicious to be stopped completely, their hatred too ingrained from the Earl's terrible rule. But with Bolt's continual thoughts of peace and love, the penguins hesitated just enough so that their battle with Blackburn and Annika came to a standstill.

Beads of sweat formed on Bolt's forehead as he increased his concentration.

We are family. Penguins are peaceful. I have an idea—let's go bowling.

He hated encouraging penguin bowling, but he was desperate.

Three or four penguins ran off, presumably to get their bowling shoes. But even without those penguins battling, it was just a matter of time before Blackburn and Annika were overpowered.

Bolt heard a howl, a mad bark, and then a large piece of blubbery mass rushed in from behind the penguins, ramming into their backsides. Some penguins tumbled into the water, some shrieked in surprise, and others, distracted, were kicked aside by Blackburn and Annika.

"Pygo?" mumbled Bolt.

Their puppy-like penguin friend was a dog possessed, barking and snarling. She bit the leg of one penguin, slammed into another, and drooled on a third. Closer to Bolt, a swordfish sword swished and a knife gleamed.

"Borscht!" Blackburn fought the hoodie-wearing poker-playing bird. Its beak shot forward, but Blackburn blocked it, and then deftly parried another peck. Another peck, another parry. Peck, parry, peck, parry. Sparks flew from the collision of swordfish blade and penguin beak. Blackburn swung his weapon. The bird ducked and swung its wing, but Blackburn somersaulted backward and then sprang up and shouted, "Tripped again!"

The hoodie-clad penguin rushed forward and Blackburn barely had time to react. The bird feinted to the left and Blackburn twirled away, raising his swordfish to block the thrust that never came. Fooled by the fake maneuver, Blackburn's body was unguarded, and the penguin's beak shot forward and pierced it. Blackburn staggered back, his hands clutching his chest.

"Blackburn! No!" Bolt and Annika cried at the same time.

Blackburn looked dazed, his legs wobbly. But he was dazed, not dead. He pulled his *Pirate Handbook* out of his vest pocket, a handbook which now had a beak hole in the middle. "First ye took me ship, and now ye've ruined me

book, ye beastly bird!" He headbutted the penguin in its belly, and the bird fell into the water.

A loud chorus of barks rose from the harbor's edge. Two dozen additional penguins soldiers waddled toward them. Reinforcements.

"To the ship!" cried Blackburn. Pygo and Annika hopped aboard, quickly followed by the pirate. As Blackburn scurried on board, he sliced the ropes still holding the boat to the deck's cleats.

The wind, as if waiting for that moment to join the fight, filled the sails. The ship lurched away from the pier. The penguins watched as the boat sailed away, the winds whisking Bolt and his friends farther and farther into the sea.

Annika hung over the railing. "Why aren't they following us? Penguins can swim, right?"

"Maybe they are under strict orders not to leave Sphen," Bolt guessed.

"You must be right," said Annika, but she seemed uncertain. Bolt was, too. He thought of the saying "never look a gift horse in the mouth," although he had never quite understood why you wouldn't look at a horse's mouth if you received one as a present. What if your horse had a cavity? Wouldn't you need to take it to the dentist? The whole expression was as odd as the unmoving penguins on the pier.

Pygo barked and hopped up and down, and Bolt patted her head. "Good girl. But how did you know we needed help? Where did you come from?"

Bolt couldn't read this penguin's thoughts. As always, he just felt a wall, although he caught a quick image of squeaky rubber toys and a bag of puppy chow. Pygo wagged her short wedge-shaped tail.

"I'm just glad this penguin showed up," said Blackburn. "After all, ye should never look a gift horse in the mouth, although I've never quite understood the expression."

"The whole dentist and cavity thing, right?" asked Bolt, and Blackburn nodded.

31.
Out on the Deep Blue Sea

A school of minnows swam alongside *The Heinous Hering* while it carved its way through the water. Bolt waved down to them, although it was hard to see if they waved back under the foamy water. Bolt felt at home here, his penguin heartbeat in sync with the crashing of the waves. He could feel the sea salt in his skin, the foam mist in his lungs, and the smell of fish in his sinuses. He wished he were swimming, rather than watching the water from the ship's deck, but he was hardly dressed for it.

This was the first chance he'd had to think in a while, which wasn't necessarily a good thing. His thoughts of the Earl turned to worries, his worries to terror. He was no fighter—the battle on the pier had reminded him of that.

He also thought of the seagull girl he had seen. A were-gull? He hadn't been aware such creatures existed, but why not? He hadn't known about werepenguins until a few months earlier.

Was she a friend? An enemy? Just a random creature of the night? He had no way of knowing what role she might play in the fight against the Earl, if any.

Meanwhile, Annika groaned, her head hanging over the starboard railing. Unlike Bolt, she was not meant for the sea.

Pygo ate fish-flavored dog chow from a bowl, a bag of which they'd found belowdecks while patching the hole.

Blackburn steered, a big grin on his face, his elation bursting out with an occasional "Borscht!" or by singing a jaunty pirate song such as this one:

> *Lock down the hatches, pass out eye patches,*
> *For new treasure we set our course.*
> *Me foes walk me planks, and I give me thanks*
> *For pirating while shouting, "Borscht!"*

His tune was halted as he pointed out to the water, the wind knocking his tricorn pirate hat off his head, and his hair standing up. "Shiver me timbers! Sharks!"

Bolt ran to the side of the boat to look. Annika stayed where she was, and threw up again.

Three sharks swam next to the boat's hull. They had large fins and, worst of all, large teeth. Great white sharks are feared by all sea creatures, but these were the dreaded great off-white sharks, which are rumored to be . . . just as big and nasty as their more famous kin.

One of the sharks rammed into the boat, nose-first. Great off-white sharks are known for their strong noses, and the boat lurched. A wave of water splashed onto the deck. Then another shark rammed the hull.

And then the third.

Bolt's birthmark tingled, as it did whenever a werepenguin was near, or he was faced with a terrible seacreature threat, like this one. He wondered if the sharks could sense him, if they somehow knew a werepenguin was on board. Sharks love the taste of penguin.

Again, a shark rammed the boat with its ramrod nose. Wood splintered. The watermelon-size hole that Bolt and Blackburn had just patched was once again a watermelonsize hole, or perhaps now the size of a large pumpkin.

"I hate sharks," muttered Blackburn as two more sharks battered the hull. More wood splintered. The hole widened, and water poured into the lower cabins. "Curses! They're going to take down this ship. And then eat our floating carcasses for dinner."

"It's closer to lunchtime," Bolt corrected him. "And I think they'll eat me first, if that makes you feel better."

"A little," admitted Blackburn. "I'd rather be a main course than the appetizer, if I had me druthers. Still, I'd rather not be eaten at all." He unsheathed his swordfish sword. "A pirate always goes down with his ship, but that doesn't mean I won't go down fighting. Are ye both with me?"

Annika responded by leaning over the railing of the ship to throw up. Pygo barked twice and wagged her tail.

Only Bolt was silent. Thinking.

Two of the sharks butted their heads against the ship again. The ship rocked, a wave of water splashed onto Bolt's feet, and he staggered back toward the edge of the ship.

He reached for the railing to keep himself from toppling over, paused for a moment, and then made up his mind. There was only one way to save the ship.

Later, he would look back at this moment with pride. He had never considered himself brave, but if bravery was measured by deeds and not fears, then maybe Bolt was far braver than he gave himself credit for.

"See you guys later," he said right before he dropped over the edge of the boat, curling into a ball as he hit the waves.

"Man overboard!" cried Blackburn, his voice tinny and faint to Bolt in the water. "Or, boy overboard. Or, boy who is penguin-like overboard, maybe?"

Bolt's eyes stung, just for a moment before they adjusted to the harsh salt water. His penguin blood kept him warm, but he wished he had thought to kick off his shoes and his clothes. They were drenched and heavy.

The sharks stopped their frenzied boat-ramming to eye Bolt. They would have licked their lips if they had lips.

"Hi, guys," said Bolt, gulping in air as he bobbed upon the waves. "You wanted me, right? Well, here I am. Lunch, or maybe the pre-lunch appetizer. Come and get me."

32.
Into the Deep Blue Sea

While jumping off the boat had been a surprising feat of bravery for Bolt, he regretted his action as soon as he hit the water. He was going to fight sharks? What had he been thinking?

But even stronger than his desire to not be battling sharks was his desire to not be eaten by sharks. At least the creatures had stopped ramming the ship with their steel-like noses. The ship's inertia had kept it moving, floating off into a mist that had settled on the water. It would be safe, unlike Bolt. As a werepenguin, he might have had a chance to fight the sharks off. But he was no match for them now.

Although Bolt was not a penguin, his penguin blood endowed him with some penguin skills, such as the ability to hold his breath longer than any human, and he could swim faster than anyone else with arms and legs. He dove under the water. The sharks gave chase.

Bolt kicked, pushing the water with his limbs, hurtling through the dark sea with as much speed as he could muster. He had the endurance of a penguin, so he kicked without worrying about tiring.

Bolt kicked down, down, down. Pink, purple, and green sea plants rose from the depths, thin and wiggly, waving in the water as if calling out, *Welcome! Your bones will soon join us!*

Up ahead, Bolt spied an old pirate ship sitting on the bottom of the sea. Its wood was rotted, and green algae was thick on it walls. Bolt couldn't help but wonder if Blackburn would have been excited to see the ship, or sad to see it resting in Davy Jones's locker.

Bolt saw a chance to survive. He dove toward the rotting craft, hoping to hide inside it. But the sharks behind him had fins and bodies shaped like torpedoes. They were faster and quickly gaining. Bolt doubted he would make it to the boat before the sharks reached him.

Bolt zigged and zagged. The sharks zigged and zagged a little better. Bolt swam a giant loop. The loop the sharks swam was a little more impressive. He spun left, spun right, and then did a giant figure eight. The sharks didn't just spin and do a more masterful figure eight; they also did a figure nine and ten, just to show off.

Only a miracle would keep Bolt from being eaten.

An army of bubbles erupted behind the sharks. Swimming doggy-paddle-style yet remarkably fast, Pygo emerged from the froth. The shark trio did not see Pygo approach—they had been too busy finishing their beautiful figure tens—until the penguin rammed into them, scattering them, her mouth open in a soundless *Arf!*

Pygo did no damage—really, what can a penguin do to a shark?—but her appearance shocked and distracted them just long enough for Bolt to reach the sunken ship, Pygo by his side.

They swam through an open crack in the hull and were soon belowdecks.

The sharks were too big to fit into the crack, but they rammed the hull with their powerful noses, splintering the wood that had softened and rotted from decades on the seafloor. Wood chips filled the water. Bolt and Pygo swatted the fragments as they dove deeper. They slipped through more cracks, but the sharks kept coming,

bulldozing through wall after wall. Jaws snapped. Wood crunched. Bolt and Pygo somehow managed to stay ahead of the monsters' choppers, but just barely.

Bolt and Pygo kicked forward, through another narrow crack. They had swum through the entire ship and emerged into the open sea once again. Behind them, the three sharks shot out of the hull, bursting through it.

Bolt and Pygo turned and swam back through a crack into the boat.

BAM! The sharks followed.

Bolt and Pygo slithered in and out of the boat. The sharks crashed after them.

Slither, CRASH! Slither, CRASH!

Fortunately, there were a lot of cracks for Bolt and Pygo to slither through. And now, thanks to the sharks, there were a lot of holes.

The sharks were slowing, tiring, but still snarling, the ferocity behind their sharp teeth propelling them onward, even as they grew weaker.

But Bolt needed them to remain strong just a minute longer.

Bolt and Pygo wiggled through another crack, and CRASH! The sharks followed.

The ship wobbled. The walls had so many holes, the entire boat looked like it might collapse at any moment.

At least, Bolt hoped so.

He and Pygo glided through another crack, and three shark holes exploded behind them, wood bending and breaking as if the hull had been constructed from Popsicle sticks.

The ship rocked.

The walls swayed.

The wooden sides of the boat crumbled.

Pygo and Bolt shimmied through a quickly widening crack. As they shot out of the boat, and into the safety of the open sea, the entire boat seemed to swallow itself, imploding in a cloud of debris and dust.

The sharks were nowhere to be seen. Whether they survived the destruction of the rotted pirate boat, Bolt would never know. As he and Pygo kicked farther away, the ocean bottom turned into a cloud of dust and floating wood.

Bolt broke through the sea's surface, desperately sucking in air. He hadn't realized how close he had been to running out of oxygen.

On the horizon, *The Heinous Hering with One R* headed toward them.

Ten minutes later, Bolt was back on the boat, drying himself with a towel while Pygo shook the water off, dog-like. Pygo had seemed almost penguin-like in the water, but now that they were on the boat, she was back to her old yipping and yapping self, chasing her tail.

"Good girl," said Bolt, rubbing Pygo's belly.

"Land ho!" shouted Blackburn from where he stood at the ship's wheel.

Annika greeted the news by not getting sick for a moment, but then got sick again, over the railing. The distant shores of Omnescia grew nearer.

The large green island featured a tall mountain in the middle, reaching up to the clouds. Atop its sandy shores stood a twenty-foot stone statue of an old, bald man wearing a toga and a pair of cheap plastic X-ray glasses with black spirals painted on the lenses. The man was sticking out his tongue with puffed lips, as if greeting every visitor to the island by blowing a raspberry.

33.

Gentoo and the Warning

Gentoo walked back to the pier, a fresh bag of worms in her grasp, her shopping at the bait store successful. She hoped these worms would attract more fish than her last bag; they had caught so few fish that Gentoo had eaten the worms for dinner. Worms were quite tasty, so she hadn't minded so much. Her aunt had even put a little cinnamon on them.

She hurried down the city streets. She didn't think much about the visitor she had met earlier that day, other than how odd it was to find a visitor in Sphen at all.

But while meeting the girl had been surprising, seeing a new werepenguin the other night had been even more so. Perhaps this was a new evil, come to rule them all?

Gentoo knew in her heart that wasn't so. This new

creature hadn't seemed evil, at least not Earl-like evil. He hadn't laughed maniacally, as the Earl was known to do, and hadn't immediately tried to peck her to death, as the Earl was also known to do.

Gentoo rounded the corner, in a hurry, and didn't see the penguin soldier standing there. Gentoo nearly ran into him, but managed to sidestep into a lamppost. The lamppost was harder and more painful than the penguin, but the punishment for hitting a lamppost was far less.

"Did you hear about the seagull who turned into a lamppost?" she asked herself, quietly so no one else could overhear. "How it turned back from a lamppost into a seagull, I'll never know."

She picked herself up from the ground and then stared at the sign posted on the lamppost. It was the same sign she had seen earlier, but someone had updated it.

Public Announcement: Hanging ~~*Next Friday*~~ *in two days!*
Town Square, ~~*10:00 a.m. sharp*~~ *8:00 a.m.!*
We've caught the greatest bandit of all time. He must pay for his crimes!*

*He must pay and so must you: 5 flumkins per person or donate a fish!

Two days! Gentoo wondered why they had moved up the date.

Gentoo looked up, just as a seagull neared from overhead, swooped down, and landed on her shoulder and then pecked lovingly at her ear. "Ha, ha!" it cried.

"Not now," she said to the gull, not wanting to draw attention to herself. Besides, she was in a rush to get back, while there were still a few hours of daylight left for fishing. She didn't have time to play. "Go peck someone else, OK?"

She didn't mean it to be rude, or harsh. But the next thing she knew, the bird was making a straight line toward the penguin across the street, beak out.

As Gentoo hurried away she heard the fluttering of wings and an angry, pained howl from the penguin. She didn't look back, but smiled.

She rushed down the street, her bait box clasped in her hand, and saw smoke rising in the air well before she reached the pier. The smell of burning wood, nearly as strong as the perpetual stink of dead fish, grew stronger and stronger. When Gentoo finally cleared the last few buildings, she looked out at the pier, where flames crackled and smoke rose from a ship.

Was that *The Beautiful Seagull?*

A lump caught in Gentoo's throat and remained there,

lodged in her windpipe. She ran closer, and didn't breathe until she saw that her ship was fine. Unfortunately another boat, one down the dock from *The Beautiful Seagull,* was aflame. Most of the other boats were out in the sea, so there wasn't a big crowd watching, but Gentoo's aunt stood at the end of the pier sobbing, along with two other fishermen, each with long black beards down their gaunt faces. Gentoo didn't know their names.

"What happened?" asked Gentoo, jogging up to them.

"Pier patrol set Noah Fredrickson's boat on fire because he couldn't pay his fish taxes," said one of the fishermen, shaking his head.

"Poor Noah!" wailed Aunt Margie.

"It's bad enough us fishermen can barely make a living anymore," said the other fisherman with a moan. "But now they're burning our boats? I should leave Sphen and try to make a living somewhere else."

"What's stopping you?" asked the first fisherman.

"A thousand penguins who will eat me if I'm caught," said the second one.

"Good reason," said the first.

As they watched the smoke rise higher and higher, a seagull flew over the boat, circling it. Gentoo waved.

Gentoo's aunt wiped tears from her eyes and then turned to Gentoo. She knelt down so they were eye to eye. "The penguins are getting worse. Once they would have

given us a warning, but now they show no mercy. Promise me you'll be careful."

"I'm always careful," Gentoo assured her aunt.

"Promise me anyway."

"I promise," said Gentoo. Why was her aunt so worried about her? Sure, the seas were almost barren of fish, but they always had enough fish to pay the taxes.

"Just don't do anything rash."

"Me?" What could Gentoo possibly do? "Don't worry, Aunt Margie. Penguins won't burn our boat. I would never let them."

34.
See Here

Bolt stepped off *The Heinous Hering with One R* and onto the sandy shores of Omnescia. The sand was so white, it nearly blinded him, and the pristine air of the island was so free of hate, it made Bolt giddy. While penguins are, mostly, creatures of the cold and wet, a bit of sunshine can make any creature happy. Bolt smiled as the warm sun beat down on him. "I can practically smell the carefree happiness."

While Bolt stood on the beach with

a wide grin on his face, Annika's eyes were narrowed in suspicion. She sniffed warily. "I don't like it," she grunted. "Bandits don't do carefree happiness."

Off in the distance, a group of penguins played on the shore. Bolt longed to join them. But he was here with a job to do, not to enjoy himself.

Past the sand lay a small village, with primitive huts made from wood and thatch, dirt paths, and no sign of electricity or plumbing. All the Omnescians wore white tunics and were bald, including the women.

One woman carried a large basket of fruit on her shoulder. Her eyes were closed and she walked straight into a house and then toppled to the ground. It looked painful. A man with a large jug of water also walked with his eyes closed and bumped into a tree. Bolt winced as the man fell backward holding his nose, and his jug landed on a rock and cracked in half.

"Welcome, visitors." An incredibly tall man approached them—he must have stood ten feet tall. Most of his height came from his impossibly long legs, although they were hidden by his long tunic. He walked stiffly. In one hand he held an umbrella, even though the sky above was bright and sunny.

"We have been expecting you," said the tall Omnescian, bowing. "The great seer, he whom we obey and honor, foretold your presence." He raised his umbrella. "Just like he foretold it would rain today."

"There's not a cloud in the sky," Annika pointed out.

The man tossed the umbrella over his shoulder. "Well, the great seer knows almost everything. I am Qvadaciuosruffinmaliwitzian." Spittle flew from his mouth.

"Thank you, Qvadcious . . . what was that again?" asked Blackburn.

"Call me Quad."

"Borscht!" replied Blackburn.

"No, *Quad*," repeated the man.

Two Omnescian women strode past them. Their eyes were also closed and they walked straight into each other, and fell. They scrambled to their feet, and then crashed into each other again.

"Why is everyone walking around with their eyes closed?" asked Bolt.

"Here in Omnescia we are all seers in training. We try to see with our inner eyes whenever possible. Someday we hope to share the great one's gift and see the world, always."

Someone howled, and Bolt turned to see four people on the ground, each holding their heads and moaning.

"Most of us still need a lot of practice," Quad admitted. He closed his eyes. "With my inner eye I see you—six people who have traveled from far away."

"Actually, there are four of us, and one of us is a penguin," said Annika.

"And you have questions," he continued.

"Sure, we want to know—" began Bolt, but Quad held up his hand.

"I know what you seek. You are curious if the groundhog will see his shadow this year. You want to know what you should buy a unicyclist for his birthday, and you seek the world's greatest recipe for pumpkin pie." He opened his eyes triumphantly. "Am I right?"

"Not even remotely close," said Annika.

"Aye," said Blackburn. "Although I do like a good pumpkin pie."

Quad shook his fist. "I'll get the hang of it one of these days. But enough chatting. Follow me." Quad stepped forward and stumbled. He cursed, sat down, and unstrapped a pair of stilts that had been under his tunic. He rolled up

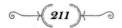

the extra fabric of his tunic and secured it in place with a button. When he stood up, Quad was now shorter than Bolt. "Ah, that's better."

"Are the stilts part of your training?" guessed Bolt. "So you can see the world from a different viewpoint, or something like that?"

"No, I just like stilts," explained Quad. "If I hadn't become a disciple of the great seer, I was going to join the circus." He sighed. "Maybe someday." He left the stilts in the sand and led the group deeper into the village, past huts and small fires where people roasted lizards on spits. Some of them tried to grab the spits with their hands, but with their eyes closed. Their moans from burnt fingers were painful to hear.

Up above, the sky suddenly filled with clouds, a crack of thunder rang out, and rain fell in torrents, drenching everyone. The shower ended as quickly as it had started, the sun reappearing and the clouds dissipating in seconds.

"Sorry for doubting you, oh great one!" shouted Quad, bowing to his right and left. He bowed a few more times before straightening up and continuing to walk forward. "Come, we have prepared tents for all of you. We will celebrate your arrival with a great feast, followed by a month-long series of Mad Libs, meditation lessons, and challenging games of dominoes."

"We were kind of hoping to talk to the seer and leave,"

said Annika with a grumble. "We're in a bit of a time crunch."

"A shame, we get so few visitors," said Quad.

"Will we see the seer now?" Annika asked, fidgeting impatiently.

"Oh, no," said Quad, jabbing a finger at Annika. "You will not see Omneseus. Never, ever."

"What do you mean?" Annika asked, mouth scowling, her hand slipping to her belt, where her knife was tucked. "We have to see him. It's a matter of life and death!" Bolt knew she was preparing to fight.

"You misunderstand," said Quad, bowing. "Only Bolt will see Omneseus. He is the chosen one."

"And I'm chosen for what, exactly?" asked Bolt, leaning in, raising his eyebrows. He had heard those words often, but he was still quite unclear about what he was chosen to do. Maybe, finally, someone would tell him.

Quad shrugged. "Beats me. Omneseus just said you were chosen. I didn't ask for specifics."

"I want to go, too," said Annika. She stepped toward the Omnescian, her hand reaching for her knife again, but Bolt put his hand on her arm to calm her. "It'll be OK." Bolt gave her a friendly squeeze. "I'll be back soon. And then we'll know how to defeat the Earl and free the people of Sphen."

Annika eyed Quad, and then she eyed Bolt, her knife

hand twitching. But after taking a deep breath, she slipped her knife back into her belt. "Just hurry, OK?"

"We'll free Sphen," said Bolt. "Whether it takes days or weeks."

"We don't have weeks," grunted Annika.

"Why not?" Bolt asked.

Annika turned away. "Just because."

Bolt was proud of Annika for being so impatient—it showed how much she cared about the people of Sphen. Why else would she be in such a rush?

Quad showed Annika, Blackburn, and Pygo to their tents, which were all quite luxurious, with full beds and ample space inside them. The covers for the beds were half on the floor. "It's hard to make beds with your eyes closed," explained Quad. To Bolt he said, "Come."

The man led Bolt away from the village, down a long path that led to the base of the great mountain. "The seer lives up there," said Quad. Bolt peered up, but the mountain rose so high he couldn't see the top, which disappeared into fog and clouds.

"Why does he live so high?" asked Bolt.

"It is easier to see the future in solitude," said Quad. "Also, property taxes are a lot cheaper up there." The two began their ascent, following a small dirt path that led up the mountain.

The path inched up slowly at first, but soon grew

steeper, and the dirt gave way to stone steps. The stones were uneven and chipped, making them difficult to walk on.

After fifteen minutes or so, they were still much, much closer to the bottom of the mountain than even the middle of it, but Bolt's legs dragged. Even with his penguin-infused stamina, it was tiring to climb up a mountain, especially after fleeing three great off-white sharks.

Eventually, the path stopped rising, and two large stone pillars, crumbling and ancient, marked the path's entrance atop a wide plateau. "Are we there?" Bolt asked, hopefully.

"If you mean are we at a large plateau halfway to the seer's cave, then yes."

Bolt sighed as Quad pointed to another set of stones rising up the mountain once again. Soon, they were walking through dense fog, or perhaps a cloud, as the uneven and chipped stone staircase twisted higher.

Bolt began to pant, but despite the distance, Quad didn't even appear to be tired. "This climb is much harder when I'm wearing my stilts," he explained.

They continued to climb and Bolt continued to pant. Finally, as Bolt feared he couldn't take another step without collapsing in exhaustion, Quad pointed forward. The path led directly into a dark cave, just above them. Two stalactites hung from the top of the entrance like fangs, making the mouth of the cave look like the mouth of a

giant and ferocious serpent. "The seer awaits. In there."

"He couldn't live in a cave that looked like the mouth of something happy, like a panda bear?" Bolt wondered.

"Panda bears are the most power-hungry creature in the world," said Quad.

"I've heard that." Bolt took a step up the path, although Quad did not move. "Aren't you going in, too?"

"The seer asked to see only you." He bowed, turned, and began the long descent down the mountain.

Bolt walked up the remaining steps and entered the dark serpent-like entrance to the cave, alone.

35.
The Great Seer

Bolt was a feared creature of the night, and he felt that feared creatures of the night should be able to walk into a dark cave without shaking legs. But his legs shook anyway. Yes, he had fought sharks. Yes, he had defeated a baron. Yes, he would fight an earl. But he was still afraid of the dark.

The dark reminded Bolt of the orphanage where he grew up. Nighttime had been when the moles would emerge from the orphanage floorboards and nibble on the boys' toes in search of food. Even now, despite the fact that he was wearing shoes, Bolt's big toes throbbed nervously as the cave's darkness swallowed him.

Bolt took only a few steps inside before he saw a small fire at the end of the cave. The flames danced and swayed, as flames do. Bolt walked toward the fire, the dread in his stomach dancing and swaying, too.

But a small fire was better than no light at all, and the glowing flames soon revealed a small man sitting in the lotus position. He wore the same white tunic as the others on the island, although he appeared older and thinner. He also wore plastic X-ray glasses, just like his statue. He grasped a staff, or maybe an old tree branch.

The man did not move until Bolt stood in front of the fire. Before then, Bolt wasn't completely sure if the man was awake, or alive. But then the man jerked his head. "Welcome, Bolt. I have been expecting you," he said in a powerful voice, a voice much more powerful than Bolt would have thought could come from such a thin man. Bolt hiccupped in surprise. "Do not hiccup. Sit." Bolt did as he was told, swallowing any further hiccups and sitting across from the man, so the fire separated them. Then the seer threw back his head and cackled loudly.

Bolt knew that fortune tellers often cackled for no reason, and seers were similar to fortune tellers. But, in the blackened cave, the cackling was still unnerving.

Bolt took a deep breath, inhaling the deep rich scent of charred wood, but also a hint of marshmallows and chocolate. The remains of a s'more clung to the tip of the great seer's staff.

"I need . . ." began Bolt, but the seer put his finger over his lips, motioning Bolt to be silent.

"I know what you need!" He pointed at Bolt. "For I see all. I see the trouble in Sphen. I see the Earl's menace. I see your ear about to itch!"

Bolt suddenly had an uncontrollable itch in his ear, and he scratched it. "Wow," Bolt mumbled to himself. "This guy is good."

"I see a gnat in a small town about to crawl under a rock!" Bolt had no way to check if that was true, but assumed the seer knew what he was talking about. "I see a boy halfway across the world about to burp!"

"That's sort of random," said Bolt.

"But, most of all, I see pain. So much pain!" A stalactite hanging from the cave ceiling cracked off and fell on the seer's head. "Ow," said the seer, wincing. "I was hoping I was wrong about that last one, to be honest." He stood up and began to rant. "I see so many things! I see the stars yawning as they scatter across the evening sky! I see clouds weeping for joy on a sunny day!"

"Can we get back to me and my problems?" Bolt asked.

Omneseus frowned and sat back down. "Fine. Whatever." He stared at Bolt so intently, Bolt almost thought the seer could see right through him. "Oh, yes, I see you. I see you as clearly as I see seashells sold by the seashore."

Bolt was impressed by the seer's enunciation. "For you are the chosen one."

Bolt leaned in closer. "I know that. But I've never been absolutely sure what I was chosen to do. I used to think it was to stop the Baron."

The seer pounded his staff on the ground. "Oh, Bolt! You were chosen for much more than fighting a baron!"

"Like what? Can you go into specifics, please?"

"You were chosen to cough twice!" Bolt coughed, and then coughed again. "You were chosen to lick your lips!" Bolt was about to lick his lip and then stopped as if to prove the seer wrong, and then, when thinking about proving the seer wrong, accidentally licked his lips. "And I can see you were chosen to say 'what.'"

"What?"

"Exactly!" shouted the seer. "But that's not all. Oh, no. You were chosen for many more things, Bolt. For you carry the mark, child."

Bolt tilted his head to his left, slightly. He was self-conscious about the large penguin birthmark on his neck. "I hate this birthmark," he groaned.

"Your birthmark is not the only way you are marked. There are invisible marks upon your soul. Oh, yes, I can read those, too."

Bolt felt uneasy, as if he weren't wearing clothes. He blushed. He wondered if this was how penguins felt when

he read their innermost thoughts. "What other marks?" he asked. "What do you mean?"

"That's for me to know and you to find out," said the seer. "For you are here to discuss the Earl, not marks."

It wasn't easy for Bolt to put aside all his other questions, but the seer was right. The Earl was the immediate problem, although just thinking of the monster was enough for Bolt's legs to start shaking again. "Do you know how I can defeat him? Can I even defeat him? I mean, he seems to be way more powerful than I am."

"Power is not the same as strength."

"It sort of is."

"The Baron was stronger than you, yet you defeated him, no?"

"Sure, but I had help, and I had the tooth of a killer whale. Is that the weapon I need now?"

The seer cackled again. "You will need something far better than a pointy tooth!"

"Like what?"

The seer cackled some more and then announced, "You will need an egg!"

Bolt, who had been leaning forward to catch every word, nearly toppled over into the fire. "An egg?" He righted himself and blinked. "Like scrambled eggs?" he asked incredulously.

The seer shook his head. "How would you defeat a

powerful monster with scrambled eggs?"

"I don't know. That's why I asked it incredulously. An egg didn't seem better than a pointy tooth. Quite the opposite, actually."

"My boy, you cannot defeat the Earl with a plate of scrambled eggs, nor even with an omelet. No, you must defeat him with the egg . . . of Shorty!"

Bolt blinked a few more times. "Who?"

"Shorty the penguin. You must climb to the top of this mountain and steal one of Shorty's eggs from her nest. Then return to me."

"I'm not at the top of the mountain already?" asked Bolt, remembering the long, impossible climb.

"Not even close."

Bolt muttered a couple of curse words he had learned at the orphanage under his breath. He would have preferred the seer to just hand him a pointy weapon rather than sending him off to get an egg. "How will this egg help me fight the Earl?"

"You will know what to do when the time is right."

"What if I don't?"

"You will! For I have seen it, just like I see that spider about to crawl on your foot!"

Bolt looked down and saw a bug about to jump on his shoe. "Actually, that's a cricket."

"Well, no one bats a thousand. But do not worry. I'm hardly ever wrong."

Bolt winced at the words *hardly ever* and he had serious doubts an egg could stop a werepenguin. Could the seer be wrong about that, too? At least, other than a steep climb, stealing an egg from a penguin named Shorty sounded like a fairly easy quest.

The sooner Bolt set off, the sooner he would complete his potentially worthless mission. So he stood up and straightened his backpack. "I guess I'll get that egg, then. Any last words?"

"Nope. Let us just hope that your words aren't *your* last ones."

With that depressing thought, Bolt waved goodbye and exited the cave.

36.
Meanwhile, Down Below

Penguins squawked merrily along the shoreline, but their barking felt unfamiliar to Annika, for there was no anger in it. Penguin squawks usually terrified her, as she expected those cries to be followed by a penguin trying to hang her, or throw her in a dungeon. These birds felt like an entirely new species.

"You should join them," Annika suggest to Pygo, who sat on the ground next to her. "Make some friends."

Pygo tilted her head to the side as if to say, *Why would I want to be friends with a group of penguins? I'm a puppy.*

Annika turned away from Pygo and back toward the boat, where Blackburn was fixing the last of the shark holes. It had been a miracle the ship hadn't sunk. One more nose-first shark hit would have done them in.

The repairs had gone quickly. The robed disciples of the seer kept bringing them wood and tools, often before they were needed. Quad had said things like, "The seer foretold you would need a joiner's mallet next." The Omnescians also brought food, cradled in heavily bandaged and burnt fingers: a hearty stew that smelled like cabbage but tasted like marmalade, a glass of a thick milk that smelled like mint but tasted like meatballs, and a plate of warm pastries that smelled like chocolate chip cookies and, thankfully, tasted like chocolate chip cookies. Unfortunately, some other dishes had been ruined when a group of blindfolded Omnesicans crashed into each other.

Annika was delighted to eat. She had thrown up for nearly the entire trip to the island and was very hungry, but soon she felt like herself again.

Her mind wandered back to the Sphen dungeons. While she wiggled her toes in the pristine white sand, her father stood on the cold stone floor of his cell. While she ate refreshing foods, he dined on burnt fish sticks, if he was lucky.

Time was wasting. She was restless to return to Sphen and save him.

Blackburn drove in a final nail and then stood back to admire his work. "Not beautiful, mind you. But seaworthy, and that's all that matters."

Without warning, he unsheathed his swordfish,

turned, and swung it at Annika. "Defend yerself, missy!"

Annika grabbed a wooden stick that lay on the ground, raising it to block the weapon just in time.

Blackburn swung his sword straight at Annika's head. She ducked, and the blade whizzed above her, grazing a bobby pin in her hair. Blackburn jabbed to the right and to the left. Annika stepped back, and then back again.

"Beware Blackburn the pirate!"

He swung his sword anew, and again Annika raised her stick to deflect it. But a stick is no match for a sword. The blade sliced the wood in half. Undaunted, Annika jumped back with her remaining stick halves raised high.

"I'd tie my shoelaces if I were ye," said Blackburn, holding out his sword.

"And while I look down, you'll stab me. Do you think I'm a fool?"

Annika started to dance away from him but tripped over her untied shoelaces.

"Always tie yer shoelaces before a fight," said Blackburn, sliding his swordfish back into its scabbard. "That's the second-most important fighting lesson."

"What's the most important?"

"Never bring a stick to a swordfight."

Annika and Blackburn had taken frequent breaks for sword-fighting lessons. Learning pirate skills might come

in handy someday. Annika's own father had become the leader of the Brugarian Forest Bandits because he had learned to waltz.

"Can you teach me any more pirate tricks?" Annika asked.

"Aye, this is me favorite," said Blackburn. He reached over to Annika's head, and then opened his palm. "Look, a coin in yer ear!"

"Look, twelve coins in your ear." Annika jutted her hand to Blackburn's ear and then showed him a stack of coins in her palm.

He grabbed the coins from her. "Hey, those are mine."

"Sorry. Force of habit."

A penguin bark, long and fierce, interrupted their conversation. The bark crawled up Annika's spine and she crouched, ready to fight, slipping a bobby pin from her hair. But there was no reason to crouch. It had just been a few penguins squawking over an egg.

The penguins, a mother and father, patted their egg. Elsewhere, penguins walked in threes: two parents and a baby. Other penguins fed their young.

There were so many happy families.

Here, among the peaceful waves of the Omnescian shore, Annika saw how penguins free from mind control could love and be loved. Maybe Bolt had not been

entirely wrong to think of penguins as *his* family.

Penguins probably don't lie to each other about why they want to defeat evil earls, either, she thought glumly.

Blackburn put his arm around Annika's shoulders and gazed at the penguins with her. "I know what yer thinking, missy. What if an elephant had the neck of a giraffe?"

"Actually, that's not what I was thinking at all. I was admiring the penguins."

"That was me next guess. There is nothing grander in this world than a peaceful penguin. But ye never want to get between a penguin and an egg. Aye, that can be dangerous. That's how me best friend lost his leg. It was all me fault, too."

"That's horrible!"

"I remember as if it were yesterday. I was practicing me swashbuckling on the beach when I fell into a penguin nest. Nearly smashed an egg, too—and ye never mess with a penguin's egg. The father, enraged, chased me down the beach to where me friend was sitting on his favorite chair. I darted to the side, and the penguin plowed straight into him. One of its legs snapped clean off. I tried to fix it, but the chair always leaned to the left after that."

"Your friend lost a *chair* leg?"

"It was a very nice chair, I'll have ye know. Soon after that, we drifted apart, or rather he drifted away, using

his chair as a raft. But that's another story."

With a frown, Annika picked up another large stick, and held it in front of her as a weapon. "Let's go again." She paused and looked down at her feet. "But let me tie my shoelaces first."

37.
Let's Break the Action Again

Shivering in the cold, I sneezed. I fumbled with my tissues and two blew away, skittering across the remains of the St. Aves Zoo. Despite the frigid air, and the former penguin caretaker's long, beak-ish nose, he didn't even as much as sniffle.

It was as if he was impervious to the cold. But then, I suspected he was. "Let's take a quick visit to Sphen, where Gentoo . . ."

"Let me get this straight," I said, interrupting his narrative, a frown curving onto my lips. "Bolt is scaling a mountain. Annika's father lies in a dark and presumably dingy dungeon. And you're telling me about broken chairs and halting the story's momentum to go back to Gentoo?"

The man nodded his head.

"I question your storytelling skills, sir."

The man shrugged. "Why does a full moon stir werepenguin blood? Why does the fate of an entire city rest on the shoulders of a young orphan boy, a bandit, and a pirate? Does adding a dash of paprika really make a tastier fish stick? *Those* are the questions you should be asking yourself."

"Those questions have all been bubbling in my head since your story began," I admitted. "Well, except the fish stick question, I suppose. I don't care for fish sticks much, to be honest."

The man staggered back. "You shock me, sir!" He straightened himself and regained his composure. "Be that as it may, I find Gentoo's story interesting. You might, too. Humor me."

"I will humor you," I agreed. "But there is no place for humor in a book about werepenguins."

The man nodded his head in solemn agreement. "So true," he said, and then farted.

38.

Gentoo, the Fisher Girl

arguerite Audouin looked greenish. Even her white hair had turned a seaweed-green. It's never good to be greenish unless you are a head of lettuce, or broccoli. She lay in her bed, a soft moan sputtering from her lips. "Water, my dear Gentoo. Water." Her voice scratched through chapped lips.

"You're holding the water glass," Gentoo said politely.

Gentoo's aunt smiled and then sipped from her cup. She set the glass carefully upon the small wooden crate next to the bed. The crate served as an end table, as they were too poor to afford actual end tables. "What would I do without you?"

"You'd be holding a water glass and not drinking it," said Gentoo.

Her aunt sat up. As she did, she winced. Her bones creaked like an old rocking chair. "It is late. We should take the boat out." Gentoo gently pushed her aunt back into a reclining position.

The sounds of her aunt moaning had awoken Gentoo that morning. Gentoo had sprung out of bed, looked briefly at the broken chains on her floor, softly lamented the lousy quality of chains nowadays, and hurried into her aunt's room. Her aunt's forehead burned, and she was mumbling about popcorn balls. Her aunt loved popcorn balls, although she didn't usually mumble about them in the morning.

It was obvious Aunt Margie was quite ill. Gentoo didn't know how sick she was, since they were too poor to afford a thermometer.

"Aunt Margie, you can't fish in your condition. You need to stay in bed. You're sick, although I can't say how sick, since we don't have a thermometer."

"Nonsense," said her aunt, starting to rise again. But the mere exertion of rising was so difficult she soon plopped down on the mattress. "Well, maybe you have a point. But what about the taxes? We have to pay the soldiers. Fish don't grow on trees, you know."

"If only they did," sighed Gentoo, imagining a sardine bush in their backyard. "I will fish by myself. I've been helping you for years. I know exactly what to do."

"I've never heard anything more ridiculous," grunted her aunt.

"A clown landed on the moon flying on a walrus," said Gentoo. Her aunt scratched her head, confused. "Now you've heard something more ridiculous," explained Gentoo, although she wasn't sure if her aunt understood her joke. She looked dazed from her high fever.

"Stay here, Gentoo. We'll get by."

"How?"

"Maybe dead fish will fall from the sky, thrown by catapults."

"Now you are being ridiculous," said Gentoo with a soft smile. "I will fish and return tonight." She kissed her aunt on her forehead, which was so hot it burned her lips. She turned to leave.

"Stay!" declared her aunt. "Something terrible will happen if you fish alone. The pier penguins are ruthless!" Her voice was so raspy and cracked, Gentoo pretended she didn't hear her. Her aunt fell back into a deep, feverish sleep. "Popcorn balls!" she bellowed, dreaming.

Gentoo stepped outside their house, her burnt lips stinging, and her head filled with so much alarm she wished she could put it on snooze. She had never seen her aunt so sick, and Gentoo felt partially responsible. If Aunt Margie hadn't gone out in the middle of the cold night

to buy chains for her, chains Gentoo broke anyway, she might still be well.

As she walked to the pier, toward their boat, Gentoo passed a penguin soldier, and her mind wandered back to the boy werepenguin she had seen on the shore. If only this werepenguin could fight the Earl so they no longer had to pay fish taxes and her aunt would just be sick, and not also sick with worry. She and her seagulls could help!

Of course the entire notion was ridiculous. Not as ridiculous as a clown flying on a walrus, or someone flinging dead fish from a catapult, but close behind them.

As Gentoo stepped onto *The Beautiful Seagull*, penguins watched her from the dock. Ignoring them, Gentoo tried to remember her aunt's routine before they sailed. It was Gentoo's responsibility to untie the ropes and unfurl the sails, and that kept her too busy to watch her aunt closely. So Gentoo took her time, careful not to make an error, although she only guessed at some of the things she needed to do.

Where did *that* rope go again? How did the radio work? What would she eat for lunch?

Soon, the boat was off, but Gentoo felt uneasy, as if there was something she hadn't done. She put her worries aside and concentrated on steering. It felt good to sail the boat herself. She set a course for the open sea, turned

to the left, and then turned to her other left. It was fun to turn, although she was so busy turning that she didn't see the fishing boat in front of her.

The bow of her boat grazed the side of the other boat, nudging it ever so lightly. "Sorry!" she shouted as the fisherman on the other boat rained curses upon Gentoo. After shouting a few more apologies, Gentoo headed out of the harbor and into the murky Deader Sea.

As always, she would have to travel far to find enough fish. She wasn't sure where she was going—her aunt always set their courses—but as the boat sailed away from land and other boats, she closed her eyes and called out to her friends.

Soon, she was surrounded by flapping wings and the cries of the gulls.

I am here.

And the seagulls

answered back, joyous, although somewhat confused as usual.

Welcome, Gentoo! Ha, ha! We love you! Zigzag-marbled saltine house giblets!

The seagulls dropped into the water and quickly emerged with wiggling trout in their beaks. They dropped their gifts at Gentoo's feet. Her aunt would never have allowed such a thing, but she was not here to stop it.

"Thank you, my friends," Gentoo shouted as she leaned back into her seat, her eyes closed. *Collecting fish will be easy*, she thought, falling asleep as the ship floated out aimlessly into the sea.

39.

Shorty's Egg

The wind yearned to throw Bolt off the mountain, or so it seemed. It whipped around, slamming into Bolt in unpredictable rushes. Quiet, calm . . . WHOOSH! Bolt pressed himself against the mountainside until the wind ceased. A large stone next to Bolt tumbled over the side and it fell down, down, gone.

The path was narrower, steeper, and the steps even more broken and uneven than on his earlier mountain climb. Bolt had to steady himself often, not only from the threatening wind but also from the crumbling ground.

Eventually, the path became flatter and, sometime after that, led through a large, flat grassland, filled with a dozen grazing mountain penguins. Mountain penguins have long mountain-goat-like beards, and their feathers are thicker and fuzzier than sea penguins. They are rare, and even rarer to run across, as they are naturally distrustful of people. These penguins were no exception. They watched Bolt skittishly while Bolt tried to calm their fears.

I mean you no harm. I am family. And, by the way, do you know where Shorty the penguin lives? I need one of her eggs.

A mountain penguin rubbed its feet against the ground, bleated twice (mountain penguins bleat instead of barking), and raised a wing. *That way. Go in peace. But I'd leave her eggs alone, if I were you.*

I can't. I need it.

It's your funeral.

That wasn't a very hopeful thing to bleat, but Bolt thanked the mountain penguin for its help and continued along the path, which wound around to the other side of the mountain before climbing up again. Bolt took a deep breath and continued onward.

Finally, the ground leveled once again and the wind slowed. The path had ended. Bolt felt like he was on top of the world. Maybe he was. His brain grew fuzzy from the thin air, but cleared quickly.

On the flat mountaintop was a group of boulders in a circle. The formation reminded Bolt of a nest, but penguins made nests with pebbles, not giant boulders like these. He slunk forward as silently as he could, which was

only semi-quietly. He was no stealthy bandit. His foot cracked a twig. He burped.

He peered over a boulder.

As he suspected, it was a nest, but a giant one. While some penguins line their nests with small twigs and leaves, this nest was covered with long tree branches and small bushes. Three speckled eggs lay inside, and they were the largest eggs Bolt had ever seen, each the size of his arm.

Bolt scurried over the shortest boulder. He walked up to one of the eggs and rapped his knuckles against its shell. It made a dull thud. The egg appeared to be solid rock.

Bolt unzipped his backpack. He tossed the two remaining fish that were inside it down his throat, then picked up the egg. He could barely raise it; the egg was not only as hard as a brick but as heavy as a dozen of them. He lowered the egg inside his backpack gently. He couldn't zip the backpack all the way up, but he raised the zipper as high as he could, so the egg wouldn't fall out. It poked out the top.

"Let's get out of here," he said to the egg, but mostly to himself. "I don't want to see your mom."

A loud, thunderous bleat shook the nest.

Bolt tripped over one of the tree branches in the nest, and banged his knee against it. He grimaced, rolled over, and looked up. "Um, hello."

A mountain penguin glared down at Bolt, standing

fifteen feet tall. It smelled like ten horses. Bolt remembered once reading about dinosaurs, and ancient penguinsauruses that ruled the arctic kingdoms of yore. Bolt didn't know whether this was a dinosaur that had survived, or a more recent creature.

"So, I guess Shorty is an ironic nickname, like calling a bald man Curly?" He wished the seer had mentioned that.

The behemoth didn't comment. She glared at Bolt with intense yellow eyes the color of bananas, and stomped the ground. Bolt got to his feet, standing on a tree branch, but the beast flapped a wing, and the wind from the wing flap toppled Bolt over again.

The monster penguin snorted and

then brayed. *What are you doing with my egg?*

What egg? Bolt answered. He looked at his backpack lying on the ground and realized he wasn't fooling anyone.

"Oh, that egg?"

The egg's mother snorted again.

"You're so big you probably eat whales instead of fish, huh?" Bolt asked. And then he added, but only to himself, *And egg stealers.*

Bolt put his backpack around his shoulders and inched away as best he could over the nest's tree branches.

I am your brother, Bolt thought, still reaching into the monster's head. *I just need your egg so I can defeat a horrible Earl werepenguin. Your egg is as hard as a rock, anyway, so I don't think it can hatch.*

The monster mother gave no indication she cared about Bolt's plan or how hatchable her egg was. She unleashed a bray so loud, so ferocious, that every hair on Bolt stood straight up, including the tiny hairs on his arms. Even if the beast could understand Bolt, she wouldn't listen. Nothing is a stronger than a penguin's bond with an egg. Bolt had only one way to get out of this.

Run for his life.

40.
A Mother of a Battle

Bolt leapt to his feet and pointed behind the colossal penguin. *Look! A box of fish sticks!*

What are fish sticks?

Bolt shook his head. Mountain penguins never ate fish sticks! It was a depressing thought, and for a moment Bolt wanted nothing more than to take Shorty out for dinner. Fortunately, he quickly regained his wits, but the fish stick question distracted Shorty just long enough for Bolt to leap out of the nest and start to run. Bolt wasn't the fastest runner, and with a heavy egg strapped across his back, he was even slower. The monster penguin waddled toward him. Fortunately, penguins can't waddle fast either, and fifteen-foot-tall penguins are only slightly faster than ordinary ones.

Bolt made it to the edge of the mountain and hurried down the steep path he had walked up earlier. He slipped on the cracked ground and skidded on bare dirt patches, and the wind once again threatened to topple him into the great abyss below.

Somehow he didn't fall, trip, or topple.

I'm family. I need the egg to help our brothers and sisters!

The mother penguin merely brayed back angrily. She crashed on the steps, too heavy for the wind to slow her. The path was narrow, but she had enough room to rumble down. The already cracked and shattered stones on the path cracked and shattered even more under her feet.

Just ahead of the beast, Bolt reached the flat ground where he had seen the mountain penguins. The trip down had been far faster than the trip up. The creatures were gone or hiding as Shorty bleated, *My egg! Give me my egg!*

I need your egg. I feel terrible about this, I really do. But the egg is as hard as a stone, so all I'm stealing is a heavy paperweight, if you think about it.

Shorty gave no indication of understanding him. She probably knew as little of paperweights as she did fish sticks.

Bolt veered off the path and ran toward the edge of the mountainside. This was a drastic mistake, as he soon ran out of room to run. *This is even worse than running into a blind alley,* Bolt thought. He could either leap off a cliff or

stand still and be pecked to death by a giant penguin.

Bolt closed his eyes. He could feel the mountain penguins watching him from the safety of their perches and from inside the mountain crevices where they lurked. And, suddenly, Bolt felt his heart slow. He was one with the penguins, part of their family. It was that connection that made him brave. It was why he could fight sea lions, and werepenguins.

I am your brother. Help me.

When Bolt opened his eyes, the monster mom stood over him, but the mountain penguins had left their secret lairs. Bolt reached into their heads. He soothed their fears.

We can do this.

The penguins came, partly out of love and partly because Bolt was silently controlling them. No, not controlling. Asking. Urging. And soon a dozen mountain penguins surrounded him and the penguin monster, forming a circle.

Together.

Now.

One of the mountain penguins jumped forward and pecked the monster mother's rear. She growled and twisted around, but the mountain penguin had already scurried back to the circle. Another penguin leapt forward.

The penguins back at the colony had practiced their tickling circle many times. Bolt only hoped these mountain

penguins were fast learners. Besides, it is far easier for penguins to peck than to tickle.

Peck.

Again, Shorty roared, enraged, and turned to lash out. But that pecking penguin had already rushed back to the edge of the circle, and was replaced by another penguin lunging forward.

Peck.

Yowl!

Peck.

Roar!

Each time a penguin ducked back to the safety of the circle, another buried its beak into Shorty's exposed hind end. Over and over, a dozen times. The colossal penguin mom raised her wings. She twirled in circles, whipping them in a terrible arc, the wind spinning around her like a mini tornado.

Bolt ducked beneath the swirling wings and leapt forward.

Peck. Peck. Peck.

Shorty screamed. She brayed and bleated. She hopped twice and wailed.

And then she leapt.

Penguins are mighty leapers, and this monster jumped higher than Bolt could have imagined possible. She rose so high, Bolt wondered for a moment if she were flying.

Twenty, thirty feet up, and then she fell, fell, fell, over the side of the mountain.

And was gone.

Bolt looked down the edge of the cliff, stricken with confusion and sadness. He hadn't meant to kill the mom, just to swipe her egg. He didn't blame her for wanting it back; it was in her nature.

But Bolt did not see her plummeting to her death, or anywhere. It was as if she had disappeared. Perhaps Shorty had leapt into some secret perch or crevice. Bolt hoped so. He had a feeling she was alive, perhaps hurrying back to her nest to keep her remaining eggs from harm.

The mountain penguins approached Bolt and nuzzled against him. He wrapped his arms around his mountain penguin brothers and sisters.

Thank you.

They hugged him back. *No problem, bro. That's what family is for.*

And another one added, *But I warned you about the egg, didn't I?*

41.

The Light

The sun had nearly set by the time Bolt reentered the great seer's cave. Omneseus sat near his fire; Bolt wasn't sure if the man had even moved since Bolt had last visited.

"You have returned," the seer said. "With the egg, and also a slight crick in your neck."

As Bolt sat down by the fire, he felt a sharp pang in his neck. "If you know so much, you could have warned me that Shorty wasn't exactly short, you know."

The seer shrugged. "I knew you would return. I saw the future, as I do always. How's your nose?"

"Nothing is wrong with my nose," said Bolt gruffly. A bat emerged from the back of the cave and soared into Bolt's nose, before flying off. Bolt rubbed his nostrils and grumbled to himself. "I have the egg. What now?"

"As I said, you will know what to do when the time comes."

"Can't you at least give me a hint about how I can defeat the Earl with an egg?"

"Seers are not allowed to give hints, unless they are chanted."

"How come?"

The seer held his palms up. "I don't make the rules. I just live with them. Do you want the chant or not?"

Bolt nodded. He knew fortune tellers often chanted in confusing rhymes that were helpful, but only sort of. He listened as the seer cleared his throat and sang a slow, funeral dirge–like song.

When all hope is depleted, when birds reign forever,
When they can't be defeated, at least, hardly ever,
When the bright full moon rises, when its power's aglow,
When your feet grow ten sizes, then there's one thing to
*   know.*
To stop the mad ruler's quest, you must go to great
*   lengths.*
And when the moon's at its crest, use a penguin's true
*   strength!*

Bolt blinked once, twice, and then five more times.

"*Use a penguin's true strength?* What does that mean?"

"You must decipher the song's meaning."

Bolt hated chants. "Oh, come on. Unless a penguin's true strength has a pointy end to stab with, your chant doesn't seem helpful. It would be a lot easier for you to just decipher it for me."

The seer shrugged and then sneezed. His X-ray glasses tumbled off his head. He growled, picked them up, paused, and then tossed them over this shoulder. "I hate those things."

"Then why do you wear them?"

"People expect seers to be blind or have strange googly eyes. I hate to disappoint anyone."

Bolt thought the glasses made the seer look silly, but he merely nodded.

Omneseus cleared his throat. He looked so intently into Bolt's eyes, Bolt imagined the man's eyes swirling as if he still wore X-ray glasses. It was as if the seer really was reading the mark inside his soul.

"Fate will guide you, Bolt. For you are chosen, for something."

Bolt felt like screaming. He hated being chosen, for whatever he was chosen for.

The seer stood, strode around the fire and toward Bolt. He bent down and laid his hand on Bolt's shoulder.

"It is late and the trip down the mountain pass is difficult in the dark. You will stay here for the night. Make yourself comfortable."

Bolt looked at the cave, which had nothing but a dirt floor strewn with rocks. "How can I make myself comfortable when I have to sleep on a dirty cave floor strewn with rocks?"

The seer shrugged. "I don't know. I can't see everything." The man backed away and bowed. He bent down, picked up his X-ray glasses and put them back on. "It is always dark for me, Bolt, or at least when I'm wearing dark X-ray glasses in a dimly lit cave. But I also see your left elbow about to tickle." Bolt scratched his elbow. "I see some spittle on your chin." Bolt chortled at this, and some spit flew on his chin. "But mostly, I see light, the light of hope. And you are that light. A lightning bolt brings light to a dark night. That is your destiny, Bolt. That is why you have your name."

"Actually, the boys in the orphanage gave me my nickname because I always bolted under the bed when I was scared." Although he had lived in the orphanage less than a year earlier, those days seemed lifetimes past.

"You were fated to have that nickname, and not because of your bed bolting."

The seer smiled and snapped his fingers. A cloud of

smoke emerged before him, enveloping him. When the smoke dispersed, the seer had vanished.

Bolt had to admit it was a very cool way to leave. With a resigned grunt, and still frustrated about the confusing chant, he curled up on the floor next to the still-crackling campfire, a rock for a pillow.

A penguin's true strength? What was that? He wished seers weren't so mysterious.

The exhaustion from his trip up and down the mountain, and from fighting the monster mother, spread over Bolt. He reached out his fingers and felt his backpack on the ground next to him. He ran his finger up the zipper until it rested on the egg, cold and smooth. He feared coming to the island had been a waste of time. He also couldn't help but feel guilty for stealing the egg.

He supposed that guilt, that love and appreciation of family, was what made him part penguin. It was also what made him human.

With those thoughts, he soon drifted to sleep, relieved that here in Omnescia, the moon was only a crescent in the sky.

42.

Gentoo and the Angry Soldiers

Gentoo steered *The Beautiful Seagull* back through the harbor. She sniffled and rubbed her teary eyes. Her day of fishing had been a failure.

Without Aunt Margie barking orders, Gentoo had slept most of the day. When she awoke, she had drifted miles from the prime fishing spots, and the seagulls were long gone, with only a dozen fish at Gentoo's feet.

Between naps, Gentoo had remembered to drop the net into the water, just like she had done a thousand times, but it was her aunt that always tied the net to the boat. She didn't realize she had forgotten that crucial step until late afternoon, when she went to haul in the net and discovered it wasn't there.

The boat had an emergency net, and for a moment

Gentoo thought she could salvage the day, until she remembered the emergency net had a big hole in it. They might have had the money to repair the net, if her aunt hadn't spent all their hard-earned coins buying chains to keep Gentoo in bed at night.

Gentoo was so frustrated, she jumped into the water, slapping and yelling at fish for not leaping into her boat by themselves, but all she managed to do was annoy two perch and lose a shoe.

She steered back to the pier, the sun starting to set, a nervous rumble in her belly. Her meager haul wouldn't come close to covering the fish taxes. Maybe she could dock unnoticed?

Not a chance. Two human members of the pier patrol stood with the birds watching her, scowling.

Gentoo looped a rope around a piling, her heart fluttering as quickly as her stomach. "A funny thing happened to me today," Gentoo said as she finished tying the rope knots, trying to quiet the worry in her voice as the penguins and patrol officers glared at her.

"Funny? Like a joke?" demanded one of the men.

Gentoo quickly backtracked. "I meant odd funny. Not ha-ha funny. I hate jokes," she added with a forced smile. "What happened was this: we were attacked by walruses. You should have seen it. A dozen giant walruses. No, two

dozen. And so I don't have my fish taxes today. But it's hardly my fault, is it? I'll just bring extra fish tomorrow."

All Sphen fishermen feared uninvited walruses climbing aboard their boats. Not only might rogue walruses eat all your fish, but they are very impolite, chewing with their mouths open and burping.

"Don't matter if walruses attacked you or not," grunted one of the officers. "You still owe your fish taxes. We need sixty-two fish."

"Sixty-two?" That was more than she could catch in a good week. Gentoo held up the bag with her dozen fish. "You can have everything I have." She jumped down from the boat and handed one of the patrol officers the bag.

The officer snarled, looked into the bag, and then tossed it into the water. "You got no tax money, you got no boat. You also owe us money for new beaks."

"W-what do you m-mean?" asked Gentoo, her tongue clumsy in her mouth.

Both officers removed their wooden beaks from around their heads. One of the patrol officers removed a lighter from his pocket.

The officer lit both of the beaks on fire. They burned quickly, flames immediately engulfing the beaks as if they were made out of paper.

Gentoo's eyes widened. "No! Stop! You can't . . ."

They could. The officers tossed the burning beaks onto the boat.

It's not easy to burn a ship. Ships usually have lots of water in and around them, and water doesn't burn well. But this was not the first boat these men had lit. One of the flaming beaks landed on the mainsail, which immediately burst into flames. The other beak was thrown into the middle of the boat, the driest part of the boat, and a second fire quickly leapt up.

Gentoo tried to rush forward, but one of the penguins held her back with its wing. She stared, mouth agape, struggling to break free as charred embers floated up into the darkening skies. The sides of the boat snapped and twisted; glowing red wood chunks fell into the water.

"Let that be a lesson for next time!" snapped one of the human patrol officers.

"But I don't have a ship, so how can there be a next time?" Gentoo asked as the penguin released her and kicked her to the ground.

Gentoo landed with a thud on the hard wooden pier.

The officer didn't answer her question. He and the others walked away, snorting with laughter. Gentoo ran to the water and scooped handfuls of it onto her boat, but it was like grains of sand trying to cover a pyramid.

Gentoo sat on her knees, sobbing, as the flames licked

the sky. The air was so hot, it felt as if the world was melting around her.

The smoke made her eyes water more. She cried so hard, her sniffles had sniffles of their own. She wailed and hugged herself, rocking back and forth, her heart melting with the fire.

After the final ember sank, Gentoo trudged home. She thought of her aunt, sick in bed. What could Gentoo tell her? That her aunt had been right, and Gentoo should never have gone out alone?

Sorry, Aunt Margie. And now our entire source of income and survival is burnt to a crisp. My bad. But want to hear a joke?

When she arrived home, Gentoo saw her aunt was in no mood for bad news, or any news. She was still in bed, moaning, her lips dry and cracking, while the bedcovers were drenched with sweat. Gentoo felt her forehead.

"You're burning up, Aunt Margie. Like our ship."

"What, my darling Gentoo?"

"Nothing."

Gentoo wiped her aunt's face with a dish towel, gave her water, and prepared some broth for her to eat. Her aunt seemed to say something about aardvark tuba plumbing, but she was just mumbling incoherently, like a seagull.

If anything, her aunt was more ill than she had been

before. Gentoo should have stayed home to take care of her! If she had, her aunt might be feeling better, and they would still have a boat. And if Gentoo hadn't snuck out all those years ago, she would never have become a were-gull, and they wouldn't be so poor.

All their problems were Gentoo's fault.

Well, it was all her fault and the Earl's fault. He was the one who forced them to work so hard. He was the one who demanded fish. He was the one who ordered his patrol to burn boats.

Someone needed to stop him. But Gentoo knew that, even with a thousand seagulls by her side, she wouldn't stand a chance against the Earl.

43.
The Uncertain Seas

The next morning, after Bolt awoke alone in the cave and found a pile of fish thoughtfully left next to him for breakfast, he climbed down the mountain. It was a slow journey—the egg on his back hadn't become lighter overnight. Upon arriving at the beach, he was greeted by his friends.

Pygo nuzzled Bolt's hand and barked, and Blackburn clasped him on the back with a hearty "Borscht!"

"Did the seer tell you how to defeat the Earl?" Annika asked.

"Not really," said Bolt. He showed them his egg.

"Can we at least make scrambled eggs for breakfast?" asked Blackburn, but Bolt told him they couldn't.

Annika grabbed her knife, spun, and hurled the knife.

The blade twisted in the air and then embedded itself into the side of a thin tree. "Let's get out of here," she grunted, walking over and yanking her knife from the wood. "I can't believe we wasted so much time coming to this island."

"It'll be OK," said Bolt, jogging after Annika, who was stomping to the boat. "The seer said I would know what to do with the egg when the time came."

"And if you don't?" she asked.

Bolt couldn't answer the question, and so didn't.

As the group went to the ship and began to prepare it for their voyage home, Quad approached. He wore his stilts, so Bolt had to crane his neck to look up at him. "I trust your voyage up the mountain was successful?"

"A complete waste," grumbled Annika.

"Do not underestimate the great seer," said Quad, closing his eyes and breathing deeply. "I can see the future, too. I see a pomegranate tree growing out of your nose, I see all of you marrying dolphins and I see you inventing soap." He opened his eyes and grinned happily. But when he saw Bolt, Annika, and Blackburn all shaking their heads and rolling their eyes, his smile turned into a disappointed frowning. "Well, I tried. Good luck."

"Keep practicing," said Annika, throwing Quad an encouraging thumbs-up.

Soon, the boat was ready and loaded with food prepared by the Omnescians, and then they were off, gliding

along calm waves. Annika was only partially green, and only threw up a few times instead of continually.

"When we land, we're going right to the castle," Annika said.

"Don't we need a plan first?"

"Sure, but we'll figure it out when we get there."

Annika looked so worried—she looked even more worried than seasick—that Bolt promised they would go straight to the castle. He still didn't totally understand why Annika cared so much, since it was against all bandit rules to rescue people. But he was glad she felt that way, as her conviction lightened his load, which had grown even heavier with the egg in his backpack.

They hit a patch of rolling water, and Annika ran to the side of the boat to get sick. Bolt looked out into the sea. A penguin swam in the water, and Bolt felt an aura of hate burning inside its head. The others on the ship were oblivious to the waves of despair weaving themselves across the Deader Sea. The Sphen moon, although hidden now in daylight, stirred inside Bolt, making his blood and his birthmark tingle. Soon, they would return to Sphen. And soon, he would face a werepenguin monster.

No, not a monster. A ruler. Maybe the Earl wasn't such a bad guy after all. Family came in all sorts of shapes and sizes, even oversize, fanged penguin ones.

Yes, Bolt. Rule!

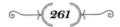

That voice! It was back! And so were those thoughts that kept bubbling up. Join the Earl? Become a hateful violent creature of the night? That twisty evil must be embedded in the layer of Sphen-hate misting around Bolt.

We are waiting for you, Bolt.

The closer they came to Sphen, the louder that voice became! Bolt couldn't quite decide if the voice came from inside him, from his werepenguin curse, or from somewhere else.

Bolt pounded his ear, hoping to squirt out the voice, along with any hate-mist that might have entered. He couldn't let any evil thoughts linger inside him. If they festered, would he ever free himself of them?

"What are you doing?" asked Annika, still looking green.

"Just hitting my ear," said Bolt. "No reason."

The closer they drew to Sphen, the louder the voice inside him spoke.

Join the Earl! Rule the penguins! You might enjoy bowling!

Bolt had to end the Earl's reign with an egg and ignore that tempting voice. He hoped he would succeed.

If only the entire mission didn't feel so hopeless. And if only his ear didn't hurt so much from hitting it.

44.

The Earl

In a room at the very top of the palace, the Earl of Sphen admired himself in a mirror and laughed. Then he frowned. Then he pouted. Then he sneered. It didn't matter what facial expression he tried: he was handsome with every single one. He looked young, too, much younger than his ninety-two years. He had stopped aging many decades earlier, after the night that had changed his life; the night when he had been bitten by the werepenguin.

The Earl's eyes were the only hint of his true age; they were filled with wisdom and insight, or at least dotted with some yellow specks that some people thought meant wisdom or insight, but really just meant his eyes had yellow specks.

He was a large man, and grew larger every day, or at least rounder every day. But rounder was good. Successful people were round, or at least the Earl told himself that.

He looked away from the mirror but continued to smile and pout, imagining how attractive he looked.

The Earl took in a big breath, sucking in the smell of old, rancid fish that surrounded him. There were thousands, maybe tens of thousands of fish crammed into this room, too many fish to ever eat. Some of the fish, the ones at the very bottom of the piles, had spoiled long ago, which only added to the pungent odor that permeated every inch of the castle and clouded most of the city.

The Earl didn't like to go more than a few minutes without snacking, so a pile of fish carcasses always surrounded the throne, his bed, his library, and anywhere else he might like to go.

He was an earl, the mighty Earl of Sphen, so it was his right to keep as many fish as he liked, wherever he liked. If the people complained that they didn't have enough fish to eat because he kept them all, and that the smell made it nearly unbearable to breathe in parts of the city, that was their problem.

Are you there?

The Earl's thoughts of confident mightiness blew out of his head, replaced by the Voice wafting through his skull. Sometimes the Voice was faint. But sitting in a

darkened room surrounded by twenty thousand spoiling fish seemed to enhance the reception.

"I am here," said the Earl. The Earl liked to answer the Voice aloud.

The Earl did not know the name of the being who spoke. The Earl just called him *the Voice*, or *Mr. Voice, sir.* Once, he had called the man *the Stranger*, but that was long ago.

It had been the Voice, or the Stranger, who had bitten the Earl, who had turned him from an ordinary earl to a werepenguin earl. At first, the young Earl thought he was cursed, but that feeling had not lasted long before being replaced by the giddy truth: it was delightful to turn into a penguin at night. Everyone feared you and did whatever you said because they were terrified you would eat their gizzards, although, if he were to be honest, people's gizzards generally didn't taste good. The Stranger had barely stayed a week, only long enough to claim the Earl as his victim, explain what was happening, and set up these weekly telepathic calls.

No one else in Sphen knew of the existence of the Stranger. The Earl didn't like to admit he reported to anyone but himself.

The boy will be there soon. The Voice was raspy, older than the hills. The Earl had no idea how old hills were, other than very.

"That's wonderful," said the Earl, although he didn't know why the Stranger was so interested in this were-penguin boy. "We will have more fish?" That was all the Earl cared about, or at least what he cared about most of all. He picked up a fish carcass from the floor and licked it.

I have promised more, have I not?

The Earl nodded, then, unsure if the Voice could understand a nod, said, "That you have."

Have I not told you that you will have what is rightfully yours?

The Voice sounded angry, and the Earl nodded more enthusiastically and then, again realizing that head nods were potentially meaningless, said, "You have, you have, Mr. Voice, sir." He almost asked if the voiceless stranger could see his head nods, as that would be helpful for future telepathic calls, but then decided against asking. "We're just running out of fish here. That's why I was wondering."

He sucked on the fish in his hand. It calmed him.

If you insist on more fish, take them! You have an army. Use it. After the boy comes, you will lead your army to the neighboring cities. Demand their seafood and then lock their people in your dungeons. The boy will be with you soon. I can sense it.

"And if he doesn't want to lead an army?"

Then throw him in the dungeon until he changes his mind!

The Earl grinned, ear to ear. He enjoyed throwing people in dungeons. Even better, though, he had been

waiting for permission to attack neighboring cities and steal their fish for years. Generally he just sent out small parties of penguins to break into seafood stores, but the bounty they brought back to Sphen was never particularly impressive.

You will hang the prisoner in the morning?

"Yes, yes, yes. Just like you told me. But, well, you know, we made a deal with that girl . . ."

A deal with a human? What do we care about humans? When the war is won, they will snivel at our webbed feet! They are to be used, sucked dry, and tossed over our shoulder.

The Earl, who had been tossing the fish bones over his shoulder after sucking them dry, smiled at the analogy, and then tossed another fish bone and picked up another fish. He had fourteen housekeepers devoted to nothing but cleaning fish bones from around the castle. Technically they were prisoners, but "housekeeper" sounded better, at least when the Earl introduced them to guests.

Not that he had guests, but maybe someday he would.

Soon, the world will bow to all the penguins. Soon, we will rule all. And you will be amply rewarded with as many fish as you can dream of.

The Earl smiled. He could dream of a lot of fish.

When their conversation ended, the Earl walked down the tower steps, around and around, down and down, and toward the throne room, the floor complaining noisily

under his weight. The Earl felt a little dizzy, which he often felt after those conversations, and especially after winding down the tower steps.

He stomped into the throne room, eyeing his massive throne with its golden spiraled edges and rich maroon upholstery. His penguin soldiers stood on the sides of the room in their fashionable fuzzy bearskin caps, along with a smattering of tuxedo-clad humans. He didn't enjoy having people inside the throne room, but they were needed to talk to the prisoners, order them about, and yell at them. Still, he didn't trust them. He couldn't read their minds and control them like he could control the penguins.

He glanced at the giant egg against the wall, a large four-foot egg, and the penguin soldier sitting on it, waiting for the egg to crack and the Earl's child to be born.

The heir! The next ruler of Sphen! Of course if the Earl lived forever, there would be no need for another ruler, but an heir was still nice to have.

In most penguin colonies, male penguin took turns sitting on an egg, but the Earl was too important for such chores. Anyone could sit on an egg, assuming they had a big enough rear end, and while no one's rear end was as big as the Earl's, most penguin rears were big enough.

And soon the egg would hatch! The Earl wasn't quite sure when, but it was long overdue. He also wasn't sure what, exactly, would come out of its shell.

But, in the meantime, he would hang a bandit prisoner and loot a city.

He raised his iron fist. He always liked raising his fist, as it reminded him of his awesomeness. Not everyone had an iron fist.

He stepped over a pile of dead fish and sat on his throne, glancing at the empty cage across the room. Its locks were unpickable and it was shaped like a giant bird-cage. The Earl enjoyed the irony—a bird owning a cage for birds! He just wished he had put the little bird swing inside lower, as it was too high for any prisoner to use. Before he'd had the cage custom-made, the Earl had kept prisoners shackled in the throne room, but it was more fun to mock and torment a prisoner this way.

"Bring up the bandit so we can mock him. And put more signs up announcing his hanging tomorrow morning. I want a big crowd!" He shouted this to no one in

particular. That was the best part of being an earl. He could just shout out orders and someone would obey them. "And some fish sticks! I want some fish sticks!"

The Earl bent down and picked up a dead fish by his feet, and licked it. He hadn't snacked in minutes.

45.
One Final Break in the Action

The penguin caretaker halted telling his story. Despite the cold, his breath made no vapor cloud, unlike mine, which emitted as much as a steam engine. I rubbed my hands before digging them back inside my coat pockets.

"It is cold," said the man. "That, and this terrible story, has left a chill in your bones. Perhaps you care to leave, warm your ears, and free them from my disquieting tale."

"Poppycock," I replied and then smiled because I had never before said *Poppycock* and it's a funny word to say. "Ragamuffin," I muttered, which is another fun word that I had never before said, and had always wanted to.

"Funny words, those two," said the man. "But there is nothing funny about this story. Who could possibly be amused by a boy who turns into a penguin? Or a pirate with a swordfish? Or a young bandit-wannabe stealing items like a wind-up chicken from a jacket pocket?"

"As a boy, I owned a wind-up chicken," I thought out loud. "I wonder what happened to it."

"No doubt it was destroyed, mangled, and discarded— just like your mind may be if we continue to dwell on the terrible past."

"I'm willing to take that chance." As I spoke those words, the angry ostrich ran up and squawked at me. I swatted at the flightless nuisance, and it ran away without another sound.

I wondered if a man who turned into an ostrich would be as annoying. "Were-ostrich," I said to myself, wondering if such a creature could exist. Why not?

"Where ostrich? Why, he went that way," said the caretaker, pointing.

I nodded and shivered again. "Go on," I commanded him. "We must be near the end of your tale. Near-ish. Complete your story and I will give your animals a new home."

The man bit his lip, bit his tongue, and then, impressively, bit his nose. He sighed. "Let's visit the dungeons of Sphen

to see what our two trapped forest bandits are up to."

"And Bolt and his friends?"

"They will be back in our story soon, fortunately for you. Unfortunately for them."

46.

Unfortunately

Vigi Lambda yearned to be free. He was a forest bandit, and not used to being cooped up in a dungeon. His cell had a bed and a toilet and not much else, and smelled like old and decaying fish. But then, the whole palace smelled like decaying fish. Vigi Lambda still hadn't gotten used to the odor.

He also thought of Annika. She had gone out in search of that werepenguin boy. Vigi hoped she never found him, and so would never return. Her life and safety were far more important to him than his own. He didn't trust the Earl to keep his word. He suspected, if Annika returned, she would be thrown back in the dungeon, and Vigi would still hang.

Unfortunately, Annika was resourceful and smart and

determined. Those were great traits to have for a bandit, but it meant she would probably return, with the boy.

"Dinner," yelled one of the guards, tossing a handful of burnt fish sticks between the bars. Vigi was sick of burnt fish sticks. The prisoners ate burnt fish stick–flavored sausages for breakfast, burnt fish stick–flavored burgers for lunch, burnt fish stick–flavored fish sticks for dinner, and packets of burnt fish stick–flavored fish stick flavoring for dessert. It felt like he had fish sticks coming out of his ears, but when he checked, it was only earwax. He grabbed the fish sticks and ate, chasing them with a gulp of burnt fish stick–flavored water.

When he finished, he listened for more of the sentries, but heard only silence. They were gone.

"Enjoy dinner?" he whispered.

"I'm sick of burnt fish sticks," Felipe moaned. "It's almost like they burn them on purpose." Vigi had been fortunate that his right-hand man had been assigned the cell across from him. They could not see each other, but they could chat when no sentries or penguin soldiers were near. They had been assigned the same fish stick frying schedule, too. Talking while frying fish sticks was strictly forbidden, but they had perfected an elaborate sign language alphabet to communicate.

Eight karate chops from each hand was an *A*. Twelve left-handed punches followed by nineteen pinkie flicks

was the letter *B*, and so on. Unfortunately, they had never spelled more than "Hello" to each other before becoming too exhausted to attempt spelling another letter. Vigi wished they had invented a simpler alphabet.

At least here, in the dungeons, they could talk freely.

"If only they would let me bake something," complained Felipe. He was a marvelous baker. His pumpkin strudel was always a best seller at the annual Forest Bandit Bake Sale. That sale was scheduled to take place in a few weeks, but without Vigi to organize it, and Felipe to bake for it, it would be a failure. That was a shame, as the bake sale was the highlight of the annual bandit fund-raising drive.

"I also wish they would clean our filthy clothes," continued Felipe. "Or at least give us hangers to hang them." Upon saying the word *hang*, Felipe's voice choked up. "Sorry."

"I still have over a week," said Vigi. "And I wish my clothes were less wrinkly, too."

Vigi could hear Felipe rattling the bars on his cell door, although the bars were sturdy and rattled only a little. "Forest bandits are not meant to be caged like animals," said Felipe, who then howled like a coyote.

"We're bandits. Being caged is, unfortunately, always a possibility," said Vigi.

"Unfortunately," agreed Felipe, who continued to shake the cage.

Vigi did not shake his own bars. What was the point?

"Move back," said a brusque, harsh voice, as someone opened Vigi's cell door. Vigi was surprised to see a guard standing at the doorway with three burly penguin soldiers. They glared at him, and one of the penguins snapped its beak.

The beak-snapping penguin soldier rushed into Vigi's cell and swatted him across the head for no reason. Vigi reeled backward, nearly falling.

"We're bringing you upstairs to the Earl," said the sentry as the penguin pushed the still-reeling Vigi out of his cell, and into the dungeon hallway.

"But why?" Vigi asked, his head spinning.

The guard spat on Vigi's shoe. "We're hanging you in the morning, and the Earl wants to mock you in his bird-cage first."

"I was expecting more time!" said Vigi.

The guard shoved Vigi forward. "Always expect the worst in Sphen."

"I just hope Annika is far away," Vigi muttered to himself, unaware how wrong he was. He should have expected the worst.

47.
The Cove

The sun had almost set, now just a hazy blur of yellow and red light over the horizon. *The Heinous Hering with One R* gently caressed a rock before wedging itself atop a strip of sand. Sails were loosened; an anchor was cast.

"A captain is always last off," Blackburn bellowed. "Unless a boat sinks, then we don't get off at all. For a captain always goes down with his boat."

Bolt was glad he wasn't a ship captain.

Annika was the first one on the shore. She lay down and hugged the ground. "Land, land, land," she sang, her green face already regaining its color.

"This cove is empty, just as I promised, aye?" said Blackburn. "Pirates, smugglers, and ruffians of all kinds use this inlet, although not so much anymore. Few journey to Sphen. I wish I had not ignored the warnings meself, all those years ago."

"If ruffians use this inlet, can we consider ourselves ruffians?" Annika asked, sitting up, brightening. "I've always wanted to be a ruffian."

"Aye, missy."

Annika beamed as she sprang back to her feet.

Bolt was half expecting to be surrounded by the pier patrol or penguin soldiers at any moment. But Blackburn was right; the cove was deserted.

Welcome back, Bolt.

The voice rammed itself into his head so abruptly that every part of Bolt immediately tensed, including his earlobes. He felt as if someone was watching him. It felt uncomfortable, like wearing underwear that was two sizes too small. At the orphanage, most of Bolt's underwear had been two sizes too small, so he was familiar with that feeling.

Perhaps Pygo felt it, too. She seemed agitated, bouncing around and growling at nothing in particular. Bolt couldn't read her mind, but some of her thoughts trickled out. They were confused and panicked.

Puppy chow . . . Dog leashes . . . Penguins rule all!

Bolt patted Pygo's head. "Don't worry, girl. We'll free your friends. We'll free all of Sphen." *You are safe.*

Pygo gave no indication of understanding. She barked twice and her thoughts remained scattered as they sprayed from her ears.

Rubber bones . . . Frisbees . . . Obey me, puny human!

Annika looked down. "Is she OK?"

"I don't know," admitted Bolt.

Annika frowned. "Whether she's ready or not, we're going to the castle."

Bolt nodded, remembering his promise, but still not completely sure why she was in such a rush.

While Annika and Bolt stepped forward, Blackburn stayed behind with Pygo.

"C'mon," said Annika. Again, only Bolt followed her.

"I don't think Pygo is coming," said Bolt as Pygo bounced in circles. "The Sphen air seems to be bothering her." Bolt's gaze shifted to Blackburn. "But what about you?"

"Aye? What about me? I'm staying here."

"You promised to fight the Earl," said Bolt.

"For chests of gold so I could get me boat. But I have me a boat now, don't I?" The pirate gestured to *The Heinous Hering with One R.*

"What about your soccer ball and gold tooth?" asked Annika.

"And freeing the people of Sphen?" Bolt added.

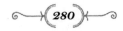

"The people can take care of themselves," said the pirate with a scowl. "The treasures are tempting, but they're not much good if I'm in the Earl's dungeon."

"But you gave your word," Bolt yelped.

"Aye, and a pirate hardly ever breaks his word." Blackburn smiled at the words *hardly ever.* "There's no profit in being a hero."

How could Blackburn abandon them now? They needed him. The penguins and people were counting on his help. Bolt's mind darkened. He coiled, preparing to leap at the pirate and force him to fry fish sticks!

Then Bolt uncoiled. He counted to twenty, letting the rage ebb, blaming the evil Sphen air for his sudden and twisted urge for violence.

Annika balled her hands into fists. She looked as angry as Bolt had felt. "What about honor?" demanded Annika. "What about loyalty?"

"Nothing in me *Pirate Handbook* about risking yer life for those things," said Blackburn with a shrug.

"There's more to life than a stupid handbook," she grunted. Bolt thought of Annika's own bandit code, and how she seemed to be constantly breaking parts of it, like by being Bolt's friend and fighting for justice. She had changed quite a bit from the bandit he had first known, and Bolt was thankful for that.

Annika reached for a bobby pin, but Bolt put his hand on his friend's shoulder. "If he wants to look out for himself, let him. We don't need him. We have an egg."

"And what's that supposed to do, again?" she asked, her eyes still burning with rage.

"I'll know when the time comes," said Bolt unconvincingly.

Annika glared at Bolt and glared at Blackburn, then turned away with an angry grunt. Soon, she was stomping and glaring down the beach again, Bolt following. He had to admit that, deep down, he should have known better than to trust a pirate. Then again, at one time he thought he knew better than to trust a bandit.

Bolt jogged to keep up with Annika. He hadn't expected to see anyone until they got into the city streets, but up ahead he spied a large boulder with a girl sitting upon it. She had been so still, Bolt hadn't noticed her at first.

Bolt's birthmark tingled as they neared her.

The girl had long hair as white as a penguin's belly, although the phrase "as white as a seagull's wings" filled Bolt's head instead. She was around the same age as Bolt, and thin, wearing a simple pink dress with a frilly collar. Instead of sleeves, the dress had two large holes.

"Do I know you?" asked Bolt, halting. She felt familiar.

The girl shook her head and frowned. Her eyes watered

and her lips trembled as she spoke. "Have the penguins taken away everything you care about? Have they robbed you of all happiness? Have they ruined your life forever?"

Bolt had to think about that. Sure, penguins had brought suffering and misery to him. But they had also brought happiness and joy. Love. Family. "No, I guess not. Not completely, anyway."

"Then we can't possibly know each other."

Bolt thought of all the anti-penguin attitudes he had witnessed in the last few days and bristled. "Penguins aren't so bad, you know. Not all of them, anyway. Most penguins are gentle and peaceful."

"None I've ever seen," said the girl bitterly.

Bolt looked at the girl again, into deep green eyes that seemed to almost glow. He had seen those eyes before. "Are you sure we don't know each other?"

"I don't know how you could know her," said Annika. She had stopped walking and stood behind Bolt. "But I do. Her name is Gentoo."

The girl on the rock narrowed her eyes, staring at Annika. "I know you, too. You're the girl I met in town." She laughed. "Or should I say 'the ruffian.' Only ruffians land in this inlet."

"We're not ruffians," said Bolt, offended.

"Yes, we are," insisted Annika, standing tall.

The girl sniffed and said, "Ha!" and it was that "ha"

that did it. That laugh. Bolt would never forget that laugh.

"I knew you looked familiar," said Bolt. "You're the seagull girl."

The girl on the rock stiffened. "I don't know what you're talking about."

"You turn into a seagull at night, under the full moon," said Bolt.

"You must have me confused with someone else who turns into a seagull," said Gentoo.

"No. It's you." And then Bolt said it—and it felt odd to say because he couldn't remember actually ever having spoken these words to anyone, ever: "It's OK—I'm a werepenguin."

"Ha!" said the girl again, but then her smile faded as she looked at him more closely. "The bushy eyebrows, the long nose . . ." she mumbled, nodding her head. "I should have guessed it. I saw you the other night." She glared and pointed a crooked finger at him. "Are you here to join the Earl? To help him in his evil rule?"

"No. Bolt isn't like that," said Annika. "He's here to stop the Earl."

"You could help us fight him," added Bolt.

"Ha! How could I possibly help you? I'm just an ordinary girl who turns into a seagull."

"That seems pretty extraordinary to me," said Bolt.

"Well, there's nothing I can do," said the girl. "Why do

you think you have a chance of defeating the Earl anyway?"

"We have a weapon," said Bolt, gesturing to his backpack.

"What is that? An egg?" Gentoo asked. Bolt nodded. "What are you going to do with that? Make scrambled eggs?"

"No, we can't," said Bolt, looking down at his shoes. He then added sheepishly, "But it's a better weapon than a cotton ball."

"I have enough things to worry about without fighting the Earl with an egg," said Gentoo, shaking her head. "Like a sick aunt. And fish taxes. And no boat. Besides, you'll never beat the Earl."

"You're wrong," said Annika, and she spoke with such confidence that Bolt puffed up his chest. "We can win. We can free Sphen. The penguins can be beaten."

"And maybe I'll grow wings!" said Gentoo, who then blushed. "Um, I mean, and maybe I won't grow wings."

"I've seen things I didn't think could happen," said Bolt, his chest still puffed, Annika's strength fueling his own. "Like me turning into a penguin. And my best friend, Annika, fighting for nothing except to help the people of Sphen."

"Yeah, about that . . ." said Annika, kicking the dirt and mumbling under her breath.

"What?" Bolt asked.

"Nothing," said Annika. With a deep sigh she strode forward. "Forget about her, Bolt. We don't need her. Or Blackburn. Or Pygo."

Bolt wasn't sure he agreed with Annika. He felt that the more people or creatures they had fighting together, the better.

"It's not too late to go back on your boat and sail away," said Gentoo, calling after Annika. "If you fight the Earl, you'll lose. You'll probably end up hanging tomorrow morning with that bandit fellow."

"Tomorrow?" gulped Annika, skidding to a stop and wheeling around. Her feet looked so wobbly, Bolt thought she was about to faint. "But we had until next Friday."

"The Earl moved up the date," said Gentoo.

"Um, what are you guys talking about?" asked Bolt.

"He can't do this!" Annika gurgled, her face turning purple.

"Sure he can. He's the Earl, he can do anything," said Gentoo. "Sorry."

"Annika, is there something you want to tell me?" asked Bolt.

Annika brushed Bolt off and strode forward. "I'll tell you later. We need to hurry. We're fighting the Earl tonight, plan or no plan."

48.
A Surprising Discovery

Annika remained steps ahead of Bolt, who kept yelling, "Wait!" and "Stop!" and "We need to talk!" She didn't want to stop or wait and she definitely didn't want to talk. She would bring that towering monster to his knees, even if she had to battle him alone.

She hadn't trusted the Earl. Not really. But there had been a drip, a slow but steady stream of hope from an otherwise clogged pipe of distrust, that maybe he would hold up his side of the bargain. Not that she had any intention of holding up *her* side of the bargain, mind you. Still, the *decent thing* would have been for the Earl to *wait for* Annika to bring Bolt, so they could *free her father and defeat the Earl!*

"Why do your eyes keep zigzagging back and forth?" Bolt asked.

"I keep thinking in italics."

But the Earl had been the one playing with Annika. He had never intended to keep his side of the bargain: that was obvious now. Why else would he have moved up the hanging?

But it didn't make any sense. He needed Bolt. He wanted him. Why would he . . .

Unless he knew they were coming. Unless they were walking into a trap. Well, trap or no trap, she was coming. They were coming.

When they reached the outskirts of the city, Annika slowed for a moment, unsure whether she should turn right or left, taking a brief beat to compute the best, shortest route, but one that allowed Bolt to catch up. He grabbed her shoulder.

"What?" she said, spinning around, fury ripping through every pore in her body. "We need to save my father. We can't stop."

"But . . ." sputtered Bolt.

"But what?" demanded Annika.

"I need you to tell me the truth for once."

She saw the hurt in his eyes. He had been so proud of her for coming to Sphen, and she had been embarrassed by

that pride, but it had also made her feel good. People feel a lot of things about bandits—fear usually, disapproval sometimes—but pride? Not often.

But that just made the sadness and disappointment in Bolt's face feel even worse. His anger she could understand. She felt anger all the time. But sadness and disappointment, too? It was almost unbearable. "Can't you just look angry?" she growled.

Bolt didn't answer her. "You didn't come to Sphen to rob and kidnap all by yourself, did you?" Bolt said. "You came with your father, and they captured you both. That's it, isn't it?"

Annika nodded. "Maybe."

"And then what?" Bolt demanded.

Annika could lie and say that was all. If she did that, Bolt would be angry, but he'd understand. He'd help her free her father, and free Sphen, or at least try. A good bandit wouldn't say anything else. A good bandit would keep whatever lies helped herself or her bandit clan the most.

But a good friend wouldn't continue to lie. And, maybe, being a good friend was more important than being a good bandit.

Annika gulped. And she told him.

She told him how she and her father had come, and why. About how they were caught. And how the Earl had

demanded she bring Bolt in exchange for her father's life, but that the Earl had lied and was going to hang her father anyway, so they had to free him now.

And at the end, Bolt looked even more disappointed and sad, and Annika wanted to scream at him, and she did. "Why can't you just be angry?" But that didn't change a thing.

"You were going to trade me?" Bolt asked, his eyes moist. "You were going to hand me over to the Earl?"

"No," said Annika. She reached out and grabbed his hands. They were limp rags, neither fighting her nor accepting. "That's just what I told the Earl. I was always going to fight him. With you."

But Bolt gave no sign of understanding her. He merely muttered, "You were going to trade me." He sniffled, and the sniffle hurt Annika more than a bobby pin in her eye. She had once sneezed while picking a lock with a bobby pin and had accidentally jabbed herself in the eye, so she knew the feeling.

"I thought we were friends," said Bolt with an extra-long sniffle.

"We are friends. You're my best friend. But they have my father!" Annika said, continuing to squeeze his hands. "If you're angry with me, you can jab me in the eye with a bobby pin. Just stop sniffling."

Bolt continued to sniffle. "I shouldn't have trusted you," he said in a near whisper. "I should have known a bandit can't change her spots."

Annika had never been ashamed of being a bandit before. But his words cut her, because there was some truth to them. Bandits were not nice. Bandits, at least those who followed the bandit code, would do exactly what Annika had done, except they wouldn't have felt guilty or blabbed the truth.

If Annika survived today, she would do some serious editing to *The Code of the Bandit.*

Annika took a deep breath. "I'm sorry, Bolt." For a bandit, few words are more difficult to say than *I'm sorry.* "When I came to you, I only thought about my father. About me. I thought penguins were silly birds. I should have been honest from the start."

Bolt's eyes grew larger. "Silly birds?" he growled.

"I was wrong about everything. Penguins aren't silly, I know that now." She inched closer to him, and now it was her turn to sniffle. "I realize a penguin family *is* important." *Sniffle, sniffle. Sob.* "But my family is important, too. I need to save my father. I didn't know if you'd come if I told you the truth. I didn't believe in you, and I'll never forgive myself for that. And I'll never do it again." She looked away, rubbing her eyes. "I understand if you no

longer want to help me. I wouldn't blame you for no longer wanting to be my friend."

Bolt wrenched his hands from hers. His eyes flashed red. "I'm going to fight the Earl, because that's why I came here. And I'm going to win, because I have a mighty weapon." He jabbed his thumb at the egg. "But I'm not stopping him for you. I'm stopping him for the penguins of Sphen. For my family."

"Because nothing is more important than family," said Annika, nodding.

Bolt nodded and looked away. "Right." His words seemed to ease some of the tension, as if maybe he understood what she had done, just a little. A little was enough, for now.

Still, they didn't speak as they walked into Sphen, although no one spoke while walking in Sphen. The only sounds were footsteps, and an occasional angry penguin bark. A couple of people laughed, which surprised Annika, until she saw it was two human soldiers, laughing at an old man who had tripped.

The penguins paid no attention to Annika or Bolt. She saw Bolt concentrating, probably sending pinpricks of distraction to the penguins they passed, so that a soldier would turn away or sneeze when they drew close.

Annika kept having to stop and wait for Bolt, who was

slower than she was. "You're walking like you have a cinder block or a brick tied to your leg," she remarked. She checked; he didn't.

"The egg isn't exactly a feather."

They didn't say another word until they saw the looming palace ahead, illuminated by the full moon rising up into the evening sky.

49.

One Hundred Penguins

Annika and Bolt hid in the alley where they'd hidden before, behind the same trash cans across from the palace gates. The scent of dead fish was stronger than Bolt remembered; it was so thick it formed a cloud that fogged the streets.

"I can barely breathe," Annika complained, putting a stiff finger over her nostrils.

"I think it smells yummy."

Annika removed a bandanna from her pocket and wrapped it around her mouth and nose to keep out the smell. She looked like a train robber.

"Where did you get that?" Bolt asked.

Annika shrugged, and also removed two pairs of socks

and a lint brush. "Sorry. They were practically falling out of people's pockets."

Bolt sighed and turned to watch the palace, where penguin soldiers marched up and down the drawbridge. When Bolt danced into their heads, he felt, as always, dense blocks of hatred. But he felt an almost giddy feeling of anticipation, too.

Tomorrow, the army marches off to steal fish! barked one penguin.

Tomorrow the army marches off to hurt people! barked another.

I thought we already got to steal fish and hurt people whenever we wanted? barked a third.

But now we get to steal fish and hurt new, different people! replied the first one.

The penguin conversation was interrupted by an unexpected wave of water splashing against the sides of the drawbridge. A leopard seal leapt into the air, snapping its jaws at the penguins and sending a current of fear and panic through them.

"Any idea how we get in?" asked Annika.

"Not through the moat," said Bolt.

"I can take them," said Annika, her eyes narrowing and her hand reaching toward her knife. Bolt couldn't see her mouth under her bandanna, but he thought she might

be grinning. "There's about one hundred of them. I'll fight those ninety, while you fight those other ten." She looked back at Bolt. "Or maybe I'll fight those ninety-nine, while you fight that short, pudgy one?"

Bolt held his hand out to silence Annika. He needed to concentrate. Maybe, just maybe, he could penetrate the mist of evil lingering inside the heads of the penguins. He sent his brain waves into the air.

Go inside. Leave your post. Let us in.

A few penguins stopped and looked around, waving their wings up as if swatting at flies.

But there was so much hate! So much despair! Peeling back the oniony layers was awful, filled with images of laughing penguins, bowling penguins, burping penguins. Bolt closed his eyes, trying not to scream with terror at the icy chill of hate rolling off the penguin minds.

Go inside. Leave your post. Go bowling!

When he opened his eyes, Annika was staring across the street and gasping.

Every penguin soldier was hurrying inside the castle as if a fire alarm had been sounded. Maybe they all really loved bowling? No, Bolt couldn't believe they would leave their posts to bowl. But a minute later, the drawbridge was empty. "You did it!" cried Annika.

"I did?"

"Who else?"

They're gone. Come in.

Bolt jumped with a start. "What did you say?"

"I didn't say anything."

Bolt slapped his palm against his head. It was just the hate mist, that was all.

Whatever the reason the penguins had gone away, Bolt knew you weren't supposed to look a gift horse in the mouth. But he seemed to be doing that a lot lately, and wondered if maybe he should start examining these gift horses more closely. "Maybe we should wait," he suggested, but Annika had already left her hiding spot and was sprinting toward the castle. Bolt ran after her.

They stepped through the gate, and no one stopped them. As they walked onto the drawbridge, Bolt expected someone to jump out and yell, "Fooled you!" But no one did.

They were halfway across the drawbridge when the water next to them erupted. A giant gray sea monster leapt from the water, its breath hot and dangerous. It smelled like death.

"Stop staring at that leopard seal and come on," urged Annika, tugging Bolt's arm.

The creature crashed back down into the water while Annika and Bolt raced to the castle, Bolt's knees knocking.

Although he was still mad at Annika, he *was* glad she was there. Her fearlessness was still contagious. He didn't

think he could have crossed the bridge without her.

They walked through the open door and stepped into an empty courtyard. A plate of dead fish sat on a small table next to a single chair, as if someone had left in the middle of lunch.

"Do you think it's a trap?" asked Annika.

Bolt closed his eyes. He could sense a massive energy of hate and evilness in the middle of the palace, like a pulsating rotten heart. It was the Earl. He was filled with so much vile, putrid rottenness that it stained everything here.

But Bolt couldn't feel any penguins nearby. "I don't know about a trap. But the coast is clear for now."

They walked forward slowly. They crossed the atrium to the main building just beyond it, and pushed open a heavy stone door.

Annika pointed to her left. "The dungeons are that way." She pointed the opposite way. "And that way is the throne room."

"You get your father. I'll get the Earl."

"As soon as I free him, we'll find you." Annika grabbed Bolt's hand, squeezing. "Thank you, Bolt. And I'm sorry. I really am. We'll fight the Earl and free everyone."

And then she was gone, and Bolt was waddling toward the Earl.

50.
Gentoo and Her Army

Gentoo's aunt slept soundly, or in other words, with lots of sound. She snored and whistled and hummed.

But Gentoo was glad she was asleep, even if she was loudly asleep. It had been a rough day for her aunt, sipping broth, muttering random sentences, and tossing and turning.

With the exception of her early evening stroll to her favorite isolated spot along the shore to clear her head, Gentoo had stayed home all day.

Gentoo never would have expected to run into a werepenguin and a ruffian, though. And the werepenguin wasn't even evil—at least she didn't think he was.

They had seemed so confident. Gentoo had only

seen people walking, slightly hunched, weighed down by oppression, for as long as she could remember. Their confidence almost gave her hope that something could be done to stop the Earl.

Now Gentoo wandered out of the house again, toward the shore of the Deader Sea. It was the only place she felt at peace. As she walked, she passed one of the many large posters of the Earl that hung in the village, this one pinned high above her on a pole. He stared down, his fish nuggets and bones wedged in his beard, mocking Gentoo. Mocking the entire city.

She picked up a stone and hurled it at the poster, where it bounced off harmlessly. If a penguin had seen her, she could have been imprisoned for such a feat, but the streets were empty. Still, she cried out, "Sorry!" just in case. She didn't breathe for thirty seconds, until she was absolutely sure no one had seen her.

She gritted her teeth and balled her fists. Her boat gone! The taxes raised! Her aunt sick! It was all the Earl's fault!

The Earl!

The Earl!

That hateful, evil Earl!

What had that ruffian girl said? *We can win. We can free Sphen. The penguins can be beaten.*

Gentoo had answered, *And maybe I'll grow wings!*

The conversation rolled around in her head. The girl and the werepenguin boy had seemed so certain things would be better.

The boy had also called Gentoo *extraordinary.*

Was he right? Could Gentoo make a difference? Was she extraordinary?

Gentoo closed her eyes and held out her hands.

Come to me, my friends.

There was no one here to see her now, no one to caution her to stop. Birds came, flying to her from neighboring streets and from the shore. They landed on her arms and in her hair, they flittered over her head, and none went to the bathroom, which Gentoo appreciated.

Yes, my friends. Come to me.

They answered back. *We are here, Gentoo. We love you, Gentoo. Marbled incisor meat loaf! Ha, ha!*

Dozens of birds surrounded Gentoo. She saw her glowing green eyes reflecting off theirs, shining through the night.

Come, my friends.

She strode onward, the birds remaining on her shoulders and head, or flapping about her. If anyone had seen them, that anyone might have run away in terror, convinced the girl was being attacked by a swarm of seagulls. But people seldom walked the streets at night and the penguin soldiers were surprisingly absent from their corners.

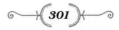

Gentoo and her band of seagulls marched toward the castle as the full moon climbed higher in the sky.

Midnight neared. By the time she reached the palace, the Earl wouldn't be facing a young girl. The Earl would be facing the wrath and might of an extraordinary were-gull.

51.

An Expected Guest

Bolt paused to gape at the opulence surrounding him. He stood in a massive entry hall. The golden handrails lining the grand staircase nearly blinded him. Room-length tapestries hung on the wall, many filled with intricate images of penguins floating in the clouds, plucking harps. Some might have considered these images *heavenly* if the penguins didn't have glowing red eyes and devil horns.

Moving forward while staring at the tapestries, Bolt collided against a giant beak, a beak as big as Bolt's entire body, its fangs ready to chomp poor Bolt's head. It took a moment for Bolt to realize he had bumped into the skull of a prehistoric penguin-saurus. "I've met one of your relatives," Bolt said quietly, and he moved onward.

Bolt had still not seen soldiers, although he could sense others in the castle, and he could feel the Earl's presence. But everything was muddied. Soldiers were somewhere. But where?

Bolt froze. Penguin footsteps plopped along the hallway just around the very next corner. He felt the penguins' anger. He smelled their fishiness. He understood their thoughts.

I like my feathers!

I like mine, too!

Their thoughts, apparently, weren't very interesting.

Bolt dipped his mind into theirs, finding their scorn for humans and delicately scrubbing at it, like one cleans mildew on a shower stall. When Bolt lived at the orphanage, the boys took turns cleaning mildew from the shower stalls with nothing but toothbrushes. The work in the birds' brains reminded him of those times. Scrubbing. Brushing. Rinsing. Flossing.

Flossing the shower stalls had been the hardest part.

The penguins turned down another corridor, and Bolt hurried onward, farther into the bowels of the castle.

The Earl's presence grew stronger, blipping like a sonar, pointing Bolt in its direction. He rushed past a room, following the *blip, blip, blip* farther and farther. Right, left, turn here.

Closer, Bolt. Closer. The Earl is waiting. For you.

Bolt scrunched up his eyebrows and his ears. He was getting sick of that voice in his head.

Bolt wondered if he was heading into a trap. Maybe. But Bolt did not bolt. He did not hesitate. He was braver now, maybe.

Just up ahead. There. Down that hallway was the throne room. Bolt felt it. The Earl's aura throbbed inside Bolt's neck, as if his birthmark had a heartbeat. As Bolt advanced, his neck pulsated and rippled.

The Earl was not alone. Bolt sensed others, but exactly who was with him, and how many whos, Bolt couldn't tell.

He inched forward until he was at the door. He needed to lean over, just peek inside, and see what he was about to face.

"There you are!"

Bolt toppled into the room, shoved by a wing in the back.

Bolt staggered upright. Two dozen penguin soldiers surrounded him, snarling and growling.

On a gilded throne sat the largest man Bolt had ever seen. The man clapped. One hand was made of iron, which made his claps particularly loud. *Clap, clap, clap.* "Welcome, Bolt. I've been expecting you."

The throne room was as big as a football field, maybe

two football fields, and the ceiling rose thirty feet high. A line of windows was positioned at the top, and moonlight bathed the timber rafters on the ceiling and the golden borders on the walls. Near the throne, just off to its side, a penguin soldier sat on a four-foot egg.

The Earl continued to clap. He had a black beard that was twisted into the shape of two horns, matching the twin hair horns on the top of his head. Those top-of-the-head horns framed a golden crown. Large, bushy eyebrows—even bushier and larger than Bolt had pictured—sat on the ruler's face, menacing in their intensity. "Welcome to my humble home." He looked around the magnificent room. "Or maybe not so humble."

The ground around the throne was littered with dead fish. The Earl leaned over, picked one up, and bit off its tail. Fish slime dripped onto his golden robe.

Off to the side of the room was a person-size birdcage, and a figure sat within. At first Bolt thought a very thin, emaciated penguin sat inside the cage, but he quickly realized the figure was a man wearing a crude and tattered penguin-like disguise. "Vigi Lambda?" gasped Bolt.

"Our hanging victim." The Earl gave a careless wave of his hand. "The birdcage was a special creation of mine. I like it, don't you? Extra-strong bars, and the locks are unpickable." He lifted a set of keys from his pocket and jangled them. "And I have the only keys." He looked down.

"But it's not so bad inside. The newspapers on the ground are extra spongy."

"They are quite bouncy," agreed Vigi, rubbing his feet on the newspaper.

"Let him go!" demanded Bolt.

"Why would I do that?" asked the Earl, sucking on a fish.

Bolt didn't have a good answer. "Just because?" His voice trailed off and the room was silent for a moment. The only sounds came from the Earl's fish licking.

"Your rule is over," Bolt finally said. "I'm going to stop you." He was quite proud of himself: he sounded brave.

"Well spoken," said Vigi. "Very bandit-like."

Bolt stood a little taller, and thought briefly of Annika. She was his friend, despite her lies.

The Earl looked less impressed with Bolt's bandit-like words. "You are on the wrong side of the fight, Bolt. Don't you understand why you are here?" The Earl picked up another dead fish carcass and dropped it into his throat, whole. He licked his lips. "You are here because the Stranger wanted it so."

"A stranger?" Bolt asked.

"No. The, and with a capital *S*. The Stranger."

Bolt knew that name. It was the Stranger who had bitten the Baron and turned him into a werepenguin. It was the Stranger who had declared war in Brugaria one

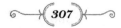

hundred years ago, although he had been defeated and driven away. "I thought the Stranger lived in the South Pole or someplace."

"I'm not sure where he lives," admitted the Earl. "I've never been invited to his home." He looked away and shook his head angrily. "I even offered to bring a vase or a toaster as a housewarming present. Have you ever had a vase or a toaster?" Bolt nodded. "Still, I am in his debt. The Stranger made me what I am today."

"An extremely large fish hoarder?" Bolt guessed.

"A powerful ruler with an iron fist!" The Earl stood up and raised his arm, light gleaming off its metal surface. The Earl pounded his fist onto the armrest of his throne. The chair grumbled, and wood splintered. "Look!" He rolled up the sleeve on his non-iron-hand arm and revealed a penguin birthmark just under his wrist. It was almost identical to the birthmark on Bolt's neck, although slightly bigger. The Earl laughed, and then dropped another fish into his mouth and burped.

52.
The Earl's Story

The Earl sat back on his throne. "Sixty years ago there was nothing special about me except that I was an earl, living in a lavish palace with riches, dungeons, and a moat."

"That sounds special to me," said Bolt.

"I didn't have a leopard seal in the moat. And really, what's so special about someone without their own personal leopard seal?" He didn't wait for an answer. "Of course, I also had the bird-shaped birthmark on my arm. I usually wore long-sleeve shirts to hide it."

Bolt leaned his head to his left, just a little, as was his habit, to hide the birthmark he was sensitive about, too.

"But then one night, when I was sleeping in my bed under a blanket of money, a tall man with jet-black hair, a large, thin nose, and bushy eyebrows came through the open balcony door. But I didn't scream. Something about the man seemed familiar, as if I had been expecting him my entire life. He said he was traveling the world in search of those with penguin birthmarks. I asked him his name and he merely said, 'Call me the Stranger.'"

"But why?"

"Maybe he doesn't like his real name?" the Earl guessed.

"No, I meant why was he traveling the world looking for people with penguin birthmarks."

"Oh, yes. That's a much better question. Because he wanted to unite us all, of course. To take over the world! A single werepenguin is powerful. Two werepenguins are doubly so. But imagine a group of werepenguins, each with his or her own penguin army. Who could stop us?"

The Earl stared at Bolt, as if waiting for an answer, but Bolt couldn't think of anyone who could stop a group of penguin armies, at least not off the top of his head.

"The Stranger knew it would take time to coat penguins with enough thick oniony layers of violent rage that they would fight. But that's the great part about being immortal: time isn't an issue."

"And you gladly agreed to his plan," said Bolt bitterly.

"Not at first. When he told me I could be a werepenguin

and torture and maim whomever I chose, it sounded too good to be true. I just laughed at him."

"That doesn't sound funny," said Bolt, shuddering.

"It turned out a goose feather from my pillow had wiggled itself under my armpit. Quite embarrassing, really. Once I removed it, I didn't laugh again for weeks. The Stranger asked permission to bite me. *Why not?* I answered. But then, after, I understood the truth. Penguins *are* meant to rule. I *was* special. Converting the palace library into a giant fish-frying room *was* a good idea. Pouring melted iron onto my arm until it created a hard, permanent cast *was* a very sensible thing to do. It was all so obvious."

"Why didn't you just make some sort of removable iron glove or something?"

The Earl rolled his eyes. "And pretend I had an iron hand? That would be as silly as wearing X-ray glasses in a dark cave." The Earl bent down, grabbed two fish, and ate them.

Bolt puffed out his chest and told himself: *You are brave! You are a bolt of lightning!* "You sound like the Baron. But he was wrong," he said, stepping forward and pointing an accusatory finger at the Earl. "And so are you. Penguins aren't meant to rule. They are meant to love one another and raise families."

"Family? What a quaint notion," the Earl said, chuckling, unfazed by Bolt's accusatory finger-pointing. "Families are quite overrated." He looked at his egg. "Well, mostly overrated. I do like my egg." He plopped another fish into his mouth, then squirmed in pleasure as it rolled down his throat. "Delicious!" He wiped his mouth with the sleeve of his robe and then raised his fist and pounded it on his armrest. It made a solid thud. He frowned, and then crashed his other hand, his iron hand, atop the other armrest, which completely broke off and crashed to the ground. "Much better," he mumbled with a smile. "Fortunately, I keep a couple dozen backup thrones in a storage room."

"What happened to the Stranger?" asked Bolt.

"He continued his quest to find more of our kind. There aren't many of us, but there are some. He is the greatest of us all, though. He talks to me." He pointed to Bolt. "And he talks to you."

"He's never talked to me."

"Are you sure?" The Earl giggled, ate another fish, and then giggled again. "You've never thought it might be fun to rule? You've never felt anger? Or violence? Or craved fish sticks?"

"Well, sure," admitted Bolt. "But that's just part of being a werepenguin."

"Is it?" The Earl shrugged, ate two more fish, and then

hiccupped. "Perhaps. Or perhaps that is him inside you. Talking."

Bolt stared at the Earl. Those voices in his head—he had thought they were his werepenguin side, or maybe the Earl, talking to him. But was it the Stranger? Had it been the Stranger from the beginning?

All his other thoughts suddenly made sense, from the fleeting sympathies for the Earl to the many gift horses he had avoided looking in the mouth during their voyage.

Bolt gripped his ears, as if to rip them off and reach inside his head and try to grab whatever Stranger-infested thoughts might be inside, but all he did was bruise his earlobes. He released his grip and groaned, uncertain which thoughts were his and which thoughts had been planted there.

Bolt had long sensed a barrier deep inside every penguin, a crusty coating that had kept him from truly being one of them. Was that crust from the Stranger, too? Had he infected every penguin in the world?

If that were true, no penguin would be free while the Stranger lived.

The Earl spat fish parts from his mouth. "But you are here now, Bolt," he said. "And that's what's important. We need you."

"Why?"

"Because you are the chosen one!" declared the Earl,

standing up. His weight was so heavy that the marble ground sagged under him. "Although I have to admit, the Stranger is slightly confused as to what you were chosen for."

"I get that a lot," Bolt admitted.

"The Stranger wanted you here, with us, and not living in some far-off colony. That was the challenge, wasn't it? How could we lure you here to join our fight? It wasn't like I could send you a plane ticket."

"I'm not a big fan of planes anyway," said Bolt, remembering his unpleasant journey to Brugaria.

"All penguins hate to fly unless it's first class," agreed the Earl. He picked up another fish, looked at it, frowned, and then tossed it away before grabbing a different fish and nibbling a fin. "Much better," he mumbled, although Bolt hadn't seen anything wrong with the first fish. "Where was I? Oh, right. You were living in a colony and we needed to get you here. It was a miracle, really. A bandit girl was captured and she mentioned you to one of my prison guards. One of my penguin soldiers overheard, and reported the news back to me."

"I know the rest of the story," said Bolt. "You made a deal for her to bring me here. But you're hanging her father anyway."

"A deal with a human is worth nothing to our kind,"

said the Earl. "But she wasn't planning on turning you over either." The Earl stuffed an entire fish in his mouth, spat out a bone, and sighed happily. "You see, we've known everything all along. We had a spy." The Earl looked at his egg, and the penguin soldier sitting atop it. Bolt hadn't paid much attention to that soldier before now. As he stared, his eyes widened. The penguin had blue eyes, a color so rare in a penguin.

"Pygo?" muttered Bolt. The soldier stared straight ahead, but Bolt had no doubt it was her. His throat tightened. "Help me," he choked.

The Earl laughed. "Help you? Don't be absurd. She was quite helpful to me, of course. Her mission was to make sure you came back in one piece, by protecting you from sharks or overzealous penguin soldiers. And since you're still in one piece, she did her job quite well."

"But she thinks she's a puppy."

The Earl laughed. "Yes, the Stranger's idea, once again. You can read penguin minds, of course. But can you read the mind of a whale? Or a walrus? Or a puppy? Of course not. So we did a little mind probe into her head, and convinced her that she was Pygo the puppy. It worked quite well! But as you can see, she's all penguin now."

Bolt reached into Pygo's head, expecting to run into a wall and maybe a fleeting image of flea powder, but

instead he was greeted by oniony layers that, when peeled back, revealed the same vicious hate that infected all the penguins of Sphen. Screaming and maniacal laughter echoed within her brain. He gasped for breath before leaping out of her brain, panting.

"We've been one step ahead of you, Bolt. I let you escape the dock in that silly boat—couldn't have you accidentally impaled or anything—but I knew you'd be back soon. I ordered the penguins to let you into the castle tonight and stay out of your way. And now you are here."

"I'll never avoid looking a gift horse in the mouth again," Bolt mumbled, angry at himself for not doing so.

The Earl threw the half-eaten fish he was holding straight at Bolt. Bolt caught it in his teeth without even thinking. The Earl chuckled. "We are not so unalike, you and I."

Bolt spat out the fish. "I'm nothing like you." He looked into the Earl's eyes and saw his own reflection: his horn hair, his white skin, and his eyes, which were softly glowing red. "Well, maybe a little like you."

The Earl lifted another fish from the ground and rubbed his tongue against its side. "The Stranger says we are one big werepenguin family. And I think you know that nothing is more important than family."

Bolt stared at Vigi, sitting in the birdcage. At the Earl, giggling and burping on his throne. And then he shuffled his backpack, with its egg. He was supposed to fight the Earl with *this*? The full force of his doubts hit him now, harder than ever. *I am a fool.*

Bolt's stomach growled. He wasn't just a fool, he was a hungry fool.

The Earl laughed. "Welcome to the family, Bolt."

53.
Welcome to the Family

F amily. The word lingered in Bolt's head like lint in a belly button.

Maybe the Earl had a point.

Bolt could finally have a family that understood what it was like to be part human and part penguin. Bolt could speak with were-people who felt the same confusing things he felt, such as never getting cold but also enjoying sweaters, or craving fish sticks but not tartar sauce. And sometimes, not often, but sometimes, wanting to wear something that wasn't black and white.

Orange. Bolt also liked the color orange.

Join us, Bolt. You look better in black and white.

That voice! Bolt wanted to scream and he yanked on

his ears again, even though they were still sore from pulling his earlobes earlier.

Ruling is fun.

It's not! He had to free the penguins!

People are your servants. Penguins will bow to you.

Never! He needed to fight the Earl!

"I couldn't help but notice that your eyes keep rolling in circles," said the Earl. "Does that mean you are ready to join me? Our blood makes us family."

"No!" The word burst out of Bolt without his even thinking it, before any Stranger-buried words could wiggle their way out of him. Blood didn't make family: love did. Caring did. Respect did. That was the strength of penguins.

The true strength of penguins.

The Baron didn't understand the power of a penguin's love for family and, in the end, that had been his weakness. And that was what made Bolt different, and why the Stranger would not control him.

Bolt felt a flit of air blow out of his ears, and he hoped it was filled with the last of the Stranger's evil thoughts. He repeated, even stronger now, "No!" He felt like nothing could defeat him now. "I will never join you."

That undefeatable feeling would not last long.

The Earl snapped his fingers, and two penguin soldiers

wrapped their wings around Bolt's arms, pinning them behind his back. Bolt struggled to free himself but he was no match for these burly birds. "Throw him in the cage with the other one." The Earl pointed to Vigi Lambda. "Maybe we'll hang the boy in the morning, too. Or perhaps he'll change his mind after we've had a long chat." He stood up, lifted his iron fist, and pummeled it into his throne, cracking it in half. "I can be very persuasive."

"If it's any consolation, these newspapers on the bottom of the cage are very spongy," said Vigi Lambda.

"It's not much of a consolation," said Bolt.

54.
Non-Burnt Fish Stick-Free Zone

Annika feared finding a horde of penguin soldiers in the dungeon, but there were none, as if the palace penguins had been called away. She dashed down the marble steps that led into the bowels of the castle, down, down, passing no one. She paused to scan a sign at the bottom of the staircase:

Welcome to the palace dungeons.
Escaping is strictly prohibited. So is happiness. And hope.
No fish sticks allowed unless they are burnt.

Torches on the walls revealed layers of dust and grime. Each cell had a solid iron door with only a small barred window—some of the windows were at eye level, others were on the bottom of the doors, and others near the top.

Annika remembered her father's cell—it was in the middle of the Ruthless Bandit wing of the dungeon. The dungeon had many different wings, including the dark and dreary Shoplifters wing, the even darker and drearier Accidentally Poked a Penguin in the Eye wing, and the worst of them all, the Do We Really Need a Reason to Jail You? wing. There had even been a joke she had heard once. It had been whispered, since jokes were illegal:

Why can penguin soldiers fly?

Because they have so many prison wings.

It wasn't a very funny joke, but being locked in a penguin dungeon wasn't a very funny situation either.

Annika took off the bandanna still wrapped around her mouth and nose and whispered now, too. "Papa?" She stood next to the cell she was certain held him.

But there was no answer, and her heart sped faster.

"Papa?" she croaked, again. Her voice cracked just a little; her knuckles tapped the door.

Still, silence.

Her heart beat even faster now, and while she knew she must be quiet, she yelped in frustration, "Papa! It's me, Annika!"

The cell did not answer back, but a voice from across the way did. "Annika? Is that you?"

She rushed to the opposite cell door. The darkness of

the dungeon made it difficult to see the man's face in the shadows until he stepped closer.

"Felipe?" asked Annika, shocked. "What are you doing here?"

"I could ask you the same." Felipe had always been like a second father to Annika or, really, like a third father, since Annika had been stolen as a baby from her original father.

"I've come to free you," said Annika. "Well, I came to free Papa, actually. I didn't realize you were here, although if I had, you would have been in my rescue plans, too."

"I appreciate that." Felipe reached his fingers through the iron bars of his cell, and Annika pressed her fingertips against his. "I tracked you both here," he explained, "but was caught by penguins."

"Where is Papa now?"

"They took him upstairs a couple of hours ago. They have him in a cage in the throne room."

"We need to rescue him."

"Forget about your father and me. You need to get out."

"Nonsense." Her bobby pin bent when she inserted it into the cell door lock. Annika yanked the pin to her left as hard as she could, hoping to loosen the metal, but the pin snapped in half.

"Please, go," begged Felipe.

"I have more bobby pins," said Annika, removing

another one from her hair and inserting it into the lock, which still didn't budge. But Annika was patient, twisting the lock slowly to massage the key pins and turn the plug back and forth. Finally, she heard a satisfying click, and the door unlocked. Felipe stepped out and wrapped Annika in an affectionate, father-like hug, or rather a third-father-like hug.

"We need to go to the throne room," Annika said. "Papa and Bolt need our help."

"Bolt? The penguin boy? You brought him?"

"Yes, and I promised him I'd help him."

Felipe hesitated. "I've never actually read the entire bandit code, but doesn't it say we're not supposed to help people?"

"Bolt is my friend and I gave him my word. Keeping your word is part of the code, too," said Annika. "And I think the code needs to be updated, anyway."

A moment later, they were running back up the dungeon steps. Felipe knew the direction of the throne room, and he led them through passageways. Just as in her journey into the dungeons, Annika passed no soldiers. "Where are those missing soldiers?" she wondered aloud. Felipe could only shrug.

As they rounded a corner, Felipe skidded to a stop, almost falling, but grabbing Annika's arm to keep himself upright. Annika banged into him and was about to mutter

an "ouch," but Felipe whispered, "Hush!" and she cuffed her hand over her mouth and swallowed the sound.

Felipe jabbed his finger toward the open door in front of them. Hot steam filled the hallway, and a cloud floated from the room. Annika and Felipe peeked inside.

Peering through billows of vapor, Annika saw the vast fish-frying kitchen. A handful of penguin soldiers stood inside, cramming fried fish nuggets into their greedy mouths. Dozens of thin, groaning prisoners toiled around them, some loading large frying baskets.

An old woman knelt in front of one of the penguins. Her gray hair fell loosely across the shoulders of her gray dungeon jumpsuit. "Please, sir, just a nibble of your fish tender. I'm so hungry, and so sick of eating burnt food." She stuck her tongue out, hoping to catch a fallen bread crumb from the coated chunks of fish meat held by the penguin. The soldier slapped her with his wing. She fell backward with a *thump!* before scrambling to her feet, her face red and swelling.

"We should help them," said Annika.

"We're bandits, not heroes," said Felipe. "Remember who you are."

Annika nodded. She'd been angry at Blackburn for declining to be a hero, but what right did she have to demand that of him? Felipe was right: bandits weren't heroes. And neither were pirates.

Annika had always wanted to be the greatest bandit of all time, and nothing else. But was that all she was? A bandit, and nothing else? Perhaps bandits could be more. Perhaps they could be heroes.

They slipped past the open kitchen door. The throne room was just ahead. From within it, they heard shouting. A hiss. A mumbled threat. And the sound of wood, perhaps from a throne armrest, splintering.

Annika crept closer. She peeked inside the room. Her father! She spied him sitting in a cage, but otherwise he appeared unhurt. Bolt was there, too—and being led toward the cage by two large penguins. And there was Pygo—sitting on an egg!

Annika immediately realized Pygo worked for the Earl, and she felt anger and embarrassment. The world's greatest bandit would never be tricked by a double-crossing penguin.

Annika just needed a few more moments to stand here, unobserved, and maybe she could figure out a plan. She silenced her breathing and stood completely still. She was one of the quietest bandits, after all.

Felipe was not one of the quietest bandits. He bent to peek into the room, too, and sneezed.

Before Annika could even say *bless you*, a penguin soldier barked and another kicked her and Felipe into the

room. As they tumbled to the floor, a dozen soldiers surrounded them. One of the penguins grabbed Felipe, but Annika spun away and jumped to her feet. She pointed at the Earl. "I demand you free my father, or else!"

The Earl sucked a little harder on the fish bone he held. "Welcome back, girl," he said. "But of your two options, I choose *else*."

"Oh," said Annika, who wasn't really sure what she had meant by *else*.

"You should have stayed away," moaned Vigi from his cage.

Annika focused her gaze on the Earl, and her defiant anger mounted. She pulled a couple of bobby pins from her hair.

"Bobby pins?" scoffed the Earl. "That's your *else*?"

"Bobby pins make poor weapons," boomed a voice behind Annika. "But how about a sword? Borscht!"

Blackburn stood behind Annika, waving his swordfish.

"Blackburn?" asked Annika, shocked. "Why are you here?"

"I thought about what ye said, missy. Maybe, just maybe, ye were right about me *Pirate Handbook*. Maybe there's more to life than what's printed there. Or, maybe, I just need to add me own chapter to it, a chapter about fighting for yer friends."

"I'm going to rewrite our bandit code, too," said Annika brightly.

In addition to his swordfish, Blackburn held a smaller, thinner sword. "Let's see if ye remember yer training," he said, flipping the extra sword to Annika, who deftly grabbed its hilt.

Annika had only had a couple of sword-fighting lessons, but she was a quick learner. A penguin soldier rushed toward her, and she parried his beak with her blade. Another penguin swatted a wing, and Annika ducked, rolled away, and sprang to her feet. Blackburn was busy fighting four penguins, but there was no one between Annika and the Earl. She raised her blade and charged.

"For banditry! For the people of Sphen! And for friend-ship!" she roared, leaping in the air. She swept the sword down, but the Earl raised his iron fist to block it. CLANG!

"Puny girl. You think you can fight me?"

"I hope so," said Annika, swinging her sword again, and again hearing a CLANG! as it struck the Earl's iron fist.

"I can do this all day," said the Earl with a yawn. "But I'm getting bored." He swung his fist at Annika. This time she raised her sword to block his punch.

SNAP!

Her sword broke in half.

Annika might have been weaponless, but she was hardly powerless. She spun to her left, rolled twice, and stopped at the foot of the Earl's destroyed throne. She picked up one of its broken legs.

"A wooden leg! Aye, we'll make a pirate out of ye yet, missy!" cried Blackburn.

"I'm happy staying a bandit," said Annika, rushing toward the Earl, her wooden leg raised. She leapt up . . .

. . . and tripped over her untied shoelaces.

"I forgot to check!" she mumbled, wincing from pain. In her fall, she had twisted her ankle. She could barely move it.

"Sorry, Papa," she said softly as the Earl marched toward her, waving his iron fist in the air. She tried to leap out of the way, but her ankle throbbed too much. She was helpless.

"Stop! I have an egg!" cried Bolt.

The Earl stopped. The sounds of sword fighting stopped. All eyes stared at Bolt, his backpack on the floor, and Shorty's egg in his grip.

55.

The Yolk of Freedom

While Annika and Blackburn fought, Bolt had been in the grip of penguins leading him to the cage. Bolt was not as strong as they were, but then again, his muscles weren't his true strength. Not even close.

Bolt reached inside the heads of the soldiers next to him, not worrying about being careful or unnoticed. *Please. This is not who you are. Let me go. We are family.*

The mist of dread and hate was as thick as a brick door. But Annika and Blackburn would never defeat the Earl and his penguins without him. He kept bombarding them with thoughts of kindness and love, family and peace. Each thought chipped the door, making a hole the way a shark would against the hull of a boat. Then, with one mighty blast, he sent a tendril of thoughts into their heads:

Tickle, tickle.

The penguins stumbled, just a little, and Bolt ripped his arms from their wings. He ran toward the throne while tearing his backpack from his shoulders.

Family was the most powerful weapon of all.

Bolt pulled out the egg, which felt heavier in his hands than it had in the bag strapped around his shoulders. He shouted that he had an egg, and all eyes stared at him.

And then the Earl laughed. "What are you going to do, make us scrambled eggs?" He snapped his fingers and pointed to the penguin soldiers, who also stared at Bolt, but kept their distance. "What are you waiting for? Throw the boy in the cage, while I finish the girl." He nodded toward Annika, who was holding her ankle.

None of the penguins around Bolt moved. Bolt felt indecision swimming in their heads. To a penguin, nothing is more important than family, and that love of family can never be completely controlled. It was buried far deeper than the Earl could ever go.

Family was their true strength. And a penguin egg is family.

The soldiers stared at Bolt, not daring to edge closer and damage the egg.

"What are you doing? Grab the brat," demanded the

Earl, but his voice echoed throughout the room, unheeded. The Earl pounded his foot on the ground, sending slimy fish nuggets hurtling into the air as he glared around the room, snarling. "If you don't get him right now, I'll mince each of you, throw you in our fryers, and bake you into penguin sticks!"

"They won't hurt me," said Bolt, his own anger simmering, but controlled. "They respect family, and the love of an egg. You can turn them into an army, but you can never change that part of them."

The Earl scowled. "I will take that egg of yours and crack it in half. And then I'll crack you in half. And I'll serve you and that egg and every other egg in this kingdom for breakfast, sunny-side up!"

The penguins gasped, and Bolt sensed a tidal wave of hate and distrust surge across the room. But those feelings were not from the Earl, but from the penguins around him, aimed at the Earl. You never mess with a penguin and an egg.

The penguins in the room bared their teeth at the Earl, or would have if penguins had teeth. So they just sort of opened their beaks in a threatening manner.

"What are you doing?" demanded the Earl. The Earl sent waves of anger toward the soldiers. Bolt could feel it, and the soldiers turned toward Bolt. He sent waves of

hope and love back, and the soldiers turned toward the Earl.

Another wave of anger turned the penguins to Bolt.

Another wave of love turned them toward the Earl.

Back and forth. Back and forth. Everyone was getting dizzy.

And then the great clock tower chimed.

One chime. Two chimes. It kept going, no one moving, no one even daring to breathe.

The clock struck twelve. A shaft of moonlight lit the room from the windows high above, and both Bolt and the Earl transformed into penguins.

56.

Clash of the Werepenguins

Bolt's feet changed first. He shook off his shoes as soon as he felt his toes twitch, and his feet grew, the sharp nails on his three large yellow webbed toes ripping through his socks. A tail quickly followed, and then a white feather belly and two black wings. Finally, a long beak erupted from his nose.

Bolt saw only blurriness as he transformed, the room spinning and his skin burning. Every feather that sprang from his flesh felt like a pinprick.

When Bolt had fully transformed, the pain was gone and he stood, barking at everyone and no one. Mighty. Confident. A werepenguin.

But so was the Earl.

The oversize ruler of Sphen was now an oversize

penguin. The Earl, like Bolt, had horns on his head and big, bushy eyebrows over his gleaming red eyes. He was nearly seven feet tall, towering over the other penguins and Bolt, who felt like a dandelion next to an oak. One of his wings was made of solid iron, just like his hand had been, and he raised it, barking, and brought it down onto the floor, chipping the marble at his feet.

The Earl's beak was twisted into a snarl, and spirals of devilish loathing spun from the beast's raging head, spilling across the throne room, out its windows, and across the land.

Bolt saw all the Earl's mad wishes in those twisting loops, his mind an open book. And what a horrible book it was, filled with grammatical errors and sloppy handwriting. Within those pages was the Earl's yearning to rule all the people in the world and force them to build impossibly large fish fryers. He saw penguins swimming in pools, filled with water from salty human tears. He saw penguins wearing tuxedos that were sewn from human nose hairs.

Penguins, who already look like they wear tuxedos, actually wearing tuxedos? What a terrifying world!

Bolt forced his own thoughts out into the room and out the windows, chasing the Earl's demented ones.

Love each other. Help each other. We are family!

The Earl's thoughts fought back. *Hate, maim, wouldn't you like to own your own tuxedo?*

No, love each other! Family!

Destroy! Hate! Cummerbunds!

No, we are family! That is our true strength!

FANCY CUFF LINKS!

That last thought slammed into Bolt's head like a mallet, actually lifting him off his feet.

He crashed onto his back, his head crammed with images of tuxedos, but ill-fitting tuxedos that were too tight in the shoulders. Bolt closed his eyes to clear the thoughts, to invite peace to fill him.

He opened his eyes, thinking of family and love, but saw the Earl standing over him, holding Bolt's egg in his wings, about to smash it on Bolt's head.

"This thing won't hatch," cried the Earl, his voice half bird and half human. "It's completely fossilized. You could have joined us, you know. You could have lived your life as a king. Instead, your life will be ended with your own egg." He raised the egg high in the air. "Who needs scrambled eggs when you can have scrambled Bolt?"

57.
Attack of the Were-Gull

nnika wanted to shriek and run, but great bandits never shrieked and ran, although there were
occasions where one of those two might be war-
ranted, such as shrieking to confuse an enemy in a fight or
running away from the law.

As soon as the werepenguin transformations had
completed, fighting broke out again. Blackburn's sword
whistled and his cries of "Borscht!" thundered across the
room.

Bolt lay on the ground, the Earl-penguin standing
over him and about to bludgeon him with that egg. The
Earl-penguin sneered and the Bolt-penguin quivered and,
despite her desire to be the world's greatest bandit, Annika
shrieked.

The crash of glass breaking drowned out the shriek.

One of the windows high above them shattered.

Glass shards rained down, and with them, a giant winged creature swooped into the room followed by dozens of dirty white birds.

Annika had never seen a were-gull before, but she knew that's what it was. The creature was a little shorter than Gentoo had been, with the face of a seagull but also large green eyes. Gentoo's wings flapped, whipping air through the room, swaying drapes and blowing Annika's hair. She wished she had brought more bobby pins.

Gentoo swooped down and collided against the Earl's unguarded backside. He dropped the egg, which narrowly missed Bolt's head and instead fell on the Earl's foot. "My toes!" he yelped in a half-human and half-bird yowl, hopping and cursing.

An injured foot was the least of his worries. The were-gull fell upon him, pecking at his head with her long yellow beak. Seagulls also flew in and pecked. The Earl swung his iron wing. The birds flitted out of the way.

Gentoo hovered above the Earl, her beating wings sending currents of wind around the room. But she was unable to dive closer without being thwacked by the Earl's mighty iron wing.

Annika didn't see the beak jutting toward her own head, but she heard Blackburn cry, "Duck!" which was

odd, because there were no ducks in the room, only penguins and seagulls. But Annika ducked, and Blackburn's swordfish whistled over her head and struck a penguin who had been creeping behind her. "Don't just stand there, missy! Free yer father!"

Annika nodded. Everyone was distracted watching the seagull fight, and a great bandit always took advantage of distractions. That was the secret to pickpocketing—nudging someone gently on the shoulder and when they turned, deftly sticking a hand into their other pocket.

As the battle continued all around her, Annika stepped sideways, gritting her teeth as her ankle throbbed. She moved slowly enough so no one paid attention to her.

As the Earl swatted his wings at the were-gull hovering above him, Annika eased her way to her father's cage.

When she reached it, her father ran to the bars. His eyes were wet. "Annika," Vigi said. "I love you, but you must go. Quickly, while no one sees you."

"Not without you, Papa."

"The locks are unpickable, Annika. Please. Leave me."

Picking locks wasn't the only thing Annika did well. Instead of reaching for a bobby pin in her hair, she lifted a set of keys from her pocket. She had deftly swiped them from the Earl's pocket during their fight. "I knew I'd never beat him," she said. "But I have a few tricks up my sleeve."

She then reached through the cage bars and pulled a gold coin from her father's ear. "See?"

Annika unlocked the door, which swung open silently.

She and her father embraced. For a moment, Annika completely forgot about murderous werepenguins and flying human seagulls, even though those are not the sort of things that are easy to forget.

"Are you all right, Papa?"

"I am now." He gave her a final squeeze, one that Annika wished could last forever. But they would have time for further hugging later. "Let's find Felipe and get out of here."

Annika and her father kept to the side of the wall as they inched their way toward the main door, still unnoticed by the penguin soldiers. They could leave this cursed city. They would be a family again. They would be safe.

Annika's dreams had come true.

Or had they?

But what of Bolt? And the people of Sphen? Weren't they part of her dreams now, too?

She paused by the door as Felipe sidestepped his way toward them.

"You're pausing?" her father asked in a whisper.

"No," said Annika. "I'm stopping." She knew how unbandit-like her next words were, and that the greatest bandit the world has ever known would never say these words. But she wasn't just a bandit, but a loyal friend, too. "I told Bolt I would help. And a bandit never breaks his or her word."

Ignoring the lingering pain in her ankle, Annika rushed into the fight.

58.
The Battle in the Palace

estroy! Maim! Revolt!

DWhile a battle raged around Bolt, another battle was in his head, as those words bounced inside Bolt's penguin skull like plastic balls in a bouncy house.

Yes, Bolt. Rule!

Bolt sat on the ground as everyone else in the room fought around him. He was not the Earl, or the Stranger. He was not like them!

Or so he told himself.

Cries of "Borscht!" filled the room. Blackburn jabbed at beaks, parried wings, and swiped at feet. Annika threw bobby pins as if they were small darts, piercing the hides of the penguins, who barked and howled. Meanwhile, Vigi Lambda waltzed—his waltzing moves were legendary—seamlessly gliding out of the way of penguin soldier blows, all while thrusting a well-placed punch or karate chop upon them, in tempo. Bolt saw Felipe punch a penguin with an odd hand movement that looked like he was preparing a pumpkin strudel.

But the penguins were mighty fighters, too, and there were more penguins than people. Eventually Annika and her allies would tire, and the penguins would win.

The Earl was busy barking and swatting his wings at Gentoo, who buzzed over his head, looking for an opening to swoop down and attack. Her seagull friends, smaller and nimbler, pecked and landed some glancing blows, but their pecks did little damage to the mighty werepenguin.

The Earl grabbed a seagull that inched too close, bringing the bird to his beak, as if to eat it whole. But Gentoo shrieked and slammed into the Earl's back. He released the small bird and it fluttered away, but the Earl spun and swatted the were-gull in her face with the tip of his iron wing.

Gentoo spun in the air once, twice, twirling like an out-of-control helicopter, and then CRASH! She smashed into the wall halfway across the room. As she landed, her wing bent awkwardly, backward. Only a moan assured Bolt she was alive.

But her fighting had given Bolt the time he needed to push away the voices in his head. He leapt to his feet and rushed forward. He would defeat the monster, werepenguin to werepenguin. He would end it.

It was what he was chosen to do.

The Earl turned, a mere instant before Bolt reached him, again swatting with his iron wing. Bolt hopped to the side, and the wing crashed down, chipping the marble floor.

It would have chipped a great deal more of Bolt.

The Earl sprang at Bolt, iron wing extended. Bolt skipped to the side, but his foot hit the cracked marble floor and he fell.

The Earl pounced. He raised his iron wing and crashed it down. BOOM! CRACK! Bolt rolled over and the wing missed his head by inches, and marble rubble flew into the air. The Earl pounded his wing again. Again, Bolt rolled out of the way.

BOOM! CRACK! Roll. BOOM! CRACK! Roll.

"Stop rolling!" the Earl bellowed in his half human, half bird squawk. "You're ruining my nice marble floor."

I'll stop rolling if you stop punching, Bolt thought.

"Never mind then."

BOOM! CRACK! Roll. BOOM! CRACK! Roll.

And then, with the mightiest punch of all—BOOOM!! CRACKKKK!!!

Bolt rolled but the Earl's wing was now stuck inside the floor. He tried to yank it out, but it wouldn't budge. The Earl groaned, pushed, pulled. He was stuck.

Bolt picked up his egg, which was on the ground next to him. All he had to do was crash it on the Earl's head. It would be so simple. He could end the Earl's reign. The man was helpless.

Bolt could feel the fighting in the room ebb as all eyes watched him.

"Do it," hissed the Earl. "The Stranger warned me this might happen, although I'd rather it didn't. Destroy me, Bolt. Destroy me, and you become me!"

Bolt did not move. Was the Earl right? Bolt had so often found himself teetering between ruthlessness and family. In a flash, Bolt saw himself ending the Earl's life, and enjoying it. He saw himself raising his hands in victory, a lust for blood and rule overpowering him, shoving him into a darkness he would never escape.

No. He would not let that happen. Bolt was chosen, but he was not chosen to rule or to kill. He was chosen to be a different kind of werepenguin. A just werepenguin.

He placed the egg on the ground next to him.

"Weakling!" The Earl sneered at Bolt, his penguin mouth twisted in disgust. "A werepenguin hurts, without mercy. A werepenguin vanquishes his enemy. You are a poor excuse for one of us."

I am not like you.

The Earl spat. "Then the world will be ours. The Stranger and his followers will not show you the same mercy. If you won't stop us, no one will."

I will stop you. Maybe not by killing you, but somehow. Sure, the Baron was eaten by a killer whale. But there has to be another way.

The Earl laughed. "Baron Chordata?" Bolt heard a scream from across the room, followed by a thud from someone fainting. "Are you sure he's dead?"

Bolt didn't have time to think about those words because, with a loud grunt followed by a popping sound, like unsticking a cork, the Earl yanked his iron wing out of the ground. He shook rubble off his feathers and stomped toward Bolt.

Before Bolt could react, Annika leaped between him and the Earl. She held her small knife. "We aren't done yet!" she cried. "I am the greatest bandit that ever lived, and Bolt is my friend." She winced when she put pressure on her leg, but stood her ground.

"Get out of my way, girl," said the werepenguin, scowling.

"Never."

Blackburn emerged from the crowd of gawkers and took his place next to Annika. "Aye, and you shall have to fight through me, too." He waved his swordfish in the air.

"You have great sideburns!" remarked Felipe, standing nearby.

"They're me calling card," said Blackburn proudly.

The Earl studied them, his beak twisted in anger. "I'm getting very angry now."

"Uh-oh," said Bolt. He knew what happened when werepenguins got very angry.

The Earl's body seemed to quake. His head rotated around his neck. Twin fangs emerged from under his lips, hanging down to his chin. He was already enormous, yet seemed to grow five more inches. His eyes, already red, were crimson. His mind, which had been filled with hate, now seemed to vibrate with evilness.

So quickly that Bolt didn't even see him move, the Earl swatted Annika and Blackburn with his iron wing and flung them across the room as if they were dolls. They landed next to Gentoo with a thud.

"It's just you and me now," said the Earl, his voice more hideous penguin snarl than human, raspy and gurgling. He sounded as if he were underwater.

Bolt crouched as the creature towered over him. The fossilized egg lay by their feet. Both Bolt and the Earl stared at the egg.

"And you thought an egg could stop me?" the Earl squawked.

Honestly, not really.

The Earl swatted the egg out of the way. Despite its heaviness, it flew as easily as Annika and Blackburn had a moment earlier.

Bolt's egg seemed to fly in slow motion, directly toward Pygo, still perched atop the Earl's egg. It appeared to hover in midair for a split second, before crashing down.

BANG! Bolt's egg collided with the Earl's egg! Pygo toppled onto the ground.

No one in the room moved or even dared to breathe. The Earl's egg remained standing, although it wobbled and had a slit in the shell, and that slit spread and formed new slits. Each crack became bigger and bigger.

Pygo backed away and everyone watched in silence as the egg split open and a gray, wet, and feathery wing emerged from its shell.

59.

Oh, Boy

A head peeked out from the crumbling shell, sticky feathers dripping with a thick slime that plopped onto the ground in globs. As the shell broke away, the creature stood, uncoiling itself. It was larger than Bolt would have thought possible: nearly as tall as the Earl. The creature had an enormous penguin head, with very small feet and two mismatched wings: one small and bent awkwardly, one long and full. With the exception of that one large wing, it was completely hairless. It opened its beak, a beak as broad as an entire penguin, and a slithery croak spilled out. "Hungry!"

Bolt tried to bite his fingernails, but remembered penguins have neither fingernails nor fingers, so instead he bit the end of one of his wings. Everyone stared at the monster, and the Earl cried out, "It's a boy! At least, I think it's a boy."

Gelatinous ooze continued to drip from the monster, its eyes—so big and bright they seemed almost human—fixed on the Earl. The beast wobbled toward the Earl, its small legs barely holding up its weighty head. "Daddy!" it wailed. "Hungry!"

"Um, there are some dead fish carcasses next to my throne," said the Earl.

"Hungry!" cried the monster once again, still tottering forward.

"Don't come closer!" shouted the Earl.

The monster leapt, its beak open wide, wider than the Earl's very wide body.

GULP!

Bolt stared in horror as the baby swallowed the Earl in one giant chug.

The room was silent, everyone too stunned to move, as the baby began to sway and jerk. Its mouth trembled. Its small, thin legs buckled. Steam misted from its ears. Its face grew blue. Its throat widened.

"Get back!" shouted Felipe. "I think it's going to blow!"

The baby monster opened its giant beak again. More steam floated out and then its stomach expanded and its face turned green.

The monster baby burped. A very loud burp. The Earl's iron wing flew out of the baby's mouth and landed on the floor with a metallic CLANG.

The baby stopped jerking and steaming. "Yuck."

Bolt closed his eyes and reached into the monster's head. The baby's head was enormous, but mostly empty, filled neither with love nor with anger, just the innocence of a child, and confusion over what it had just done. Bolt

compelled it to move forward, through the soldiers who scattered out of the way. Bolt thought:

Extra-spongy newspapers in that cage. You'll like it.

Slowly, the creature walked toward the now-empty birdcage, its open mind easy to command. It stepped inside the cage, and when it did, the door silently closed behind it with a soft *click*.

The penguin soldiers stared at the creature, no longer a threat, and at Bolt, their anger melting, their viciousness ebbing. They were not horrified by the baby monster, but saw it as part of their family, although admittedly family that needed some babysitting.

Family, one of the soldiers barked.

And that's when Bolt knew the penguins of Sphen would be fine.

60.
Chosen for This

nnika, who had recovered from the Earl's blow,
hugged her father. Blackburn had also recovered
and hugged Felipe. Penguins hugged other penguins. There was a lot of hugging going on.

Bolt didn't hug anyone, for a couple of reasons. First, he
was still a disturbing werepenguin monster, and so wasn't
very huggable. Secondly, he was busy sending peaceful
and loving thoughts across the room and out the window,
into as many bird brains as he could.

The Earl is gone. Cherish your families. You are free.

Bolt could feel the deep walls of hatred crumbling like
a broken eggshell under his feelings of love, but he also
knew it would take more than a few moments of happy
thinking to set the penguins of Sphen right. They would

need to relearn how to be penguins again—true, peaceful penguins. And it would take time for the people of Sphen to trust their former tormentors.

Bolt's thoughts were interrupted by two arms circling him, and then two more. Blackburn and Felipe wrapped him in a joyous victory hug, and then Annika and her father embraced them, too. "Yes, we're hugging you, even though you are a disturbing werepenguin monster," said Annika.

"You have saved me, my daughter, my trusty left-handed right-hand man, and all of Sphen," said Vigi Lambda. "The Brugarian Forest Bandits give you our eternal thanks, and our lifelong loyalty."

"The forest bandits don't give their loyalty easily," said Annika. "It's a great honor."

"Thank you," barked Bolt. He wasn't quite sure what perks he received from having lifetime bandit loyalty, but he was glad to have it.

"You may be wondering what perks come with life-time bandit loyalty," said Felipe as the group ceased their hugging. "For one, you save twenty percent off any item bought during our annual Forest Bandit Bake Sale. It also means we'll never kidnap or rob you, at least probably not."

"No, we will not," said Annika. "The bandit code has strict rules about robbing and kidnapping those to whom you have sworn loyalty." She faced her father and added, "But there are some parts of the code I want to rewrite.

Like the parts about friendship, and heroism."

A bark interrupted their tight circle. Bolt immediately recognized Pygo. Bolt tensed, unsure if she was interrupting them to attack, but Pygo had no fight in her. She bowed.

Thank you. We owe you everything. You are our leader.

And all around the room the other penguins bent their heads in submission. A few saluted Bolt, and there is no greater honor in the animal kingdom than a penguin salute. Waves of respect and gratitude filled the room, emanating from their bird minds.

No, Bolt thought. *I am your brother. You must lead yourselves. Follow your hearts. Be penguins. That is enough.*

And I will stop the Stranger, he added, but only to himself.

Bolt now knew, without a doubt, that he hadn't been chosen to free the penguins of Brugaria. Or Sphen. He had been chosen to free the penguins of the world. For every penguin had a hateful crusty core deep inside it. Only Bolt could get rid of that crust forever.

He would never know exactly why fate had given him the birthmark, or that responsibility. It was Bolt's curse but also his good fortune, because it meant he had a family of penguins. Every penguin. His family numbered in the millions.

And they were all counting on him.

61.
Gentoo and Her Hope

Gentoo was puzzled by the odd curvature of her mouth for a moment, until she remembered that smiling was something people did when they were happy.

"Help me hoist the nets!" her aunt shouted. Marguerite Audouin's fever had broken the morning after the great palace battle, and now, a few days later, she was back to her old self. Gentoo was not back to her old self, as one of her arms was sprained and in a sling, but all things considered, the injury had been minor.

The ship was nicer than their old one and, while it had a few poorly patched and leaking holes in the side, Gentoo and her aunt had already repaired them and turned the fixer-upper into a sturdy fishing vessel. It had been a gift from the fearless Blackburn the Pirate.

They had painted over *The Heinous Hering* and renamed it: *The Beautiful Seagull II.*

The fish in the sea were still scarce, and the people of Sphen had been appalled to discover tens of thousands of dead fish filling the palace rooms. Expert fishermen agreed that the fish would repopulate after a couple of mating seasons, as long as no one else hoarded them.

As Gentoo hoisted the nets with her one hand, Bolt waved to her from the pier. Gentoo couldn't wave back since she was busy hoisting with her one good hand, but she shouted out a friendly greeting and asked, "When do you leave?"

"Today. I wish you'd change your mind. We could use you. Please come with us?"

"As I've told you already, my aunt needs me more. Sphen needs me more." Running around fighting monsters was something for a werepenguin to do, not a were-gull. This was her home. "You could always stay with us. You could help heal our city."

"Sphen doesn't need me. The world does."

Gentoo knew he was right about Sphen. After the battle, the penguin army had immediately disbanded and many penguins had left Sphen to start their own rookeries. There was distrust between people and penguins, and Gentoo knew that distrust would linger for a long time.

It would take years to overcome decades of bitterness and hate. Still, seagulls and penguins were natural enemies, so if Gentoo—a were-gull—could befriend a werepenguin, then people and penguins could find a way to live in peace, too. Even that horrible penguin baby seemed peaceful, despite its terrible first few minutes.

"I'll miss you," she said to Bolt. "But we'll keep in touch. After all, birds of a feather should flock together. Ha, ha!" It felt good to laugh, and now there would be plenty of time for better jokes, and more laughter, because jokes were no longer illegal in Sphen. She threw in a couple of additional "Ha, ha!"s.

Gentoo closed her eyes and held out her unsprained arm. She could feel the gulls flocking to her, their wings beating around her, landing on her arms and shoulders. Maybe she was meant to bring others together: gulls, people, and penguins. She didn't necessarily believe in fate, but she believed that was what *she* was chosen to do.

Birds of a feather *did* flock together—and all of Sphen was her flock now.

Above her, the gulls called to Gentoo:

We love you, Gentoo! Ha, ha! Candy-striped moose gum!

"Gentoo, stop standing around and help batten the halyards and lackshire the jibs!" called Aunt Margie. Gentoo sighed as the seagulls around her dispersed. She turned to help her aunt, and waved farewell to Bolt.

62.
A Pirate's Song

The waves lapped against the sides of the pirate ship. Annika, looking a particularly deep shade of seasick green, leaned over the side. Blackburn stood at the ship's wheel, humming a jaunty pirate tune:

> *We pirates are ruthless, and we're nearly toothless.*
> *We conquer by wits and by force.*
> *Raise yer hand and yer hook, and yer* Pirate Handbook,
> *As we sail the seas yelling, "Borscht!"*

Blackburn had been in a great mood ever since they had found his old pirate ship docked behind the castle. The poker-playing penguins had been so happy the Earl was vanquished, they forgave Blackburn for beating them in poker and gave him back his boat, which was in nearly perfect condition. Penguins can't sail ships anyway; it's hard to turn a wheel with wings.

Upon stepping onto his ship, Blackburn had kissed the deck and explained that pirates always kissed the decks of their ships, which was one of the reasons why so many were nearly toothless. He had also told Annika that her debt was forgiven, but if she ran across an extra gold tooth or a soccer ball, he would gladly accept them.

And now they were off to Omnescia to see the great seer and return Shorty's egg, now that it had served its purpose. Bolt hoped they would get answers, find out where the other werepenguins were, and, hopefully, learn how to defeat them with something better than another egg. Then he would find the Stranger and free the world's penguins.

"How's your ankle?" he asked Annika. Her leg was wrapped in bandages, although it was just a sprain.

In response, Annika threw up over the bow.

Blackburn had promised only to sail them to Omnescia, although Bolt hoped he would decide to stay with them longer. Annika vowed to stand by Bolt's side for the entire mission, no matter how long it took. The bandits had sworn lifelong loyalty, and Annika said that meant she

had no choice, but Bolt preferred to believe she was going on this journey because it was the right thing to do, and because they were friends.

Bolt was glad they were friends. He had forgiven her for lying to him, and she had vowed never to do it again.

"Land ho!" shouted Blackburn as the shores of Omnescia and the raspberry-blowing statue of the seer emerged from the mist.

Near Midnight at the Place Formerly Known as the St. Aves Zoo

Silence surrounded us, as did the ruins of the once-lively zoo. Even the angry ostrich no longer screeched; I could only assume it had found a place to sleep, hopefully free of the troubling dreams I knew I would have for the rest of my life.

The caretaker looked up at the sky. "It is late. Almost midnight."

I suspected the penguin caretaker would not remain human much longer.

The full moon shone over us. Once upon a time I did not fear midnight and full moons, but *once upon a time* is for fairy tales, and this was no fairy tale. Oh, how I wished it were!

"Tomorrow I will be back," I promised. "And I will take you and the penguins with me to your new home. You will all live happily, hopefully *ever after* but who's to say? Still, you deserve a better tomorrow, after all the horrible pasts you've survived."

"Thank you, my friend," said the man, bowing. Again, he looked up at the moon shining overhead. "I will stay here for the night." He stepped toward the maintenance shack behind him.

"You will be transforming, then?" I asked. The man did not respond. I smiled at him. "Good night, Bolt."

The man looked back, staring at me, his eyes flickering red, but only for a moment. "Excuse me. What did you just call me?"

"Bolt, of course. Or do you prefer your full name: Humboldt? Or should I call you Mr. Wattle? If so, please forgive my familiarity."

The man's eyes flashed red again and his skin seemed to ripple. He opened the door to the shack and said, "You have made a mistake, my friend. My name is not Bolt."

"Then how can you know his story so well? If you're not Bolt, then who are you?"

Without answering my question, the man stepped inside the small building, closing the door behind him.

TURN THE PAGE TO
BEGIN READING . . .

THE BATTLE OF THE WEREPENGUINS

THE EPIC CONCLUSION TO
THE **WEREPENGUIN** *SAGA*

1.

Omneseus

Bolt sat on the frozen ground in a dimly lit cave high up in a mountain on the island of Omnescia. Despite the cold, he wore just a simple white T-shirt and a pair of ratty gray sweatpants. A rainbow-and-unicorn backpack was strapped across his shoulders that held two more white T-shirts and two more pairs of ratty gray sweatpants. It also held some dead fish, in case Bolt got hungry.

A small campfire crackled. On the other side of the flames sat a bald man in a tunic and cheap plastic glasses. Black spirals were painted on the lenses, which made the man look strangely mysterious, or maybe mysteriously strange. This was the great seer, Omneseus.

Bolt sniffed. He could make out the scent of freshly

baked s'mores from the end of Omneseus's long staff. Apparently, Bolt had interrupted the man's snack time.

Closing his eyes, Bolt thought back to a week earlier, when he had sat in this exact same cave. Then, the seer had told Bolt how to defeat the Earl, the ruler of the city of Sphen and a werepenguin. Bolt had defeated him with the help of a large egg, and the Earl had been eaten by his newly born son. You sort of had to be there.

Omneseus raised his arms, his powerful voice echoing through the bowels of the cave. "Welcome, Bolt. You are back, just like I foretold. For I see all!" He waved his fingers above his head as if casting a spell. "I see a band of bunnies about to eat dinner. I see a girl eagerly picking wax from her ears. I see a little silhouetto of a man!"

Bolt nodded. The seer did see all, but a lot of what he saw tended to be somewhat random. "I'm here to . . ."

The seer held up his finger to quiet Bolt. "Oh, I know why you are here. I can see it as plainly as I see the nose on your face! There!" He pointed at a spot four feet to Bolt's left.

"Um, my nose and I are over here," said Bolt, waving.

The seer blinked a few times. "Right. Sorry. I can barely see anything while wearing my strangely mysterious X-ray glasses. Or mysteriously strange, perhaps." He removed his glasses and blinked a few times. "Ah, better." He stared at Bolt as if he were seeing him clearly for the first time, which he probably was. He cackled.

"Can you please not cackle? It sounds evil and spooky and there's nothing particularly funny." Fortune tellers and seers cackled all the time, which was annoying.

Omneseus cackled one more time anyway. "I know why you are here. Yes! You are here for . . ." The man jumped up and held out his hand. "You are here for salmon-flavored corn chips!" The seer held a bag of corn chips.

"Actually, I'm here for a totally different reason. But, well, I guess I'm sort of hungry." Bolt stood up and reached across the fire to grab a handful of fish-flavored snacks. They were delicious.

"You are also here to learn how to find and defeat the Stranger, aren't you? He is the mightiest of your kind. The father of all werepenguins in the world."

As the seer spoke, Bolt switched from chewing chips to chewing his lips with fright.

"You shouldn't bite your lips," said the seer. "It's a bad habit."

"Sorry," said Bolt, picking his nose.

"Tell me, Bolt. Are you up to the task of stopping the Stranger?"

"I have to be." Every penguin in the world had a slim coating of evilness inside them, implanted by the Stranger. That coating made them cruel and vicious. But if Bolt could stop the Stranger, he would free the penguins from that hate. The world's penguins would once again be happy, kind creatures. "I'm ready—at least I think I am."

"You *think*?" the seer demanded. "You must know! Do not doubt or you will no doubt lose!" Bolt gulped. "The Stranger does not doubt. He lives in the South Pole under a great magical moon, where he is invincible. And immortal. Unless."

"Unless what?" Bolt was glad to hear that there was an *unless*.

"I will sing you a chant." The seer sat back down and closed his eyes. He lifted up his palms and began to softly hum.

Bolt groaned. Seers gave advice coded inside cryptic, confusing songs just as often as they cackled. Bolt had figured out the meaning of other chants he had been given, but he would have much preferred simple, printed directions.

Still, he waited politely as the seer sat humming, perhaps channeling an invisible spiritual realm, likely the same realm that gave him his mystic, all-seeing powers. Finally, the seer chanted, slowly and off-tune:

> *Remember your code—yes, embrace it you must.*
> *Turn away the bloodlust. It's love you must trust.*

The hunger inside, it's so strong and so real!
Its threat you'll repeal with the tooth of a seal.
But you won't win unless you take this advice:
Born from love may suffice, but a bite's twice as nice.

Bolt's hair stood up in the shape of two horns, and he pulled them in frustration. "You've completely lost me."

"What part?"

"All of it," Bolt admitted, continuing to pull his hair until he accidentally yanked out three strands and yelped with pain. "What does it mean?"

The seer shrugged. "How should I know? I'm a seer, not a translator."

Bolt went back to pulling his hair. He knew the chant was important. The fate of the world could be hidden inside it.

Acknowledgments

When I sat down to begin writing the first book in this series, many years ago, I imagined a book about were-aardvarks. I'm not sure why, completely, other than the term "were-aardvark" seemed funny to me, funnier than a "were-anteater" anyway, just like pickles are funnier than cucumbers and borscht is funnier than gazpacho, although gazpacho is still reasonably funny.

But I hadn't gone far in my writing when I decided a were-aardvark wasn't the best fit, because Bolt longed for a family and aardvark families aren't particularly memorable, at least not from the very small amount of research I did, which consisted of reading an article on Wikipedia for about three minutes. But that seemed like enough research. I invite you to write a were-aardvark book, though. If you do, please include me in your acknowledgments. And I will include you in mine:

Thank you to _____. (*Please write your own name in the blank.*)

With my next were-animal, a penguin, I hit the jackpot. Their lifelong mating habits, their lack of fierceness, and my love of fish sticks all came together. It was meant to be.

So I wrote *The Curse of the Werepenguin*, and proceeded to write approximately one hundred redrafts of it. This book, the sequel to *The Curse of the Werepenguin*, was a much easier path, with a significant reduction in redrafts. I knew the story, you see. Even when writing *The Curse of the Werepenguin*, I was aware of where the story might go, although at the time I didn't know if there would be a *Revenge of the Werepenguin* for certain. Still, the facts and details were already imagined, mostly. The pirate came later—a comment by my wonderful editor brought him to life—but mostly everything else was already there, if not on paper then in my head, hiding.

Things often hide in my head, you see, including proper acknowledgments, which is why I have to keep hitting my left ear as I write this, hoping to jar them out of my right ear (I'm a righty, otherwise I'd have to hit the other ear). So Kendra Levin, the editor I alluded to in the previous paragraph, gets a big acknowledged thank-you, as does Hannah Mann, who I suspect played a bigger role than she would admit, even if that role was an avalanche of positive thinking, which is something I always need more of.

Thank you also to Dana Leydig, who came late to the party but ended up sticking around and helping clean up. People who help clean up after parties are always welcome, and thankfully she's already RSVPed to my next shindig. Thank you to Scott Brown, whose illustrations are beyond words, which I guess is the point of illustrations. I also must thank the copyeditors, as copyediting always makes me look much better than I would otherwise, so thank you to Janet Pascal and Laura Stiers. Also thank you to Krista Ahlberg, Abigail Powers, and Marinda Valenti.

I would also like to thank everyone at Viking, including, and this is in no particular order, Sarah Moses, Kim Ryan, Ken Wright, Kate Renner, Tessa Meischeid, and Friya Bankwalla. They all played different roles, from art direction to helping spread werepenguinism around the world, but each was important and appreciated more than they will ever know.

Lastly, I want to thank my family: Lauren, Madelyn and Emmy, my parents, my sister Deena and her family (a shout-out to Mike, Alyssa, and Kyle! Hi!), and, well, anyone else that puts up with me. It's not always that easy to put up with me but hey, at least you get to see your name in an end-of-book acknowledgment, and that's pretty awesome.